HERSHEL, The ENEMY, And ME

By

Dana G. Rumbaugh

ISBN 978-0-7414-7359-2

Printed in the United States of America

Published March 2013

INFINITY PUBLISHING
1094 New DeHaven Street, Suite 100
West Conshohocken, PA 19428-2713
Toll-free (877) BUY BOOK
Local Phone (610) 941-9999
Fax (610) 941-9959
Info@buybooksontheweb.com
www.buybooksontheweb.com

So the great dragon was cast out, that serpent of old, called the Devil and Satan, who deceives the whole world; he was cast to the earth, and his angels were cast out with him.

Revelation 12:9 (NKJV)

The enemy boasted, "I will pursue, I will overtake them. I will divide the spoils; I will gorge myself on them. I will draw my sword and my hand will destroy them."

Exodus 15:9 (NIV)

For the enemy has persecuted my soul;
He has crushed my life to the ground;
He has made me dwell in darkness,
Like those who have long been dead.

Psalm 143:3 (NKJV)

CONTENTS

Introduction

Since the hour was early when I entered Giordano's, Luigi was able to place me at a table in front near the window that looked out onto the street. From there I could watch for the arrival of someone I had not seen in every bit of twenty years. Actually, Hershel Feldman and I had not seen each other since our high school days, when he had ruled over our relationship in his typical tyrannical fashion. As one of a minority of *goyim* in a predominantly Jewish high school, I suffered the misfortune of being dragged along behind a tall, handsome, and wildly popular Jew named Hershel Feldman. His mission was to inflict upon me my daily allotment of humiliation, while my function was to assume the role of his punching bag. Being a non-Jew, pudgy, fair of skin, and ordinary looking at best, I had absolutely no defense against Hershel's abuse, so I simply absorbed it with the best grace I could muster throughout my teen years, until we both graduated and left high school to attend different universities. From that point onward, until this morning at the ghastly hour of three-fifteen, I had heard absolutely nothing out of my teenage tormentor. As far as I knew he had simply dropped off the edge of the earth.

The phone's persistent clamber tore me away from a tantalizing dream and into the realm of the real and, when I picked up, cleared my throat, and croaked, "Hello", I was shocked even further by a voice with a distant, but otherwise familiar character; a voice that somehow took me back in time but, beyond that, gave me no additional clues about its origin; at least not right away.

The voice persisted: "Elvis? Is that you, you *goy* son of a gun? I had a heck of a time finding your number without knowing your last name. Had to get drunk before I could remember it. Did I wake you?"

It seemed to me as if the preterit twenty years melted away as soon as I heard the familiar mutilation of my name. Just as I had done a thousand times before, I corrected the perpetrator: "Hershel, my name is Ellis, not Elvis; you know that. Please don't call me 'Elvis'. And, it's the middle of the night. What's the matter? Are you in trouble?"

"Trouble? Am I in *trouble*? Why else would I call a *goy* jerk in the middle of the night, if I wasn't in trouble? You're my last resort, Elvis, and I need you to help me out of this mess, and I don't want any of your measly excuses." Hershel's usually sonorous voice had taken on a squeaky character in his distress, whatever that might have been. "Ever since I saw you on TV—this big-shot preacher or evangelist or whatever you are—I started to wonder if you had somehow sopped up some brains from somewhere, and had actually begun to amount to something. Of course, you'd never be smart enough to be a rabbi but, as I always say, 'You can fool most of the people some of the time.' So I thought I'd give you a call and maybe give you a try. I figure, what the heck? Everyone else I know has failed me."

(This is probably a good place to mention the fact that, as I relate my experiences with Hershel, I'm having to re-phrase the preponderance of his comments. Hershel was prone to have a filthy mouth, and I mean with no consideration for the company in which he found himself. Even in grade school, Hershel swore like a drunken sailor and he never, at least up to this point, repented of it. This, of course, is in no way a criticism of Jewry; it simply applies to Hershel alone.)

I couldn't resist but *had* to fall back on our ancient relationship: "The name's **Ellis**, not **Elvis**! How would you like it if I called you 'Hershey' or 'Herbert' or something else that wasn't your name?"

Completely ignoring my question, Hershel resumed his tirade without skipping a beat: "So, how's about meeting me somewhere so I can give you all the gory details of the troubles I'm having? You big-time preacher types are always noising about how compassionate you are and all that crap, so now's your chance to put your money where your mouth is. Meet me tomorrow night at Soonie's Place over a gin and tonic and I'll spill my guts to you. How's nine o'clock sound?"

"It sounds impossible to me, Hershel. I don't show my face in bars these days and nine o'clock is when I go to bed. I'll meet you at Giordano's Ristorante at three in the afternoon. Take it or leave it." I could hardly believe I was standing my ground against Hershel Feldman! It was exhilarating! Hershel agreed to my terms, but very reluctantly, it sounded to me.

So there I sat, in Giordano's, at the window table, nearly four-thirty, and no Hershel. Actually, I wasn't too concerned about his tardiness. Being late was pretty much Hershel's *modus operandi*. My concern was, since he had been 'four sheets in the wind' when he called me, that he had forgotten altogether. I resolved to give him until five o'clock and not one second beyond; then, if he didn't turn up, I'd forget the whole thing and go home. Sure enough, at twenty past five Hershel came walking jauntily around the corner and burst into the restaurant. If I had not been practically Luigi's high priest, it is doubtful whether or not he would have allowed me to hold his best table hostage for two and a half hours. Even so, he threw me the occasional haughty look, as if to put me in my place.

Brushing Luigi aside, Hershel strode over to my table, a big grin plastered across his face. He looked like an Italian crime boss or something, dressed in a five hundred dollar pinstripe suit and sporting Gucci loafers. He had on one of those pastel blue shirts with white collar and cuffs, and his wristwatch looked as if it must have cost thousands. Uttering not the slightest greeting, he merely sat down at my table and began to regale me with his problems as though we had seen each other only the day before. There was not a woman in the place (and there were some really fabulous ladies in attendance) whose head he did not turn. With his rich, dark, and wavy hair, his angular handsome face (nicely tanned), and his tall, athletic figure, Hershel had them all staring. He hardly took notice.

Hershel came across as so upper-class that his profanity seemed oddly out of character: "I thought you would have grown more attractive-looking after twenty some years," he sneered, "but I guess some people are destined to be homely. Aren't you married or something? What woman in her right mind would...? Oh, well, she's probably pretty much a mud fence herself. Takes all kinds." (All this is cleaned up considerably.) "Listen, you *goy* pinhead, I got some big problems and I guess I'll have to fall back on you, even though you probably never had a decent thought in your whole miserable life. Order me a drink! So, here's the deal...."

Thus, Hershel Feldman proceeded to fill me in on the previous twenty years of his life, and how he had come to be in big trouble. If you will indulge me, I'm going to do my best to relate the entire story to you, minus the filthy language. I should explain, however, that I found it necessary to interview several other persons who were or are involved with Hershel's life in order to fill in the gaps that his knowledge and experience did not cover; or that Hershel himself did not see fit to mention to me. Here, then, is the account of the last twenty-odd years of Hershel's life, replete with all the details supplied by both Hershel himself and others who were participants.

HERSHEL, THE ENEMY, AND ME

(As told by Rev. Ellis Keaton)

PART ONE

Chapter One

Even though Hershel Feldman graduated valedictorian in his high school class, there are those who have their doubts that he earned the title academically, but rather that he must have either purchased it or extorted it somehow. In any case, this prestigious appellation, along with the Feldman family's falsely presumed affluence, precluded Hershel's entering any university but the most highly regarded within Jewish society. Thus, the very next spring following his graduation from high school found Hershel residing in Miami, occupying a posh suite in his 'aunt' Yetsye's (Yetsye being Hershel's stepmother's sister) lavish villa, and attending the aforementioned highly regarded university. There he remained until more suitable lodgings became requisite.

Aunt Yetsye's estranged husband, Nathan, though he had strenuous misgivings about it, agreed under extreme duress to take Hershel on as an assistant in his clothing business. 'Uncle' Nathan, being uncommonly insightful, could detect no redeeming features in his 'nephew' Hershel, but took him on rather than suffer the consequences. Even so, he would live to regret his decision. The prearranged plan was that Hershel would begin at the very bottom, say, as a warehouseman; then he would (ostensibly) progress through the ranks of employees until one fine day, perhaps after having learned the business top-to-bottom, he would attain the position of vice president. It was put to Hershel that this process would take quite some time and would involve much hard work and dedication. The fact that Hershel had no intention, right from the start, of wasting years of his life in the clothing business, was a point that never seemed to surface during the initial discussion of the plan. It may be that Hershel did grace the warehouse with his presence for a day or two, but all it took was for Uncle Nathan to leave on a business trip three days after Hershel's first day on the job, and the latter never set foot in the warehouse again. When in a week's time Nathan returned from his business trip, he found Hershel not in the warehouse but in a private, albeit small, office in the accounting department, having appointed himself (on behalf of his uncle) office manager. Before Nathan could voice any serious objections, he was informed jubilantly by the vast majority of the girls in the office that Hershel was already doing swimmingly well as office manager. In spite of himself, Nathan was impressed by the spirit of harmony among employees that Hershel seemed to have fostered in an incredibly short period of time. Still, he had always had it in the back of his mind to put his son Jerome in charge of the accounting department; but he had to admit that poor Jerome, with his lisp and rather effete demeanor did not seem to motivate the girls particularly well. Perhaps this move by Hershel, though he, Nathan, had no part in it, would prove to be the better course of action. He would try to soften the blow to Jerome's ego, if indeed the poor fellow had any.

Apparently, Jerome did possess some vestige of personal esteem because, on being summarily bypassed for the job of office manager, a position his father had led him to believe was all but his due, the poor wretched fellow seemed to recede further and further into himself to the point that he became virtually uncommunicative. Ultimately, he left the building one Friday afternoon and never came back, returning instead to the bosom of his mother Yetsye, where he remained in a state of limbo at the villa; and there he spent his days reading and attempting to learn to play his mother's white grand piano. Sadly, he could never master the instrument, nor did he ever seem to finish reading a single volume. By the time Jerome reached the age of fifty he was rotund, totally bald, and so insecure that his only course was to live the life of a recluse. His sole achievement in life was that he became a competent cook, preparing most meals for his mother and himself, unless there were to be guests, at which point he would repair to his room and leave the cooking to Yetsye's housekeeper (who was a better cook than he anyway). Jerome's entire life was spent on the grounds of the villa, where he grew fatter and more pallid, less and less articulate, and ultimately he rarely if ever spoke, even to his mother.

Nathan and Yetsye had produced another offspring, a plump and jovial girl named Rose, who was twelve years younger and far more outgoing than Jerome. Even though her mother was a handsome sort of woman, Rose inherited, rather, her father's meaty jowls, hawk nose, and nondescript eyes, as well as his volcanic complexion. In an attempt to compensate for these unattractive features in her daughter, Yetsye had the girl's crooked and discolored teeth crowned, every single one, so she did have a dazzling smile. To further compensate, Yetsye threw in a deluxe nose job, but neither of these could offset the effects of Rose's obesity. Unfortunately Rose, not in her very young life, found the means to reduce her body weight to match up with her height, so she was normally possessed of a girth that was approximately that of her height. For some time it had been all too obvious to Nathan that he would have to produce no inconsiderable dowry in order to entice even the most indiscriminate of men to marry his daughter. Being an orthodox Jew, and traditional as well, Nathan had originally planned to pass on his business to his son and to find a well-placed gentleman to wed his daughter; but, given the fact that Jerome seemed to have no interest whatsoever in his business, and that Rose was turning out to be nearly impossible to marry off, Nathan was hard pressed to predict his own and his family's future. Consequently, Nathan had taken to living his hectic life from one day to the next, hoping that at some point Jerome would wake up and take charge of his life and that Rose would suddenly and miraculously morph from her homely state into a comely butterfly. Sad to say, at the point in time that Hershel entered the picture, neither Jerome nor Rose had managed to bring off the hoped-for transformation. Ever the optimist, Nathan continued to plod along, trying to grow his struggling business and hoping to reconstitute his marriage.

Pursuant to this goal, Nathan paid a visit to the villa where his wife and children dwelt in relative luxury while he, incidentally, found it necessary to 'batch it' in a dreary and stuffy flat on the fringe of the commercial part of the city. After verifying Yetsye's complete aversion to reconciliation, he made for Jerome's rooms to discuss business matters with him. He found his son squinting through his perfectly round lenses, which were set in black plastic frames, at a tome bound in tattered and scuffed leather.

"Jerome, my son, come greet your Abi." Nathan strove to sound as jovial and familiar as the situation permitted. When Jerome looked up from his reading only briefly, then returned to it without comment, Nathan went and sat beside his son on the sagging couch that was the younger man's preferred roosting spot. He waited, knowing that eventually Jerome would respond to his persistent huffing and throat clearing.

When the son at length closed his book and laid it against his thigh; and then looked up at the father, his eyebrows raised in query, Nathan proceeded: "Son, it is high time you came to your senses and made something of your life. For the last time I'm offering to make you ready to take over my

4

business. All you have to do is come back in and I'll fix you up with an office of your own, and maybe even your own secretary. You got to remember who you are, you know, the son and heir to your old man's fortunes. What's the matter with you, my boy? You got no backbone? Come on, now. Tomorrow you should put on a suit; you know, that new blue one I got you, and get yourself a nice briefcase—you can charge it to my credit card—and come on in and claim what's yours. That's all you got to do, my son! Just think, Jerome Mandel, the big boss, awright?" The joviality had become pleading instead.

Jerome regarded his father with an unsteady gaze for some minutes, his pinkish eyes watering profusely and his eyelashes fluttering in confusion and discomfort. Finally, barely audibly, he replied, "Abi, I don't want to be a big boss. I don't want to be any kind of boss. I don't care for the clothing business. Besides, I have too much going on here, what with the piano and all my books." He picked up the volume he had been reading and returned to it, granting it all the attention he could muster, given his agitated condition. He said no more to Nathan, refusing thereafter to acknowledge his father's presence.

Rising to his feet with a sigh, Nathan sought out his daughter. He found Rose in her *boudoir*, filing her nails. The brisk motion of filing set her ample body to jiggling in sympathy, and when she spoke, her voice took up the jiggle as a sort of vibrato. She dropped the file and ran, as best she could, to meet and hug her father. "There's my Abi," she crooned melodramatically. "Come, sit. We should talk. Are you well, Abi? What brings you here?" She patted the seat of a flowered and ruffled upholstered chair next to her dresser, a chair upon which Nathan could not possibly make himself comfortable.

"Hello, my Dollink. How's my lit'l goil?" He hugged as much of his daughter as he was able to encircle with his arms. Her smile was indeed impressive, he concluded.

Nathan thought it best to get right to the point without dwelling too much on Rose's appearance. It occurred to him that, because of his anxiety about how she looked, he had never really gotten to know his daughter. Recalling vaguely that she seemed rather clever and bright, he determined to attempt to delve into her personality and to lay aside, for the time being, the fact that she would be unlikely to attract a suitable husband. Shifting uncomfortably in the ridiculous chair, he asked, "What does my lit'l goil think of the clothing business?"

Rose appeared startled by his question. She answered, "Why, Abi, I didn't know you cared. But, to answer your question, I think it's remarkable and vitally important. You must know that I've always been fascinated by fashionable and stylish clothing, both for women and for men. Well, for children, too, although I haven't really put much thought into children's attire. Why do you ask? In case you haven't noticed, I'm not such a 'lit'l goil' anymore." She chuckled about that last, setting up some more sympathetic vibrations.

"Well, Dollink, I've been thinking about our future and the future of the company, and I'm afraid that me trying to put your brother in charge would be the worst thing I could do. Besides, he won't do it. What about you? You wanna take charge when I retire? Think you could do it? I don't want that Hershel in charge—you know what I mean? He's too slick or something, if you know what I'm saying. I wanna retire, but I ain't gonna do it without I find somebody besides Hershel to run the whole thing. So, whad'ya think?"

Patting her father's shiny bald head, Rose declared, "You've got yourself a successor, Abi. Let's do it!"

It took Rose Mandel less than a year to whip her father's failing business into shape. She summarily dumped his non-progressive suppliers, turning instead to venders who could provide garments with leading edge style and competitive pricing. She added emphasis to women's clothing, realizing that clothing for women yielded better profit than did men's.

Furthermore, she researched children's clothes and took on cautiously a few select lines until she got a better feel for what would sell and what would not. Finally, she brought on board a line of stylish clothing for full-figured women; a line that practically exploded in popularity right from the start. This was her most profitable product line. Rose left Hershel in charge of the accounting department for two reasons: He turned out, it seemed, to be really good at running the department; and, of course, she had fallen in love with him.

To celebrate the successful completion of her first year as C.E.O. of MANDEL FAMILY APPAREL, Rose leased a suite of offices in the New York City garment district, designed for herself a posh, contemporary office, and hired an administrative assistant (a personal secretary) whose name was Arielle. She created a nationwide system of warehouses, the main one remaining in Miami, then she opened a large number of discount outlets scattered throughout the eastern United States; and finally, she established first telephone, then subsequently, computer networks that provided instant and continuous communication between her office and all other locations in the company. Initially, the offices in New York were devoted to management and marketing, while the accounting department remained in Miami under the direction of Hershel Feldman. It was at about this time that Nathan Mandel took partial retirement, remained on the company's payroll as a consultant, and purchased for himself a luxury condominium near Coral Gables, Florida, where he spent his now idle days socializing at a local country club.

Chapter Two

Ms. Rose Mandel, C.E.O. of MANDEL FAMILY APPAREL sat in the high-backed plush office chair in her spacious office overlooking busy New York City streets, tracing with a pudgy forefinger columns of figures on the printout of a profit-and-loss report she had just that day received from Miami. Occasionally, she would interrupt her focus on the report in order to turn her attention to the scene outside her eighth story windows; the snowflakes the size of half-dollars pinwheeling down on pedestrians and motor traffic below, accumulating much too fast, so that soon enough the entire city would be transformed into a frenzied crush of home-bound traffic in the dark and snow-blanketed winter night. Rose was not in the least concerned, for she had all she needed to keep herself comfortable for days at a time in the tiny apartment that adjoined her office. There were a comfortable daybed, a gas log within a small artificial fireplace, a kitchenette fully provisioned, a magnificent recliner in her sitting area, and multiple means of entertainment to keep her engaged. All of these notwithstanding, Rose's primary means of occupying herself was business. She sighed and, turning her attention from the snowstorm outside, resumed her analysis of the figures before her. Something was just not right. When she considered the volume of business her company was doing, as well as the margins of profit she had painstakingly negotiated with her suppliers, she reckoned that there should be much, much more profit thrown off from all this activity than the report in front of her indicated. Where were all her profits going? It was nearly midnight before she finally caught on to what was taking place. Pushing back from her desk, she yawned and made for her kitchenette, planning in her head what she would eat before retiring for the night. Rose had already resolved in her mind what her initial action would be come morning.

When Arielle arrived the next morning, stomping the snow from her fur-lined boots, Rose was just finishing her second cup of coffee. Tapping gently on the office door, Arielle waited a few seconds, opened the door slightly, and then stuck her head through the opening just far enough to remark, "Sorry to be late, Ms. Mandel, I got stuck in the ice on the bridge. It's a mess out there. Did you spend the night here?" She began to pull the door closed but Rose stopped her.

"Come on in, Arielle, I have something for you to do first thing." Rose's mouth was a grim, straight line across her face; and she had that set, determined look she sometimes took on when she was none too happy about things. She continued, "Let's see, it's just now nine-thirty and I want you to ring Miami and get Hershel Feldman on the line for me."

"I'll need to wait a while before I call Mr. Feldman. He doesn't get in until after ten most days. Should I call about ten-fifteen?" In her uneasiness, Arielle began to fidget with her car keys.

Treating Arielle to a wry smile that showed off her excellent dental work, Rose answered, "No. Call him right now, please. I want to speak to him immediately."

At twenty-five after ten, Arielle pressed the TALK button on her intercom and announced, "Mr. Feldman on the line for you Ms. Mandel."

"Thanks, Arielle. I'll get it in a minute. Leave him on HOLD." Rose sauntered to her private bath and re-did her face. There was a little something between two of her front teeth and she worked on that for a bit, too. Finally, she walked slowly back to her desk and picked up the phone.

Although there was only a dial tone to greet her, she was not in the least surprised. She had only to swivel slightly in her chair in order to face her laptop computer on which she pulled up her email account. The message she sent to Hershel read:

Hershel,
Referencing our failed telephone conversation today, I offer you two alternatives. 1) Report to my office in New York **PROMPTLY** at 10:00AM tomorrow for a conference, or 2) Retrieve from your mail drop a dismissal notice severing your employment with Mandel Family Apparel. Take your choice.
Rose Mandel, CEO.

At 11:26 the following morning, Hershel Feldman strolled down the hall leading to Rose Mandel's office, waving to, and smiling engagingly at, all the women he encountered. Walking briskly by Arielle without comment, he opened the door to Rose's office and went right in, flopping down in a leather chair facing the latter's desk. He pitched his fedora onto the pile of reports Rose had been analyzing and, with a flash of his winsome smile, greeted her, "This is quite some place you got here, Rosie! Your old man would be proud, or maybe appalled. It gives me some good ideas on how to redecorate my office in Miami. So, what's up?"

"Certainly not our profits, *Hershey*. Where have you been? I specifically instructed you to be here in my office at ten sharp this morning. Since you were not here at that time I assumed you had chosen my second offer and I sent an email message to Howard Katz instructing him to prepare your dismissal notice and to place it in your mailbox. Did you not check your mail this morning?" Rose was finding it difficult to sound authoritative while simultaneously regarding this roué sprawled before her.

Hershel's smile stayed fixed on his handsome face as he answered, "Well, now, I couldn't have checked my mail while on the way to the airport, could I? You asked me to come on up, so I did."

"No, you don't have that quite right. I **told** you to be in my office at a specific time, and you arrived an hour and twenty-seven minutes late; hence my assumption that you had chosen not to follow my instructions. If you had intended on complying, you would have been on time." Rose made a point of scribbling some notes on a legal pad.

"Hey, I tried, didn't I? I missed the first flight and I caught the very next one. What more do you want?" Hershel looked hurt.

Rose was having trouble sympathizing with him. "That's strange; I come up here from Miami once a month on the flight you missed and I never have trouble making it. Of course, you have to get up a little early, but I guess that sort of thing is beneath you. Never mind that, now. I have a question for you: Where did you learn to cook the company's books?"

Hershel looked even more hurt. What's more, he looked put-upon as well. Raising his eyebrows almost to his hairline, he asked, "What in the world are you talking about, Rose?" Now he was not only hurt and put-upon, he was also extremely uncomfortable. The fact that he had neglected to pique Rose by calling her 'Rosie' bore out the fact that he was squirming. He went on, "What's that supposed to mean, anyway?"

Rose answered with no inconsiderable satisfaction in her voice, "There is only one meaning that I know of to the term 'cooking books'. I'm asking you where you got the smarts to alter our books to try and cover up the fact that you have been embezzling a great deal of money from my company. I can't imagine what made you think you could get away with it. Not only did I gain my degree in accounting, but we also retain an excellent auditing firm to keep watch on our accounts. It ought to be quite interesting to see the results of the audit I have requested; an audit, I might add, that is already in progress as of this morning." Rose not only sounded satisfied, she looked pretty pleased with herself as well.

Hershel was having none of this. "Wait a minute, here. Who do you think you are, accusing me of embezzling? I ought to sue you for defamation of character!"

Rose leaned a little further back in her chair and replied, "I'd wait until the audit is complete before I did any suing, if I were you. Remember, you took charge of the accounting department and you are responsible for the proper administration of it. Even if you aren't the one who is doing the embezzling, you are still culpable. But, that's not the case, and the audit will bear me out. You are the one who actually altered the entries and that will be easy to prove. You might as well own up to it and take the consequences." By this time Rose had interlaced her fingers across her ample middle.

Hershel was left speechless, but only for a moment or two. "So, why did you call me up here to New York? Why didn't you just wait for the auditors to blow the whistle on me and watch me fry?" He didn't know what she was up to, but he was certainly willing to wait and see rather than to confess. He didn't have long to wait.

"There's a way out of this for you, Hershel, and you might want to give it serious thought." Rose sat upright in her chair and fixed Hershel with a steady gaze. She was nodding her head slightly, moving her entire body in the process and causing her chair to emit a tiny squeak with each nod.

Not knowing what else to do, he went along with her for the moment. "So, what is this way out you're proposing?" He decided that if he looked mildly amused, it might shake Rose's confidence. He put on his best mildly amused look.

Rose was not shaken, but answered, "I'm not proposing anything, but I will state a fact: A wife cannot testify against her husband in court." With that, she went from nodding to swiveling back and forth in her chair. This was terribly annoying to Hershel.

"So, I get it; if I were to marry you that would shut you up and you couldn't put the finger on me. But, how do you propose to call off the auditors?" He still couldn't quite figure out what she was getting at.

Leaning forward, her palms flat on her desktop, she rejoined, "One thing at a time. Are you going to marry me or not?"

"Okay, okay, you got me; but, what about the auditors? How're you going to get them outa my hair?" Hershel was sweating.

"We can talk about that after you propose." Rose could not conceal her delight.

Barely below a shout Hershel answered, "Awright, awright; Rose Mandel, will you marry me?" He looked sick to his stomach.

"Yes, I will!" Rose giggled. "And, don't worry about the auditors, I was just kidding about calling an audit. I was pretty sure you would listen to reason." She ran around to the front of her desk and hugged her fiancé. "There's just one other thing."

She held Hershel tight in her embrace until he asked in a muffled voice, "Oh yeah? What's that?"

"My name is Rose, not Rosie, or any of your other clever, annoying names. You slip up just once and the whole deal's off. Got it?"

"I got it; you win," was his morose reply.

Pinching Hershel's cheek between pudgy forefinger and thumb, Rose cooed, "Now that we've got all that ironed out, what do you say we make some plans for moving your office up here to New York." She could not conceal the glee in her voice as she continued, "Ma and I will take care of the wedding plans."

It was necessary for Yetsye and Nathan to set aside their differences temporarily in order to put on the wedding production that their daughter demanded. Though Yetsye was anything but a woman of faith, Nathan was an orthodox Jew who lived out his faith and required those around him to make the obligatory adjustments. *Ergo,* Rose and Hershel's matrimonial ceremony must embody strictest Jewish tradition if they were going to expect Nathan to cooperate in the disposal of his daughter. After all, Nathan was none too fond of Hershel in the first place. Accordingly, it was decided by the kallah (bride) and her mother that the wedding would take place in Miami, on the grounds of Yetsye's villa, where there was a suitable site on which the chuppah (wedding canopy) could be erected. Even before she left New York to make her wedding preparations, Rose employed the services of a rabbi, who was also a qualified attorney, in order to have crafted for her a most comprehensive and iron-clad ketubah (marriage contract), which would stand her in good stead later on. In addition to being a binding legal document, this device was also a beautiful work of art, suitable for framing. When he was confronted with the invoices for all of the legal, religious, and festive services that the wedding demanded, Nathan, for a fleeting second only, considered renouncing his faith and refusing to give Rose a Jewish wedding. After all, he maintained, they would be just as married if the deed were done by a justice of the peace in a courthouse office. Eventually he relented but nearly fainted when he totted up all the numbers.

In keeping with Jewish tradition, the kallah and chatan (groom) were not allowed to see each other for an entire week prior to the wedding ceremony. Hershel regarded this as one of very few bright spots in an otherwise disagreeable and stressful experience. Even so, the wedding ceremony itself was to him an agonizing and embarrassing incident in his life, what with having to greet dozens and dozens of celebrants whom he had never had the pleasure of meeting, clumsily carrying out the Badeken (veiling of his plump kallah), and the extreme discomfort of having to share the chuppah with Rose, the rabbi, Yetsye and Nathan, and his own parents as well. He felt caged in and several times the structure threatened to collapse on being nudged by one or more of the portly occupants. The rabbi was none too slender himself. Adding to Hershel's discomfort was the fact that traditionally the kallah and chatan are to wear no jewelry while they are under the chuppah. He felt naked without his diamond ring and his Rolex. He took to fidgeting while the rabbi read the ketubah, primarily because this was his first hearing of it; and later he was calmed somewhat by the drinking of a cup of wine while the rabbi recited myriad blessings. He nearly polished off the entire cup, leaving precious little for his kallah to drink. She need not have worried, as a second cup was provided to them later while the Sheva Brachot (seven blessings) were read by the same rabbi. Such was the quality of the wine that the chatan (Hershel) had no little difficulty zeroing in on the glass that he was to shatter with his foot. Since he had no interest whatsoever in the symbolism of this act, Hershel was not to know it represented his 'putting his foot down' for the final time. As he and Rose walked erratically (the wine) away from the chuppah, to the varied shouts of "Mazel Tov" from the guests, Hershel was anticipating his escape but was gravely disappointed to learn that the wedding was far from over. First, there was the Yichud, in which the then married couple were escorted to a private 'yichud room' and left alone there for a few awkward minutes; an act that signified their new status of living together as husband and wife. While Rose chattered gaily, Hershel uttered not a sullen word. Though the couple had been required to fast since morning, they were finally allowed, at this point, something to eat. This tiny symbolic snack led them immediately into a horrendous Seudah, or festive meal, which more properly resembled a banquet. There were barrels of wine and tons of food consumed, much music and dancing indulged in and, it seemed to Rose at least, a great deal of scandalous behavior exhibited by the vast majority of the guests. By the time the kallah and chatan staggered into Yetsye's guestroom it was after two in the morning, and they both were dog-tired. Perhaps this was the reason it took large Jewish families a while to get off the ground.

Two days subsequent to the nuptial activities, the bride and groom traveled leisurely up the east coast in Rose's Mercedes, with the bride doing the preponderance of the driving while Hershel steamed with chagrin. In anticipation of her success in capturing Hershel for her husband, Rose had had the foresight to lease a modish home in an affluent neighborhood on Staten Island, in the Rosebank area, where the home, even though expensive, had a small-town feel to it along with a spectacular view of the New York skyline. Here the newlywed couple settled into a routine of hard work coupled with an uneasy home life.

A year passed swiftly by, during which Hershel's office was relocated to the same building as Rose's, but on a lower floor. This single act, placing Hershel's office on a floor lower than the eighth, was probably the initial event in the coming apart of the couple's marriage. Though Hershel, as far as his job was concerned, had repented and was applying himself to his work with some diligence, his accounting department was nowhere near as efficient and productive as the other sectors of Mandel Family Apparel. It was with the greatest effort that Rose resisted chastising, or even criticizing, her husband on the poor performance of the part of the company that was his responsibility. However, the fact remained that her company was suffering at the hands of her husband, and she was at a total loss as to what she should do about it. Several times her auditors had informed her that the accounting at Mandel Family Apparel was sloppy and dangerously errant; a situation that had developed only in the few months prior, and one that she must remedy before too much damage resulted.

Rose Mandel-Feldman sat at her desk idly shuffling reports from one side to the other, when she abruptly jumped from her chair and literally ran to her bathroom, arriving in the vicinity of the toilet just in time to hurl the contents of her stomach into the bowl. Anyone who had not seen her in the previous six months would not at that time have recognized her. No longer was she roughly as round as she was tall. No longer did her hair hang in straight, oily strands down to her cheeks; but now, with her weight reduced to just over half her former bulk, her hair stylishly done every day, and her complexion somehow miraculously cleared up, she actually looked quite attractive, albeit not truly pretty. But, the results of her efforts to appeal to her husband were more than apparent, and it was to her credit that she had literally transformed her appearance by the arduous weight-loss process of diet and exercise. The improvement in her diet most likely was the root of the like improvement in her complexion. In any case, Rose had put formidable effort into making herself more attractive to her husband, and the results were impressive indeed. The consequence of her physical transformation was also the cause of her current morning sickness. The poor girl retched and heaved for some minutes before finally returning to her desk where she touched the TALK button on her intercom and summoned Arielle into her office. When her assistant stood before her, Rose spoke, "Arielle, Honey, I think I need to go home. Try to hold the fort as best you can and don't take any guff from my husband. If he gives you any grief, just hand him the phone and tell him you're not authorized to deal with him." Rose rode the elevator down to the lobby and signaled for Bernard, the doorman, to hail her a cab. When Hershel arrived home at seven-fifteen, Rose was in bed asleep, her faint snoring being the only sound in an otherwise silent house. When Hershel peered into the bedroom, Puffy the poodle ran and hid under the bed.

Seven and a half months later, Isabelle Feldman entered the world, screaming at the top of her lungs. From the first moments of her life onward the daughter of Hershel and Rose Feldman had a full head of rich, dark hair and a lusty, commanding voice. As Hershel drew closer and closer to his daughter in the ensuing months, he also grew farther and farther distant from his wife. This seemed to suit Rose just fine, and she set out to immerse herself in motherhood, doting on Isabelle with a passion she had heretofore given over only to business. The child seemed somehow to be able to take in stride the extreme tension between her mother and her father; and she emerged from infancy a well-balanced and even-tempered girl despite the quarrelsome environment in which she was required to live.

Chapter Three

The sleek, silver corporate jet climbed steeply out of Zurich airspace and leveled off, temporarily, at eighteen thousand feet, heading for Long Island, New York's MacArthur Airport. A stunning young Eurasian woman sat in a window seat in the lounge of the craft and watched as Lake Zurich slipped by under the wing. The woman's completely black hair, gathered in a bun at the back, matched very closely the virtual blackness of her large, expressive eyes. Clad in a dress of Asian style, red in color, with Mandarin collar and black trim, she was stunning not only due to her hair, eyes, and dress, but also because of her clear, tawny skin and striking figure. It hardly seemed possible that one so beautiful could be uncommonly intelligent, but she was that as well. Having attended first, at a very early age, the Sorbonne Paris, and later taken post-graduate degrees in business and law at the University of Greifswald in Germany, the young Hong Kong-born woman had spent much of her recent life traveling about Europe. The daughter and only child of a Swiss banker and a Chinese opera star, she was given the birth name Nhung Karen (pronounced *'Kahren'*) Boschert.

The layout of the jet's cabin was such that Karen needed only to swivel in her seat in order to face a conference table that was centered in the cabin and could be addressed by the seats on either side. Seated across from and facing the young woman was a man of fifty plus, with wavy silver hair and hazel eyes. He, too, was in Asian attire; a suit of pale beige that must have been tailored in Hong Kong, having lavish, flamboyant lines and made of lush material. Beside him was a slight man of Korean birth, impeccably dressed and clean-shaven, his gleaming black hair combed in perfectly straight lines, front-to-back. His black suit jacket was unsuccessful in concealing a handgun at his side, the butt facing forward. The two men spoke quietly in German, the Korean, Lee Min-jun, having great difficulty with pronunciation. When the woman turned to face the other two, the gray-haired man spoke to her in clipped German, spitting his words through clenched teeth, and drumming perfectly manicured fingers on the conference table as he asked, "Am I to understand, my dear Karen, that you have indeed made contact with this Hershel Feldman person?" The gentleman's German was impeccable, as his English would later prove to be.

Her answer was just the least bit disconcerting to the man, "In a manner of speaking, I would say so, Eminence." Karen so addressed the man facing her, knowing no other way to do so. How does one who was educated in Europe, without sounding obsequious, address a former statesman who is also the president of a worldwide banking and investment company? She continued, "I have thus far managed to form an alliance with the auditing firm that serves his employer, and I am assured that I am to be involved in the upcoming audit of that same firm. At that time I plan to befriend Mr. Feldman and gain his confidence. I hope this is sufficient for your purposes, Sir." She also expressed the hope that her English, though a bit halting at times, would not prove too clumsy-sounding in the company of Americans.

Apparently it was acceptable because the gentleman, who was known internationally as the Hon. Anton Klausman, and acknowledged as the last word in banking and investment matters, nodded with what seemed to be acceptance, if not total satisfaction. "Very well," he offered; then continued, "I trust, My Dear, that you will not find this assignment too distasteful. It has been conveyed to me that the subject, Hershel Feldman, that is, possesses a certain magnetism as well as what one might call an American attractiveness.

These two assets are offset, unfortunately, by a typical American super-ego that could, if you allow it, turn you against the entire project. He is, furthermore, a hedonist and a profligate, given to avarice and calumny; obstreperous in the extreme. You must stay focused, I pray, on the matter at hand and resist all temptations to become otherwise involved. Have I made myself clear?"

"Most assuredly, Eminence," was Karen's instant response. She went on, "If you have nothing else to discuss with me, I have a great deal of studying to do." Klausman turned from her without another word signaling to her that the discussion was concluded.

Swiveling back to face forward in her seat, Karen opened a pigskin attaché case and rifled through a stack of documents, attempting to put them in some semblance of order so that she could begin her study of the financial and accounting particulars of Mandel Family Apparel. From what she had gathered so far, the antics of Hershel Feldman, though abstruse to all but an expert accountant, should not require undue effort or extraordinary wisdom for one such as herself to apprehend. All she needed was some time and diligence and she should easily be able to confront Mr. Feldman with his malefactions.

Moments later she heard the pitch of the plane's engines increase, and at the same time felt the vessel begin to accelerate and climb to higher altitude. In the cockpit, the pilot and copilot exchanged grins as they experienced the impressive performance of the newly acquired aircraft. Both looked forward to career record Atlantic crossings. Neither was disappointed. Save for the unprecedented luxury and efficiency of the airplane and crew, the flight was otherwise uneventful, ending with a silky-smooth landing at the field on Long Island; and forty minutes ahead of schedule at that. Karen, Klausman, and his bodyguard deplaned first, followed by a half dozen assorted employees of the firm. Last off were the crew, with the entire retinue heading on foot to the main terminal building, where a black limousine awaited Klausman and Lee Min-jun. They would be whisked in grand style to a luxury hotel in Manhattan while Karen and the other lesser personnel would make their way to their ultimate destinations by various means. Karen took the train into the city of New York and hailed a cab to her apartment in the West Village. She was to report to her new job in four day's time.

Mabel Carter had once met Jaclyn Smith in person, but she had to admit the famous actress and beauty of "Charlie's Angels" fame had nothing on the girl with whom she was presently shaking hands. Karen Boschert, the young woman who stood facing Mabel as the two shook hands, was so strikingly and sublimely beautiful that the latter found herself even more astounded than she had been when she met the actress. Perhaps the Asian element of Karen's loveliness, adding an element of mystery as it did, further impressed Mabel; or could it have been the exquisite juxtaposition of innocence and sensuality that went to make up Karen's mien? In either case, Mabel was so stunned that she was momentarily rendered speechless. She gestured for Karen to take a seat in front of her desk, behind which she seated herself in her own well-worn chair. For some moments Mabel studied the girl facing her, asking herself rhetorical questions: Why had the parent corporation of the auditing firm with whom she had been employed for over eighteen years seen fit to send an auditor from their headquarters in Switzerland all the way to New York to perform an audit that she herself could accomplish with aplomb? If, for some reason, they found it necessary to do so, why send such a ravishing beauty? The wisdom of such a maneuver escaped her. She vowed she would not be tempted to resent the intrusion of such a formidable influence, and that she would do her absolute best to cooperate with the girl and with the authority that had sent her.

Regaining her usual composure, she addressed the girl before her, "Miss Boschert—may I call you Karen—do you currently reside in the United States?"

Karen colored just slightly as she responded, "Of course I do not mind using our first names but, if you will not mind, I would be more at ease if you would pronounce my name *Kahren* rather than the American way. I am accustomed to being so addressed, you see." Her smile was so engaging that Mabel could find no offense in Karen's request. The girl continued, "I have taken a flat in the Village and had the last four days to find my way about. I am now settled in and feel quite at home already. Originally I had thought it would be necessary for me to travel by taxi but I find the subway system to be adequate under most circumstances. I am relieved to find I will not need to taxi very often."

Mabel reacted in her usual friendly manner, "I'm only too glad to comply, Karen." She pronounced her name as the girl had requested. "I look forward to working with you and I want us to be friends, not just co-workers. If you need any help finding your way, please ask any of us in the office. So, why don't I introduce you to the rest of the staff?" She was amazed and gratified by the way Karen handled the admiring stares afforded her by women and men alike. When the introductions were concluded, Mabel had a few more questions, "Karen, will there be times and circumstances when you will require our assistance? We want you to know we are at your disposal. There was no mention made of what your requirements might be so I took the liberty of setting up a small office for you. Is that okay with you?"

Karen checked herself before answering. She had been instructed to appropriate 'Miss Carter's' office, but thought better of it. She believed it would be far more important to establish a good working relationship with the indigenous staff than to maximize her working conditions. After all, she certainly did not need an office as large as Mabel's in order to conduct an audit by herself. Her answer reflected her attitude, "All I really need, Mabel, is a desk, a chair, a filing cabinet, a small table, and an Ethernet connection—or are you wireless? I have my own computer, you see. Actually, I might need occasional help in gathering data, but I shouldn't think that will be much of an imposition for you. Do you know? I think we are going to get along famously." Her smile sealed the deal.

The office Mabel had assigned to Karen was perfect. It was small but comfortable as well as fully furnished and equipped. No more than a dozen steps from the elevators, and equally convenient to the ladies' room and a cheery break room, the office was more than satisfactory. Thanking Mabel and patting her forearm, Karen withdrew into her office and set about establishing her networks with her home office in Switzerland along with the accounting office of Mandel Family Apparel. It was with considerable difficulty, requiring several tense telephone calls, that she established any sort of connection with the latter. It seemed that Hershel's whereabouts were unknown, or possibly held in confidence, so that none of the personnel could obtain permission to establish a network connection with a party unknown to them without the participation of their department head.

To Anton Klausman, staying at the Ritz-Astoria Hotel near Central Park was simply a given. If there were a better choice, he was disinterested, because his regular suite stood ready for his arrival on practically no notice. Further, he was on first-name speaking terms with all the staff members with whom he would normally be involved, and all their gifts as well as their foibles were well known to him. Klausman was not favorably impressed by surprises; he much preferred to know ahead of time with precisely what he would be confronted. Yet, the Ritz was not only Klausman's hotel of choice, it was, for all intents and purposes, his New York 'office', where he set up his headquarters while he was in The Big Apple. In anticipation of Klausman's arrival, the hotel staff always brought in skilled technicians who would test and verify all private communication lines and equipment so that their esteemed client could get right down to business as soon as he pleased. To Klausman, these services on the part of the hotel were merely assumed, and he took them for granted as due one of his lofty station. All of these factors notwithstanding, Klausman's primary purpose in heading straight for the Ritz-Astoria when he arrived in New York was the absolute necessity for him to be available should Mr. Daemon desire his company. This present visit was no exception. As he took the private V.P. elevator up to his suite, he dispatched a bellman to Mr. Daemon's modest room (if a room at the Ritz could be so described), where the latter would be informed of Klausman's arrival. Invariably, the same emissary would then return to Klausman's suite bearing an invitation to dine in Mr. Daemon's room.

Klausman was ready when the bellman returned and remembered to read the invitation only as an afterthought. Due to the lateness of the hour, the dinner invitation was for the following evening, giving Klausman the present evening to himself. He thought of ringing up Karen but dismissed the idea as a show of excessive interest in one of a station lower than his own. Better to leave the girl in suspense for the time being. He elected, instead, to change into a cashmere smoking jacket, silk shirt, and ascot; then summoned the elevator, which he rode to the mezzanine where he exited the car and strode briskly to his favorite lounge. He was instantly recognized and greeted by the veteran barman, Elliot, who directed him to his favorite table. There he settled into a comfortable chair with a sigh and, when Elliot stood at his side, ordered an expensive cognac. No more than half an hour later he was joined by an elegant lady wearing a revealing frock; one who smoked cigarette after cigarette through a ten-inch cigarette holder. They parted company shortly after midnight.

Eight o'clock the following evening found Klausman boarding alone the V.P. elevator, bound for Mr. Daemon's room. Rather than ring the bell, he knocked gently and waited through the inevitable lengthy delay. First, there was the distinct sound of the chain lock, then the rotation of a deadbolt, and finally, the tentative opening of the door until the chain restrained it to a gap of an inch or two. A barely audible voice asked, "Yes, who is it?"

Hardly more audibly was, "Klausman here, Excellency. May I come in?" The former had dressed for the occasion in wool slacks, a beige silk shirt, and a camelhair sweater. On his feet were Gucci slip-ons.

As he slipped the chain from its slot, Mr. Daemon replied, "By all means enter, Anton." The door swung wider, revealing a timorous and diminutive man of perhaps seventy-five; certainly no more than five feet-four inches tall, nearly white hair growing in wisps scattered in patches over a pink scalp. His face flushed from rosacia and pocked from sun damage, he appeared ill and feverish. The hand that he extended to Klausman bore a slight tremor and felt soft and dry to the touch. As he shuffled back to his easy chair, Mr. Daemon looked none too steady on his feet and, when he reached the chair, he seemed to just crumple up and collapse into a bent-over sitting position. As he leaned back against the chair, he wheezed, "Well now, Anton, what brings you to New York?" The question seemed to deplete the supply of air in his lungs.

If he didn't know better, Klausman would have been alarmed at Mr. Daemon's apparent condition but, as it was, he knew that this was perfectly normal for the old man and he proceeded to answer, "Perhaps you have forgotten momentarily, Sir, but you had previously instructed me to come across from Zurich on this date in order that we might confer. I regret that I arrived so late yesterday that our meeting had to be delayed until this evening. Will we be conferring before or after our dinner, Sir?"

Mr. Daemon coughed gently and blinked pinkish eyes before replying, "Ah, yes, of course, Anton, how forgetful of me. I tell you, in the words of Winston Churchill, 'Old age is intolerable.' I had hoped that my mind would not go before the rest of me did. Well, in any case, let us dine and relax a bit before we get to business. You are hungry, are you not?" Not waiting for Klausman's reply, Mr. Daemon, with much huffing and puffing, heaved himself out of his easy chair and walked unsteadily into his dining area where a table was set for two to dine. From in front of his own place, he picked up a tiny brass bell and gave it a little shake, causing it to tinkle in sympathy with his tremor. In no more than ten seconds, a wiry Asian man, probably Chinese, slipped into the room bearing a large tray on which were two covered dinner plates, two crystal fruit cups, and two empty china cups on saucers. Also on the tray was a matching teapot, a thread of steam curling from its spout. In no more time than it takes to tell it, the man, whose name was Yong Se (a made-up sobriquet because his actual Chinese name was virtually unpronounceable to most Westerners), had set down and arranged the two places, this taking place before Mr. Daemon and Klausman had a chance to seat themselves. In fact, Yong Se had time left over in which to hold Mr. Daemon's chair for him. As usual, Klausman was disappointed in the meal set before him. There were a miniscule piece of boiled chicken breast, two steamed asparagus spears, and what appeared to be about a tablespoonful of brown rice. As usual, none of it had any flavor whatsoever and, what was worse; there were no salt and pepper shakers anywhere to be seen. The fruit cups contained strained applesauce. There was, however, ample tea for them both. This was hardly what Klausman considered dinner, but then, he always left these meetings with Mr. Daemon famished. Yong Se left the room without Klausman's noticing.

While Klausman polished off his meager fare in a minute or two, Mr. Daemon never seemed actually to finish his, but merely wiped his mouth elaborately and pushed himself back from the table, signaling to Klausman that it was permissible for him to do likewise. It was Mr. Daemon who spoke first, "Tell me, Anton, how are you getting on with this Feldman fellow? I am informed that his malicious behavior has resulted in the endangerment of his marriage. Does this cause you any consternation?"

Klausman began his reply, but was unable to complete it, "Not at all, Excellency...."

Mr. Daemon interrupted him, saying, "Really, Anton, I prefer that you not be so formal at our intimate meetings. My surname is perfectly acceptable in the present circumstances."

"Yes, of course, Mr. Daemon." Klausman resumed, "As I was saying, I am not at all concerned. We have, as of this meeting, made an excellent beginning. Only last week, I was able to retain the services of an outstanding agent—outstanding in many ways—yes, indeed. She is an absolutely stunning creature, name of Nhung Karen Boschert, and she is eminently qualified for the work we have for her. In addition to her astonishing beauty, which should accelerate her gaining Feldman's confidence, she is certainly no one's fool, having gained her master's at the Sorbonne, and her doctorate at Greifswald. At a mere twenty-three, she is a virtual genius. Well, perhaps I exaggerate, but she is intelligent, to say the least. Before I had completely explained her mission to her, she had grasped the situation and offered a few suggestions of her own. For instance, she suggested that, if we had positioned her say, in a bar in order to meet Feldman, he could easily become suspicious; but rather, we should place her in a position from which she could make contact on a business level, then he would be far less likely to suspect her. Her rationale here is that Feldman spends so much time socializing in bars, that would be the natural scenario in which one would be most likely to attempt to infiltrate his life. On the other hand, since he spends such an inordinate amount of time out of his office, that is hardly the place one would choose to make contact with him. Clever, no?"

During Klausman's discourse, Mr. Daemon appeared to have dozed off but, as soon as the former paused a moment, Daemon, his eyes fluttering open, remarked, "Hmm, well, yes, she sounds suitable, but that name—what was it—Nhung; it seems a bit of a mouthful, does it not?"

"Precisely my sentiments, Excel...er...Mr. Daemon. That is why I suggested to her that she use her middle name. The way she prefers to pronounce it, *Kahren*, retains a certain mystique, don't you think? That should appeal to Feldman's—ahem—romantic side." Klausman was unable to conceal his satisfaction with himself. He went on, "This very day Miss Boschert has begun her temporary employment with Klausman, Walther, und Hahn, GmbH; the New York office, of course. Her first assignment has been to conduct a thorough audit of the accounting department at Mandel Family Apparel, this department being under Feldman's management.

Before Klausman was able to elaborate, he was interrupted, once more, by Mr. Daemon, "Ah, yes, Mrs. Mandel-Feldman is the C.E.O. of said corporation; founded, I believe by her father, Nathan Mandel. I must say, she rather pulled his carcass out of the soup, eh what? Almost anyone with any business acumen would have written that company off while the old man was tinkering with it. The smartest thing he ever did was to turn it over to his daughter. What would you judge that firm to be worth these days, Anton?"

Klausman, a bit piqued at being trumped on the subject of the details of Mandel Family Apparel, merely assented, "Just so, Sir. I would not even hazard a guess. Perhaps fifty million dollars?"

"You are an incurable pessimist, Anton. The last reports I read indicated nearly double that. Of course, the company, with a properly managed accounting department, would doubtless be of even more worth than it presently is, you see. I need not point out to you that this very fact should—and must—be brought to Mrs. Mandel-Feldman's attention at the very earliest possible opportunity, in order that her husband's incompetence may be seen by her as perfect justification for your intervention. Perhaps you would be good enough to implement that very notion within the next day or two. Now, if you will pardon me, I must retire. You can find your way out, can you not? Good night, then. Oh, by the way, Anton: beware, my friend, lest you tumble into the very trap you are setting for Mr. Feldman. She sounds irresistible." With that, Mr. Daemon simply staggered out of Klausman's presence and into his bedroom, closing the door behind him.

As he rode the elevator to his own floor, Klausman reflected on his various encounters with Mr. Daemon. It seemed to him that, although he had entered every meeting with the resolve to assert himself and to gain the advantage over the feeble old man, he invariably walked away from every one having been vanquished and subjugated even further. Who was this Mr. Daemon, and from what source did he derive his power? Klausman vowed he would some day gain the advantage over Daemon, even if he had to wait for the moribund old codger to expire. For some reason, he didn't fancy his chances otherwise.

After many attempts and several hours of trying, Karen finally reached Hershel Feldman on his cell phone. Background noises suggested he was in some sort of restaurant or bar. She had to speak up to be heard, "Mr. Feldman, this is Karen Boschert of the home office of Klausman, Walther, und Hahn, GmbH. I am here in the New York office attempting to set up network connections between K.W.H. and Mandel Family Apparel; and I understand, from some of your staff, that your approval is required before this can be implemented. Would you please be so kind as to provide your staff with the requisite permission so I can go about my work? I have wasted nearly an entire day trying to locate you."

Hershel's reply was a bit slurred, "Who did you say you are? I don't get it. What kind of networks are you talking about? I don't want any networks and I don't know who Walter Santa Claus und Lipshitz is. I'm busy right now. You'll have to talk to my secretary who happens to be out at the moment. Ta Ta." His phone beeped when he pressed END.

Karen re-dialed and got Hershel right away. Her tone led him to conclude she was in no mood to play games, "Listen to me, you drunken idiot! I am going to audit Mandel Family Apparel with or without your permission; so you would be advised to sober up and meet me in your office in exactly one hour. Do you comprehend what I am saying?" She pressed END on her phone and placed it carefully in her purse.

"HEY! Hold that elevator, OK?" As he called out toward the elevator whose doors were beginning to close, Hershel discovered his voice had taken on a squeaky character due, possibly, to the four martinis he had swilled for lunch. When he saw that someone in the elevator car was holding the doors open for him, he sauntered toward the open car, taking his own sweet time about it. Why should he hurry just so some peon wouldn't have to wait for him? He entered the car, which was populated by a maintenance man, the one who had held the door for him, and two middle-aged women who looked like they may have been order-pickers. He stared at the ceiling of the car. Both of the women sniffed and gave him dirty looks, but he ignored them. So what if he smelled a little bit of vodka? What was so egregious about having a little drinky-poo at lunchtime? It tended to steady the nerves. He kept his eyes glued to the ceiling of the car.

31

When the elevator lurched to a stop and the doors burst open, Hershel nearly passed out. Heading right for him, her head held high and her heals tapping sharply on the marble floor, was the most fantastically gorgeous creature he had ever laid eyes on. Swaying a little from the effects of a surfeit of alcohol, he tried to smooth his jacket while simultaneously putting on his best irresistible smile. He had never in his life seen a girl so sublimely beautiful and desirable, yet so pristine and innocent looking. As he stepped from the elevator car, and the girl stepped toward it, he greeted her through his smile, using his very best and prurient pick-up line, "Hey, Babe, you going up or down? You probably need an escort. Don't worry, Hershel Feldman's here to help." He tried to capture her gaze but she looked straight through him as she entered the car, thanking the maintenance guy for holding the door for her. The maintenance man was incapable of speech. He was no worse off than Hershel who was left standing in front of the closing elevator doors, his mouth hanging ajar and his pungent breath coming in gasps. Finally, after having recovered a small measure of his composure, he headed for his office where he sought out his secretary-assistant, Kevin. Rose had hired Kevin for her husband knowing full well that if she had left the task to Hershel that there would be a total knockout, probably a ditzy blonde, sitting at the secretary's desk. As it turned out, Kevin was not only a man, but also a very competent and conscientious one at that. To Rose, the best part of Kevin was his love for and devotion to his wife and two kids.

Rounding the corner into his office, Hershel called out, "Hey, Kev, did you see that positive love-goddess that just got on the elevator?"

Kevin was already grinning when he replied, "She's something else, isn't she? That's *Kahren* from the home office in Switzerland, and she was here looking for you, you lucky dog! I think she's gone up to your wife's office—

'cause you weren't here on time, I guess." When he realized Karen would probably not return anytime soon, Kevin looked crestfallen. He would have given up his lunch in order to witness Hershel's being taken apart piece by piece at the hands of the sumptuous Karen.

Rose Mandel-Feldman regarded the exquisite creature facing her across the gleaming mahogany expanse of her desk. Her mind racing with distress born of suspicion, she could not imagine how she would be able to prevent her husband from becoming involved romantically, albeit temporarily so, with this girl. It seemed to her so inevitable that she fell into despair from the mere contemplation of it. Summoning every ounce of cordiality that she could, she addressed Karen, "So, when do you propose to begin this audit, Miss Boschert?"

Karen began, "Well, I had initially thought I would be able to begin this morning, but your husband being unavailable to give his employees permission to turn over to me certain files and documents, Mrs. Mandel-Feldman..."

"Whoa, there, young lady, we need to start over here. Suppose you call me Rose and I'll call you Karen and we'll go on from there. Mandel-Feldman is much too cumbersome to allow smooth conversation." For some strange reason she could conjure up no dislike for this girl.

Karen answered and said, "What a relief! The only thing I ask of you is that you pronounce it *Kahren*, which is the way I have heard it pronounced from my youth and the version to which I most easily respond. Is that, ah (the Eurasian version of 'uh'), acceptable to you, Rose?" She pronounced the name perilously close to '*Rosa*'.

Smiling broadly, Rose replied, "Excellent! Please continue."

"As I was saying, Rose," Karen could not help but smile as she went on, "I was forced to wait until I could reach your husband on his mobile phone, no mean feat, mind you, before I could access the necessary data from your accounting department so that I could proceed with my audit. I am rather surprised to learn that it is he rather than yourself whom I was required to contact initially. Is this a custom unique to America, that of giving accounting department managers that authority; or is it due entirely, in the case of Mandel Family Apparel, that the department manager is also your husband? I must say, this is unusual for me."

Rose sat quietly looking at her hands, trying mightily to check her temper, before she could form her answer; and this she did carefully, "I, I must apologize to you, Karen, for the inconvenience you have suffered. I'm afraid my husband is a little on the insufferable side, but that doesn't give him the right to impede the progress of your audit. The responsibility is completely mine and I promise you I will see to it that you have full cooperation from all of our employees, including my husband. I'm sorry, Dear. Could I offer you something— perhaps coffee or tea? I also have soda."

Karen gratefully accepted a Coca Cola but, having spent so little time in the U.S., was surprised at how cold it was. She sipped it slowly, waiting for it to warm a little. Also, she held the glass to her lips in order to allow it to tickle her nose, a sensation she rarely experienced at home. Together, later on, the two women walked down the hall to the elevators on their way to the accounting department offices. They chatted while they awaited a car. When the doors swept open, there stood a breathless Hershel, looking a bit harried and damp with perspiration.

Rose spoke first, "Darling! Here you are! We were just coming down to your office. You must meet *Kahren* Boschert of the home office of Klausman, Walther, and Hahn in Zurich." Turning to Karen, she said proudly, "This is my husband, Hershel Feldman." Then, to both, she suggested, "Suppose we all go back to my office. It may not be quite as luxurious as Hershel's, but it's adequate, I think."

The sarcasm of this last may have escaped Karen, but certainly not Hershel. He glared at his wife, but only for a split second, before he turned on his most winsome smile as he faced Karen. As the two women preceded him in the hallway back to Rose's office, Hershel was able to size up Karen from the rear. As a result, his gait was unsteady at best. As they all took seats in Rose's office, Hershel maneuvered their selections so that he was able to settle into a seat facing Karen, thereby enabling himself to establish eye contact with the girl; at least, that was his intention. Karen would allow him only fleeting, short-lived continuity; rather, she made certain her own attention was fastened primarily on Rose. During the course of a half hour meeting, it was decided among them that Karen would meet Hershel in his office at nine o'clock each weekday morning, for the purpose of conducting a thorough audit of Mandel Family Apparel's books, until such time that Karen was satisfied that her audit was accomplished. In order to minimize Karen's travel expenses, in terms of both time expended and subway fares, Rose assigned her the use of the office of one of the girls who was currently on maternity leave. Rose also stipulated that she would make herself available to Karen for consultation at the latter's bidding. The reasoning behind this last was perfectly transparent to Hershel, and he resented it. After all, didn't she trust him?

Chapter Four

With a snort, Mr. Horace Daemon abruptly sat up in bed. In the space of a half-second he went from a sound, dreamless sleep to a state of complete alertness. The transition was instantaneous. Glancing out into the night through a billowing curtain, he saw in the distance occasional flashes of lightning, the jagged streaks smeared by the curtain's gauze. Rain, which had been coming in torrents during a late winter storm, was diminishing in intensity to a steady, icy downpour. If daylight did not come soon, ice would begin to form on power lines, car roofs, and anything else not warmed by the earth or the heat of the buildings. As his gaze swept across the room to his bedside chair where his clothes lay, he caught a glimpse of the digital clock's citrine numerals: 3:32 AM. Pulling the sheet and blanket from his lower extremities, he slipped out of bed and reached for his black, nondescript trousers. On his feet he put tattered gray wool socks under scuffed and worn black, ankle-length lace-up boots. Over his long undershirt he wore an iron gray, long-sleeved work shirt; and, on top of that, he wriggled into a black wool coat of fingertip length, a coat that faintly resembled a Navy P-coat. It, too was frayed and badly worn. The door to his room emitted a barely audible rasp as he let himself out and turned the key in the lock, dropping the key and its attached plastic tag into his side coat pocket. For some reason, even though his boots squeaked and thumped on the carpeted floor, not a soul saw him as he made his way to the emergency stairway. Concrete steps echoing with his clumsy descent, the old man stumbled his way down fourteen flights (seven stories worth) of stairs into the service area in the hotel's basement. Even the clang of the service door went unnoticed as Daemon exited onto the asphalt parking lot in the rear of the building. The security guard standing by the service entry looked right through him and saw not a thing.

Daemon stumbled hatless into the night. The rain was constant and driving but the wind had died down, and the lightning and thunder were now distant and silent, save for the occasional felt but not heard rumble of thunder. Daemon turned right, out of the parking lot and headed toward the East River, plodding along like a mechanical toy, his cadence not altering and his head bowed in determination. Soon, what had been silver wisps of hair sprouting randomly from his head were wet cords transformed into dull gray, plastered all over his scalp. Hands jammed into his pockets and feeble-looking legs pumping in fixed cadence, he plodded doggedly on with his face absolutely devoid of expression, looking neither to the left nor to the right. Three times he was passed by patrol cars and went unseen; one time even being caught in the spotlight's beam of a patrolling officer. Still, he seemed not to exist. At last, when he had almost reached the riverfront, Daemon turned into the near blackness of an alley situated between two buildings, out of range of the purplish streetlights at either end. About halfway down the alley, his path took him alongside a rusty steel railing, which guarded a stairwell that led back in the direction he had come and down into the depths below street level. At the bottom of the stairs he turned to his left, took two more steps, and stopped in place, addressing a stained and peeling wooden door right before him. Producing an ancient-looking iron key from a pants pocket, he pushed it into the door lock and twisted. The lock complained with a shrill squeak, but yielded to the pressure of the key and the door opened, dragging on the debris at its base. The noise startled a large, fat rat and it charged Daemon's foot. An old black boot rose up and came back down with speed unbecoming such a feeble old man, and thereby Daemon pinned the filthy vermin to the threshold in front of the door. As the beast bared its yellow-brown teeth and screeched, digging at the boot with its claws, Daemon held it fixed to the concrete, adding his weight gradually until the poor rodent suffocated. When the rat went still, Daemon kicked the carcass aside and, pushing the door fully open, entered into the blackness beyond. Before he allowed the door to close completely, he reached up to his left and felt along a wall until his hand touched an oil lamp hanging by a nail. Taking a wooden match from his shirt pocket, he struck it with a cracked and dirty thumbnail, the flame flaring up and then subsiding to normal. He lighted the lamp and looked about him.

He was in an ancient factory of some kind with rusted and decaying machinery, still arranged in rows, mutely decaying after decades of non-use. The lamp projected a faceted ring of amber light around the room, revealing ages of accumulated debris, heaps of rat and bat guano, as well as the skeletal remains of various creatures. Here and there he could see stained and dusty bottles, some contained dried and hardened substances and others apparently empty, but nearly all of a barely discernable green glass. The sudden illumination by the lamp startled literally hundreds of rats and as many bats, all hell-bent for some sort of haven or other. Treading straight on, Daemon encountered another stairwell, which led to the chamber directly below. The steps were of stone, many of which were either loose or missing and, that combined with the fact that the lamp's light was not directed downward, made his descent hazardous and precarious. Even before he reached the bottom step he was aware that the lower chamber was dimly lit and, looking to his right, he saw the source of the light. Standing on a rough-hewn table of oak stood a single candlestick holding a yellowish stub of a candle, the flickering light from which cast dancing shadows about a room of the same dimensions as the one above. At the end farthest from the stairs on which Daemon stood were a large pile of coal on the right and an even larger pile of ashes on the left. Shuffling to the table, he seated himself in one of the two rotting and pealing chairs that were there waiting. The air was damp and fetid. Occasionally, drops of murky moisture would fall from the ceiling, leaving odd little spots in the dust on the table. For the most part, the room was silent; but every now and then he would swear he could hear eerie mumbling or whispering, none of which he could decipher, and all of which he could trace to no apparent source. From time to time, a being of some sort or other, part carnal and part spirit, would skitter across the room, making dry and brittle scraping noises. Or, were they not really sounds at all but figments of Daemon's imagination? Were these really creatures or were they simply vaporous notions, induced into the old man's consciousness by the ambient conditions? In either case, he simply accepted them and paid them no mind. Before long, his eyelids grew heavy and, his chin dropping to his chest, Daemon dozed. A minute, or perhaps an hour, passed and he was awakened by the intrusion of an acrid stench; and he opened his eyes to the sight of what could have been a ghastly apparition. The putrid aura told him this was no wraith but something tangible and real. Huge hands, grimy and bony, lay on the table, the nails more like talons; and the stringy arms they were attached to disappearing into the armholes of a filthy and bedraggled gown of black sackcloth. Out of the top of the gown sprouted a veined and sinewy neck atop which was perched an enormous head, from which sprang filaments of greasy black hair of shoulder length. The face was nothing short of horrifying, gray and pallid, with wild, flaming eyes, a hawk nose replete with enormous and hairy wart, and a sneering, snaggle-toothed mouth.

"Wake up, Daemon!" it snarled. The owner of the head wheezed and rasped, its breath coming in whistling gasps, with attendant puffs of smoke and yellowish flames issuing from the gaping maw. There was a most appalling, malodorous, and repugnant figure seated at the table opposite Mr. Daemon.

The latter was fully awake and alert now as he responded, "Ah, Mr. Abaddon, Your Highness, I must have dropped off." Daemon rubbed his eyes with bony, grimy knuckles. "A thousand pardons, Your Majesty. How may I be of service?" Daemon's bushy eyebrows twitched as he blinked and trembled with awe. Lifting his gaze up to address Mr. Abaddon, he saw that the latter was beginning one of his extemporaneous transformations, the sackcloth slowly fading into a fine wool suit of midnight blue, the hands taking on a refined and manicured appearance, and the face no longer monstrous but sleekly handsome, with gleaming, even teeth clutching a long cigarette holder. Abaddon's face had taken on a clear complexion and his eyes, no longer fiery but coal black, regarded Daemon with what seemed an approximation of reason.

In a voice matching his new oily and dashing appearance, Mr. Abaddon crooned, "No need for alarm, Daemon; I simply wish to know how you are progressing with the final control of our hero's life." When Abaddon emitted a polite cough, he inadvertently allowed a few sparks and a thin trail of smoke pass through his lips. "I must say, I cannot agree with your choice of bait for our Mr. Feldman. The lovely Miss Boschert strikes me as an onerous case, one whom I suggest you will experience great difficulty in corrupting. However, you have made your choice and now it remains for us to wait and see if we can mould the child into an instrument appropriate for our purposes." He coughed once more, this time allowing a few small tongues of flame to pass through his teeth. He continued, "Perhaps I myself shall undertake to bring her along; a most pleasurable prospect indeed."

Lifting his gaze to the slightly more agreeable features of the transformed Mr. Abaddon, Daemon asked, "But, Your

Highness, did we not enlist Herr Klausman for the purpose of supervising the girl?" Daemon shuddered at the thought of what arcane atrocities this archon might inflict on such a young and guileless maiden, even as the former proceeded to transmute itself into yet another figure; that of a writhing and odious, stinking dragon.

In its sibilant, crocodilian voice, the monstrous, scaly serpent assailed the old man, "Are you questioning me, Vermin? In this world I reign—I do what I wish. No chattel of mine usurps my power! You have committed two errors thus far in selecting the instruments we shall use to bring down our hero, Feldman. I have already told you that the girl you have chosen will prove to be incorruptible; and I warn you now, also, that our Mr. Klausman is full of calumny and deception. His motives are none but self-serving and rapacious. Even now he plots to vitiate and enslave the child. He will fail and I shall succeed. I will deal with him and you must immolate yourself—I no longer require your services." Having finished its invective against Daemon, the dragon flew into a spasm of hissing and writhing, eructing long tongues of flame and billows of smoke from its wide-open mouth. Effluvia of the most disgusting kind seemed to ooze from under its very scales, accompanied by the rankest, the most putrid and execrable stench imaginable. An acrid miasma pervaded the entire chamber. Mr. Daemon cowered under the attack, but made no move to leave or to defend himself, believing the assault on his fealty to be unjustified. The ephemeral dragon faded back into the initial ogre of Mr. Abaddon, wart and all; then made its exit, an evanescent, numinous ghost. As he mounted the crumbling steps, Daemon wondered if the adamantine Mr. Abaddon might be persuaded to rescind his accusation of perfidy. It was borne in upon him that the dragon never was known to renege. As he made his way back to the hotel through the drizzly, predawn morning, he reverted to his vapid attitude, plodding along mechanically, until he reached the hotel's service entrance. By rights, the sun should soon be rising but the heavy clouds blocked out any evidence of imminent dawn. The old man's body was so weary that he had no patience with it or with the locked door, but simply passed on through to the other side and, trudging to the freight elevator, made his way to his room. Yong Se, who seemed never to sleep, greeted Mr. Daemon and helped him to undress and to tumble into bed. Nevertheless, the old man slept poorly.

By eight o'clock in the morning Mr. Daemon had showered and shaved, picked at his breakfast, and had summoned Anton Klausman to his room. The latter, who truly resented having been called out so early, was surly and hardly communicative. Daemon, while he held no real sympathy for Klausman, (Indeed, under the surface, theirs was an inimical relationship at best.) felt disposed to warn him about their sovereign's intent on his subaltern's dispossession: "I say, Klausman (He could no longer address him 'Anton'.), you might want to mind your Ps and Qs regarding the scrumptious Miss Boschert. His Excellency has caused me to know in no uncertain terms that we erred in selecting her in the first place, and that you are amiss in your intentions toward her. He has vowed to present his—ahem—most attractive side to her and to woo her for his own—ah—consumption. I counsel you to keep your hands strictly off the girl." If Daemon's tone lacked conviction, it was due to the fact that he cared not at all whether or not Klausman lived or died; but, on the other hand, he deplored any successes or triumphs that might be garnered by the one who had previously that morning so derided and debased him.

Klausman didn't even attempt to conceal the contempt in his voice, "If you weren't such a decrepit old curmudgeon, I would suspect you of trying to grab the girl for yourself. But, what good would it do you, eh? You are as good as dead and His Excellency is finished with you, is he not?" Somehow, Klausman had surmised from Daemon's tone and inference, that the old man no longer need be feared.

Daemon regarded Klausman with watery, pinkish eyes and replied, "Perhaps so, Mr. Klausman, but I would not, myself, wager great sums on your survival either. The difference between us is that, while I have run the course and have no aspirations for further conquests you, in turn, have quite deceived yourself into believing that you stand even the slightest chance of winning Miss Boschert's favor. Goodness, what a terrible and tragic undoing awaits you! At any rate, I have had my say and you are free to take it to heart or not, as you see fit. Good day and farewell." The old man lifted his head proudly and, leaving Klausman standing in his living room, strode unsteadily to his bedroom and closed the door behind him.

On attempting to rouse Mr. Daemon for his lunch, Yong Se discovered his body, still dressed, lying atop the bedclothes. An ambulance having been summoned, the old man's body was examined by an EMT who opined something seemed to be amiss, adding, "This is not right. I'm going to bring in the medical examiner on this one."

The M.E. who arrived in less than an hour's time was hardly more than an intern and, in addition, had a rather poor command of the English language. He remained puzzled for quite some time before settling on an inconclusive report that stated in part: "The deceased exhibits all the characteristics of having expired at least four or five days prior to our having been called onto the case. Rigor Mortis had already set in completely and the cadaver had begun to decompose to some considerable extent. There are no signs of trauma or terminal disease, which could have caused recent death. The only conclusion that can be reached is that the subject must have perished from natural causes while asleep, and that several days before. One wonders why the event was not reported earlier." Mr. Daemon's death was never explained nor did any authority ever solve the mystery of his demise.

Chapter Five

To Hershel Feldman the New York City streets had taken on an otherworldly appearance since the last time he had paid them any mind. Could it be due to the fact that it was still dark at ten until seven in the morning? Actually, darkness had nothing to do with it. He was accustomed to roaming the streets of Manhattan in the dark hours of the early morning, but on this occasion he was 'roaming' hours later in the morning than usual. If the truth were known, Hershel was experiencing something quite new to him: going in to the office before ten or eleven in the morning. So captivated by Karen's beauty and charm was he that he found himself motivated by forces that had never before even disarranged his senses. He found himself agreeing to things to which he never before would have assented, let alone considered. After all, what reasonable human being should be required to be out and about at the unheard of hour of six-thirty A.M.? He suspected it could seriously affect his health, and in an adverse way, no doubt. The issue that piqued him most was that all of this disruption and inconvenience was being brought upon him by a mere slip of a girl—no more than a child, really—but a very, very attractive child at that. When he realized what she was doing to his reputation, he felt an utter fool. He had *never* before allowed himself to be so manipulated. Even his forced marriage to Rose had behind it a threat of serious repercussions; but this, this absolutely and incredibly untouchable beauty, offered no similar threat at all; only the promise of complete indifference to him. Not one single item in Hershel's vast repertoire of pickup lines, flirtations, showings off, or any of the other antics he considered irresistible to the opposite gender had the slightest effect on the unmovable Karen Boschert. She simply told him when and where she wished to find him and he was to report to that place and at the time specified, and that was that. To her, there were no valid excuses, nor was she impressed by his opposing reason. He was simply required to accommodate her. It was driving him mad. He had not the resources to combat her. She was a much more attractive woman than he was such a man. She was *far* more intelligent than he. She could out-stare him, out think him, bluff him into submission, and dominate him at will. Finally, he had fallen into a state of despair that had threatened to undo him.

When he exited the elevator and rounded the corner on the way to his office, Hershel became aware of a sickening anticipation that had begun to afflict him in recent days. Without even raising his eyes he knew what he would see before him: the striking, poised figure of Karen waiting outside his office door, making notations on a yellow legal pad. Somehow she had contrived to look even more devastatingly beautiful than she had the previous day. In spite of this, he found himself resenting her presence. How early would he have to arrive in order to unlock the door and enter into his own office without his doing so under the scrutiny of this angelic taskmistress? His guess was that she must have come in so early herself that the night watchman had to admit her. He was beginning to hate her nearly as much as he desired her. Another thing: how can a woman possess a voice that is both childlike and sophisticated? It defied all sense of decency.

"Good morning, Mr. Feldman," the child sophisticate greeted him. "I will not be troubling you long, but I do need some figures from you that you alone can provide." Karen followed so closely behind him as they entered his office that the scent of her caused him to reel off course a time or two. She added, "Could we go back to the month of

November....?" Thus began yet another day of tension, suspense, and frustration; a day filled with the same anxieties that had marked the preterit week; the entire period, in fact, that had comprised her first week's audit of Mandel Family Apparel.

Rose looked upon her husband's plight with a mixture of emotions. On the one hand, she was infinitely grateful that Karen had absolutely no interest in Hershel, romantic or otherwise. But there was, in Rose's relationship with Hershel, a certain maternal aspect that stirred in her a current of distress at the latter's frustrations regarding Karen. After all, these were totally uncharted waters for Hershel. No one had ever done him this way—not even Rose herself with her calumny in getting him to marry her. But, all in all, she was pleased with the situation. Hershel was completely cowed and under control, and their marriage was, apparently, unthreatened by the young goddess to whom she had taken a distinct liking. To this point, she did not see how it could have turned out any better. At length, it began to dawn on her that, if Karen were to succeed in carrying out the audit of Mandel Family Apparel, thereby exposing the mischievous procedures her husband was using to gradually drain off funds from her company, she would have to face an entirely different, and perhaps more debilitating, crisis in Hershel's life; a crisis that may very well prove to be far more damaging to his ego than that of being rejected by a beautiful girl who was little more than half his age. Rose was caught in the horns of a dilemma: On the one hand she may have to deal with a husband whose manly ego has been totally demolished. However, on the other hand she may also find herself able to avail herself of her husband's company solely during prison visiting hours. Without a doubt she must endeavor to parley some sort of compromise with Karen. Did she dare, even, to suppose that Karen would be willing to consider some sort of negotiation, especially concerning matters with which her employer had burdened her with grave responsibility?

Rose had lost the train of her conversation with Karen due, no doubt, to the fact that she simply could not drag her eyes from the girl's hands. How was she supposed to wield any sort of influence against this person? First of all, her regard for Karen was not too far removed from that which she had for her own daughter. Admittedly, Isabelle and Karen were separated in age by twenty or more years, but both embodied the same sort of wise yet reckless innocence. Both girls had the capacity to melt Rose into butter with a single guileless glance. For some reason, one that Rose could not fathom, Karen would return her look with a simple, unconniving love that Rose found altogether disarming. Why would such a beautiful and sensational creature care one whit about the wife of the man she was investigating? Naturally, Isabelle loved Rose because she was the mother who loved and nurtured her. No such bond held Karen to Rose. The very idea that Karen seemed to care about her, in a perfectly natural and innocent way of course, pushed Rose deeper into the grasp of her dilemma. Even so, she decided she must at all costs raise the issue of Hershel with this amazing new friend of hers.

"I sent Hershel, kicking and screaming all the way, down to Miami on a trumped up errand on behalf of the company. He probably suspects collusion, but I don't care; I need to talk to you with him out of the way." Rose spoke as she and Karen sat facing each other across the polished expanse of Rose's desk. "Karen, Dear, there is a matter I need to discuss with you in private, without my husband's knowledge or his interference. I really don't know how to begin, though, because it's very difficult to explain how I feel."

Karen looked steadily at her for some time before replying, "Perhaps I can help by speculating how you must feel. I suspect you already know what the outcome of my audit is going to be; that I am most certainly going to be forced to expose your husband as an embezzler, and that you want somehow to protect him from such a fate. I would not respect you as I do, Rose, if I thought you had no loyalty for your husband; nor would I respect you if I thought you were willing to abet a criminal. It would seem that, because I am very fond of you and because you are loyal to your husband, we are both caught in a terrible dilemma. What are we to do? It must seem to you that I am taking far too long to reach a conclusion to the audit but, in fact, I have known for some time what Hershel has been doing, and that it is he who is culpable. I simply have no idea what to do about it, so I have been procrastinating. Unfortunately, before long I will be forced by my employer to file my full report." As she made this final remark, Karen reached across the desk and touched Rose's hand tenderly, her eyes filling with tears. She added, "I only regret that my sadness does not extend to Hershel himself, but only to you and Isabelle. It seems to me—but perhaps I am mistaken—that he is very unkind to you, but dotes on Isabelle; an additional barb for you to endure. I deplore this because you seem so undeserving of this kind of treatment." Karen's voice was uncharacteristically tremulous.

Touched by Karen's concern, Rose said, "I'm hardly what you'd call an angel, myself. After all, I tricked Hershel into marrying me."

"How so?" Karen asked.

"Well, I caught him four years ago cooking the books and I threatened to expose him unless he married me. How could he refuse, unless he believed being married to me would be worse than a prison sentence?" Rose smiled wryly, thinking about what a trial their wedding was to Hershel. She went on, "But how else could one such as I manage to land a man like him? I'm afraid he has never forgiven me for trapping him into marriage."

Karen looked a bit bewildered as she asked, "But I do not understand. Why would he not want to marry you? You are attractive, bright, witty, and affectionate. Are not these the things of which good marriages are made?"

Rose had to laugh before she remarked, "Out of the mouths of babes...." The two women regarded each other silently for a moment, then they both laughed, but at different thoughts. Rose went on, "I wonder, sometimes, why I put up with him. I suppose I love—no, I know I love him—but I certainly do not understand my husband. Why must he be so cruel and unkind, and so full of appetites and lusts?"

Karen hesitated, then asked, "My Dear, do you not know? Of course, you would not, would you? I recognized it the moment I first met him; Hershel is demon-possessed. I thought you must know, but I see now that you are unfamiliar with the demonic world. You must discuss the issue with your priest—he will know how to explain it to you."

Rose was aghast: "But, how would a sweet little thing like you know about demons and, uh, dragons and such? My Dear, I seriously doubt that my rabbi—if indeed I have one—would be conversant on the subject of demons. Matters of the world, now, that I could believe, but demons? I doubt it. And, how about you?"

Karen explained, "When my parents married, my father was an atheist and my mother was Buddhist; but after a few years they both converted to Christianity, and both became very devout, so I grew up in the Christian faith as well. My parents have taught me about the spiritual domain and the demonic world, too. I find that I am able to recognize Satanic influence in a person's mien and behavior. It is a burden, sometimes, rather than a blessing."

Rose hastened to change the subject: "I have been invited to a great formal ball in the ballroom at the Ritz-Astoria, but I'm afraid I don't know personally the one who invited me. Who is this Anton Klausman? And, I am to bring a friend. I suppose I must bring my husband, wouldn't you say?" This time her laugh carried a slight nervousness with it.

Karen brightened and said, "Oh, Rose, I am so glad you are coming! Not so glad Hershel is coming, I suppose, because I anticipate some unpleasantness; but we shall see. Herr Klausman is the president of the banking firm with which I am now employed, and a worldwide celebrity, as well. I was hoping he would invite you. We, you and I, shall have a wonderful time dancing with other women's husbands and flirting. But, I promise to stay away from yours!" They both found this amusing in the extreme. Karen asked, "Have you a suitable gown? Oh, my, I must go shopping at once!"

Hershel fussed and fumed at Rose as she, reaching her plumpish arms about him from the rear, struggled with mastering the newly acquired art of tying a dress bowtie. "Why do I have to wear this stupid thing, anyway?" he whined. "I could have snapped on my regular ready-made bowtie and we'd already be on our way to this moronic party, and I could even have a few drinks in me, and I'd be happy for a change."

"It's not a party, it's a formal, full dress ball; put on by some elite Europeans who would be horrified by a ready-made bowtie," Rose answered. "And, besides, Darling, how could I show off my handsome husband if he refuses to dress the part of a successful American businessman? If I left it up to you, you'd wear that old stained gray suit of yours, and that loud tie with the gravy stains on it. Ugh!" When she finished adjusting the bowtie, Rose began brushing imaginary lint from Hershel's tux, finally concluding her fussing over him by licking her fingers and wiping a phantom smudge from his forehead. He brushed her hand aside cruelly with a snarl and strode out to the car without waiting for his wife to accompany him. When Rose reached the car a few minutes later, he was listening to the ball game on the car radio.

When Hershel and Rose reached the hotel ballroom, fashionably late due to their couple's spat, the orchestra was playing a waltz, a dance that Hershel utterly despised. As Rose urged her husband into the great hall, a couple whirled by directly in front of them, the man dashing and superbly handsome and the woman lithe and incredibly beautiful. All eyes followed the expert dancers, as they glided across the floor, their feet scarcely seeming to touch the polished oak. Hershel immediately recognized Karen, and so did Rose, but the identity of her partner was a mystery; and so it was to all in attendance. When Hershel flatly refused to dance the waltz, Rose led him to a tiny table near one wall where a waiter joined them and took their order for drinks. Rose ordered champagne and Hershel a large whisky on the rocks. When the dance ended, Karen broke away from her partner and headed quickly over to join Rose and Hershel. She wore a gown of shimmering black with but one thin shoulder strap; a tight-fitting affair that clung to her lithe form down to her knees and then flared out from there so that, when she twirled around, the skirt revealed only her trim calves and ankles. It was impossible to ignore the perfectly faultless olive skin of her arms and shoulders. On her feet were the simplest possible black patent high-heeled shoes. Her only jewelry consisted of a pair of tiny diamond earrings, and her jet-black hair was piled high on her head in a bun, pierced through with four or five red enameled stickpins resembling miniature chopsticks. The effect was positively breathtaking.

As Karen approached, Rose took notice of an uncharacteristic grim paleness on her face, a visage of some anxiety, displacing her usual calm look of confidence. Hershel, stunned by her beauty, saw nothing unusual in her countenance. Rose, reaching out her hand, spoke to the girl, "Karen, my goodness, you look ravishing! You have to be the belle of the ball. Who is that gorgeous man you were dancing with?" She nudged Hershel with her elbow, signaling him to get a chair for Karen. Until she pointed to a chair against the wall, he had no idea what she meant by the nudge. Why were women always nudging anyway, he wondered bitterly. He experienced considerable difficulty in retrieving the chair without taking his eyes from Karen.

As she sat in the chair Hershel held unsteadily for her, Karen answered, "His name is Lucifer Abaddon. Aside from that, I have no other information about him. Herr Klausman introduced us, but he gave out nothing but the man's name. He is quite a dancer, as you must have seen, but I found him to be a bit disturbing. Every time I asked him about himself, he would change the subject; and he seemed to know a great deal about me without having asked. I can only guess Herr Klausman had told him about me, but I rather did not like the fact that he seemed terribly intimate almost from the moment we met." Because Karen had chosen to sit right next to Rose and a bit distant from Hershel, the latter had some difficulty, because of the ambient noise of the ball, in hearing Karen's remarks. It seemed to Hershel that the two women were conspiring to exclude him from the conversation. This was not too far removed from the truth; and Karen continued, "There is something about that man that is very, very disturbing to me. Perhaps it is his secretive attitude—yes, that is what it is, an attitude—that puts me on my guard. And, Rose, there is this other odd thing: there is an essence, an aroma about him that is otherworldly. Oh, I do not know, it is very strange. There is a definite magnetism or an attraction, but there is also some sort of strange, arcane numinous quality about him. I sensed an inimical force coming from him, I think." While Rose held the girl's hand and nodded, Hershel simply looked puzzled, not understanding the meaning of most of Karen's words. Spotting a voluptuous blonde woman sitting alone at a nearby table, he leapt up from his chair without excusing himself and strolled over to her and asked her to dance. She agreed quite readily but, after Hershel discovered she spoke not a word of English, he hastened to abandon her after only one dance. He did appear, however, to be very agreeably impressed by her cleavage. As he returned to his table, Hershel heard Karen remark, "After that he asked me out to dinner Friday evening, but I shall have to think about it a while. He did not seem too pleased when I told him so."

Mr. Abaddon, when he had reluctantly released Karen to escape to Rose and Hershel's table, pressed through the crowded dance floor and headed to some double doors which led out onto a grand verandah. There he leaned against a concrete railing and preceded to light up a cigarette. This he accomplished without the use of a lighter or a match, but by the simple expedient of allowing a small flame to exit his mouth to ignite the cigarette's end. Naturally, he exercised extreme caution in not allowing himself to be observed performing this operation. He didn't even want to consider the sensation *that* would cause. Turning, he observed Anton Klausman approaching from the far end of the verandah. He exhaled rather a large volume of smoke considering the fact that he was smoking only one cigarette, and raised his eyebrows in question as Klausman faced him.

"How did you find the girl?" Klausman asked.

Abaddon considered his reply a moment, forcing himself to care whether or not Klausman would be satisfied with his answer, "She is extravagantly beautiful, of course, but I am by no means certain she is a good choice for our use in this matter. I believe you could well have located a woman who has more suitable qualifications."

Klausman was hardly accustomed to being questioned in his judgments, but he suppressed any resentment he might have had, at least for the present. He said in return, "I am afraid I do not see your point, Herr Abaddon. She has already proven herself irresistible to Feldman; in fact he is falling all over himself attempting to gain her approval. What more could you ask of her?"

Abaddon's eyes bored into Klausman's as he replied, "I would require no more of the girl; only of you, Klausman.

This girl is but a child, and a problematical one at that. I do not expect the likes of you to discern such things, but I do expect you to pay close attention to one who *is* able to do so. If you had heeded my initial advice, you would have found a woman of adequate beauty but of a more mature nature. Perhaps you did not observe just ten minutes ago the degree to which our hero was impressed by Mrs. Petersen and her pulchritude. Her ample endowment did not escape his notice for a moment, and a woman of her ilk is uncomplicated and easily manipulated. Such is not the case with Miss Boschert. I perceive nothing but problems and complications with this girl. It strikes me, Klausman, that your selection of Miss Boschert was more for your own benefit than for those of our cause. However, I warn you, Klausman: Hands off the girl! She will be your undoing. However, the deed is done, so let us put the matter behind us for the present. Perhaps you would be good enough to fetch me a glass of champagne, there's a good fellow." With this, Klausman was thoroughly and completely humiliated. He had never in his life been treated in such a manner, and he vowed to get even. As Klausman turned reluctantly to find a waiter Abaddon, holding a menu close to his face, surreptitiously released a few small tongues of flame from his classically formed mouth, along with a tendril of smoke from each nostril.

As the evening wore on Hershel became drunker and more resentful of the two women at his table. Rose and Karen sat close together in animated conversation, chatting about myriad subjects of which his knowledge did not exist. He heard the names 'Milton', 'Dostoyevsky', and 'Mahler' pass with much animation between the two, but could make nothing of the conversation. At one point Karen hummed a little tune in response to which Rose declared, "Ah, La Sonnambula, isn't it?" Even though the women needed to sit close to each other in order to hear, they had no real intention of excluding Hershel from their conversation. The result was no different, however, than if they had shut him out purposely; he perceived their action as a haughty female tactic of debasement. Accordingly, he ordered another large whiskey on the rocks. It was for this reason that, when the Messrs. Abaddon and Klausman approached the table together, Hershel regarded them through the hazy filter of intoxication.

Klausman had in tow a contingent of waiters and busboys, all of whom carried among them another table and extra chairs and, gesturing for Hershel to move out of the way, they pushed the table against the one at which the two women sat chatting. Before Hershel could offer a protest, Klausman had conspired to seat himself next to Karen, whom he then proceeded to regale with anecdotes of his many remarkable exploits. Regarding this with some measure of amusement, Abaddon took a seat between Hershel and Rose, this arrangement allowing him to peer straight into Klausman's eyes. It was with considerable difficulty and reluctance that the latter tore his gaze away from Karen and yielded to the terrible attraction of Abaddon's focus. The second their eyes made contact, Abaddon locked his victim into a powerful spiritual embrace from which Klausman was unable to extricate himself. None of the others at the table could possibly have observed the effects Abaddon's stare had upon his prey, at least not initially. Only Karen was able to perceive a subtle change in Klausman's mien as Abaddon's gaze intensified, although she took little conscious note of it. Presently Klausman turned to the girl and, laying his hand tenderly on her forearm asked, "Raken, Dy Mear, you we be asting hiss mite anong?"

Having cast her eyes down to her arm, Karen had already begun to try to twist free from Klausman's grasp but, when he uttered such strange gibberish, her eyes went to his face in reflex, hoping to find in his eyes some explanation for the utterances. The eyes revealed nothing at all but seemed to belong to some subspecies completely devoid of intelligence. She addressed Klausman, "Pardon, Eminence?"

Klausman said, "My esses, Read, low tundra heppa nong labortia!" By the time he had finished this declaration, he had captured the attention of all of those at the table except Hershel, who could divine no significant anomalies in Klausman's speech. Even though Klausman had failed in his apparent hortatory utterance, he leaned back in his chair and, interlacing his fingers, he rested his hands on his ample belly; his beaming face flushed with self-satisfaction. After a few seconds of reflection he added, "Lee, lee, Fy Lear, lane forror song tee." Having uttered this last, he looked about the table for affirmation, of which he received not one tiny morsel.

Suddenly, Hershel began to roar with laughter, then fell to hiccupping violently. He shook a forefinger, wet with something vile, at Klausman and yelled, "This clown is nuts! First he's all over our little Karen, then he, he...." At this point Hershel, who had been leaning back a bit in his chair, abruptly fell over backwards with a clatter and a string of expletives, finally passing out briefly as he struck his head on the floor. Rose stood up and, strolling leisurely over to her husband, slowly poured a large tumbler of ice water over his gray and greasy-looking face, whereupon he rose to his feet unsteadily and, taking his monogrammed handkerchief from his breast pocket, mopped his face and neck. Encircling his waist with her right arm, Rose cooed, "Come on, Darling, you've had a little bit too much fun for one evening; let's get you home and to beddy-bye. Good night, all. Karen, Dear, I'll see you tomorrow morning."

Through all the commotion, Klausman seemed supremely pleased with himself and could not fathom why Karen was not impressed with him beyond all measure. Lifting his eyebrows to their maximum elevation, he declared, "Lang toor leesay aflig, Dy Mear!" He rose from his chair and, turning on his heel and saluting her, stalked out of the hall and to the elevators, his head held high.

Mr. Abaddon regarded Karen with an admiring glance, as he said, "Can't imagine what came over the old boy, can you? Seems he may have had a bit too much of that expensive cognac he cherishes so much. Pity! Well, My Dear, perhaps you would allow me to escort you back to your flat. Taxis will be in short supply if we delay our departure much longer, I fear. If you will give me your check, I will retrieve your coat and we can be on our way presently." Abaddon fastened the girl with a gaze so powerful that she was hard pressed to conjure up a reply suitable to reject his offer. Ultimately, she smiled and accepted his offer, vowing to herself to be on guard every second she was in the presence of this man, no matter how handsome and attractive he might appear to her. It turned out that Mr. Abaddon had no need of a taxi and that his car and driver had been parked in readiness at the curb, much to the chagrin of the police officer charged with traffic control in front of the hotel. As the Lincoln limousine glided along, ostensibly across town to the Village, Abaddon offered Karen a nightcap from the bar in the rear passenger compartment.

Smiling nervously, she said, "Thank you, Mr. Abaddon, but no. I have been more than sufficiently refreshed for one evening. I say, your driver does not appear to know the way to my home. It is in the West Village and we appear to be traveling in the wrong direction. We ought to be going across town."

"Yes, I know, My Dear, but I thought we could drop by a small, intimate club I know and take up where we left off dancing." Abaddon's voice was silky smooth as he fixed the girl with a gaze calculated to hypnotize; and then he added, "Surely you are not going to give up on a pleasant evening simply because Mr. Feldman cannot hold his liquor and poor Klausman has lapsed into some sort of driveling spell. The night is yet young for those of us who are also young at heart." He put on a smile crafted to ensnare her. When he attempted to take her hand, she moved it deftly away and placed it in her lap.

Trying to keep alarm from her voice, Karen protested, "I hope you will forgive me for insisting on being delivered immediately to my home. I really must get to bed in order to rest myself for an early rising. Mrs. Mandel-Feldman and I have a meeting scheduled for first thing in the morning and I must not be late. There is much preparation required on my part." Her manner of speaking was intended to end the matter.

Fortunately for Abaddon, while she was speaking this last, Karen was peering intently out of the car window, watching enormous raindrops leave silver dollar-sized wet spots on the otherwise dry pavement. Soon it would be raining in earnest, but while Karen was distracted, Abaddon allowed his appearance to change from a handsome young man to the dragon, and back to the man again, in the space of a fraction of a second. He was at his greatest ease when in his natural state: that of the inimical dragon. The girl never even noticed the brief transformation, but it gave Abaddon a split second of respite from the frustration she was causing him. However, her resistance to his overtures did puzzle him. Where was she finding the strength? Did she already suspect the prurient nature of his advances? Her restive manner produced in him a caution that checked his temerity and caused him to put off until another occasion his wanton plan for her enslavement. His voice fairly dripping with ardor, he crooned, "Of course, My Dear, I quite understand. I will direct Jean to reverse course and take you directly to your flat. Perhaps we can do this another time." Both settled back in their seats for the ride, Abaddon smoking cigarettes rapaciously and Karen staring idly out of the car window at nothing in particular. Although she appeared to be daydreaming, Karen was in fact praying her heart out.

On exiting the ball at the Ritz-Astoria, Anton Klausman experienced the worst possible difficulty in hailing a cab. On the one or two occasions he managed to get a taxi to pull over, he found it impossible to articulate to the driver what his destination was to be. Finally, after several unsuccessful attempts, and after the spell Abaddon had cast upon him had worn off, he was able to clearly state, "The Ritz-Astoria, and make it quick!"

Rolling his eyes back in his head, the driver cracked, "Right behind you, Buddy. You ain't had a little too much to drink, have you? I got other fares, y'know. Go sleep it off!" Gunning his engine, he sped off.

By this time Klausman was totally exhausted and furious as well. Having finally returned to his room, he was in bed and well into his plan for vengeance against Abaddon before he came to the realization that apparently Mr. Abaddon had complete power over him; power that gave him the ability to take control at will of anyone he wished. For the first time Klausman seriously questioned Abaddon's identity. Up until this evening, he had made the erroneous assumption that he, Klausman, was in control of this venture. He began to question in his mind the origin of all the plans and details for the takeover and control of Hershel Feldman. If Abaddon was in charge, who then was he, and from whom did *his* orders emanate? Who exactly was Lucifer Abaddon? (Unlike Mr. Daemon, Klausman had never witnessed any of Abaddon's transformations.) Klausman picked up his cell phone and entered the number of a rabbi friend of his in Switzerland, a man he knew to be a scholar of ancient Hebrew history.

After only one ring, Dr. Moeshe Weiss answered in German, sounding far off and tinny, "Ja?"

"Ah, Moeshe, my friend, this is Anton Klausman calling. How are you?" Klausman, speaking German, forced himself to sound jovial.

Moeshe replied, "I am well, Anton, how have you been? It has been quite some time since we last spoke. Where are you and what is the nature of this call?"

Still sounding cheerful, Klausman replied, "Well, my dear friend, I wish to ask you the origin of a certain name; the name of an acquaintance here in New York, where I am staying for the present. Have you ever encountered the name 'Lucifer Abaddon'?"

Aside from a slight hiss caused, no doubt, by the distance between New York City and Lucerne, there was complete silence lasting for several seconds. At length, Dr. Weiss spoke, "Surely you are joking, eh, Anton? Are you telling me that you have actually met someone who calls himself 'Lucifer Abaddon'? You must know, certainly, that these are names for the devil himself. 'Lucifer' is the name of the angel thought to have been the one who fell from God's grace because of his rebellion against Yahweh and was henceforth known as Satan. The name 'Abaddon' is actually the Hebrew for Satan. No doubt this person is having you on, my friend." He chuckled, as he was known to do frequently.

Klausman was not at all relieved, though he caused his voice to convey that notion to his friend. "Of course, I see," he said, "I'm afraid you are correct, Moeshe, the man has made a bit of a fool of me; not the first time this has been done, nor will it be the last." After passing a few pleasantries, the two friends closed their connections.

Anton Klausman could scarcely believe the fact that he had not caught on to the implications of the name 'Lucifer Abaddon'. Be that as it may, could it be that Horace Daemon knew all along? It would certainly explain many things about Mr. Daemon, such as the likelihood that the old man was one of Abaddon's minions. Why did Daemon not inform him of Lucifer Abaddon's real identity? No doubt both were highly amused at his naiveté. He cringed at the thought. Klausman resolved to conduct himself henceforth in accordance with his newly acquired knowledge.

For Rose, the drive home could not have been pleasant regardless of the weather conditions because Hershel took advantage of this occasion to pour out upon his wife every device at his disposal in order to make a total wreck of an evening he never wanted to happen in the first place. The very thought of participating in a full dress ball put on by the accounting firm that was in the process of uncovering his misdeeds was to him a daunting prospect indeed. Therefore, it was with considerable ingenuity that he contrived to spoil every effort Rose put forth in order to eke out some measure of enjoyment from an evening that was otherwise doomed to complete disaster. From the moment when Rose literally dragged her husband out of the great ballroom until she finally, with the help of a bellman, got Hershel situated in the Mercedes beside her, the latter managed to feign semi consciousness. He somehow willed himself to vomit on the bellman's uniform and Rose's gorgeous gown and still to appear unable to keep his feet without assistance. Only when Rose promised to pay for the bellman's dry cleaning bill were the two of them finally released to exit the parking garage and allowed to proceed homeward into the cold, rainy night. Visibility was poor and the traffic insanely heavy, requiring every ounce of concentration Rose could muster; and so she wished even more ardently that they had taken the train into the city and a cab from the terminal to the hotel. On reflection, she wondered what tactics Hershel would have used on the train and taxi to make everyone miserable. Her mind boggled at the thought. Ever since they had left the hotel, Hershel appeared to have passed out again, but Rose could only focus intently on her driving. What horrid conditions she must endure in order to get home this night!

About ten minutes into the drive, Hershel abruptly sat up and began to wail piteously, begging Rose to forgive him for ruining an evening for which she had looked forward with such excitement. Shedding what appeared to be actual tears of contrition, he sobbed, "I don' know why you pu' up wiff me like I am, hoo, hoo, Dear. I'n no goob, no not one li'le bish! hoo, hoo! Preeze don' hate me! I'n a bad boy, alri', hoo, hoo! You, poor li'le thin' got ever' ri' to hate ol' Hershsh, hoo, hoo hoo!" As he concluded his juicy tirade Hershel, putting on his guilty puppy demeanor, looked pleadingly up at Rose for forgiveness.

She was having none of it: "Oh, come on, Darling, you know very well you set out to ruin my evening, and I'm darned if I can see why. I mean, surely you must know that I've been onto you for some time now. Why else would I be keeping my peace while Karen drags her feet in her audit unless I'm hoping to find a way to keep you out of trouble? If I thought you were innocent, I'd be urging her to get on with it and get herself back to Switzerland and out of your sight. Do you think I haven't noticed how you gape at her with your tongue hanging out? You and every other red-blooded male in the universe! I guess I can't really blame you, but you don't even know the worst of it, do you, you silly fool. Karen is a whole lot more than skin-deep beautiful; she's a sweet, wonderful girl who feels genuine compassion for the likes of you. I know, you probably think she is consumed with desire for you; but you're dead wrong. She feels sorry for you because you've stepped in the manure pile and you think nobody is aware of it but you. What a genius you are, Pet! If you had any sense at all you'd be kissing up to the honorable Herr Klausman, Karen's boss, trying to negotiate some kind of terms of surrender. But not you, my Sweet; no, you think making passes at Karen will turn out to be the solution to your predicament. I'm sorry to burst your bubble, Darling, but that's not the way it works. Just wait and see! If you knew what's good for you, you would be sucking up to me instead of the one person who really has the goods on you."

All during Rose's discourse, Hershel's countenance was morphing slowly from the remorseful puppy into the fuming tiger, his breath coming in short gasps and his face turning puce. Finally, turning toward his wife he exploded, "She-devil! You've been planning this all along, plotting how to turn Karen against me! You're up to your old tricks, aren't you? Well, it's not going to work this time. She's going to see right through you, see how petty and suspicious you really are. You go ahead and try and play her against me—you'll see—she won't fall for it. And, I'm not going to put up with it, either! You'll be sorry, you dried up old prune! I'm sick of you!" With this last Hershel hauled off and punched Rose feebly in the face, the blow lacking much force due to the confined space of the front seat of the car. Even so, Rose found it extremely challenging to keep the Mercedes under control; and when she did finally regain command, she brought the machine to a stop in front of an all-night bar. Screaming at Hershel through tears of bitterness rather than pain, she began pushing at him, pummeling his arm and side with her fists, trying to get him out of the car.

"You going to leave me out here in the middle of nowhere? How'm I supposed to get home, anyway?" Hershel was bellowing back at Rose, his rage combining with self-pity.

By now, Rose was sobbing along with her yelling as she cried, "What's the matter? Can't you see the bar right in front of you, beckoning for you to come in and pickle your brain some more? Anyone who is brave enough to hit a woman ought not to have any fear of going into a bar to call a cab." With that, pushing against his hip with her foot, Rose attempted to complete the ejection of her husband from the car. As he slid from the seat, Hershel attempted one final swing at his wife before scrambling to his feet and, spewing a string of expletives, stumbling toward the bar's neon-illuminated entrance. Not even casting a glance back in Hershel's direction, Rose jammed the accelerator to the floor and the big car slithered off down the gleaming wet street and toward home. Hershel shouted filth at the diminishing image of the Mercedes; his tux becoming shiny from the pouring rain and his sopping, stringy hair clinging to his skull.

Still trembling from her confrontation with Hershel, Rose stood silently in the nursery, allowing her gaze to rest on the sleeping figure of her sweet, innocent Isabelle. "You don't know what life's all about, do you, Baby?" she whispered, "How in the world am I going to protect you from men like your Abi?" In spite of herself, Rose began to weep anew. Reaching into the child's crib, she pulled a fluffy pink blanket up to the little one's chin and, sniffling a bit, tiptoed from the room. In fifteen minutes, no more, she was in her bed trying desperately to sleep, but to no avail. When Rose passed the grandfather clock in the hallway heading toward the kitchen, she noted the hour was extremely late and allowed herself a moment of anxiety on Hershel's behalf. How in the world could she summon up any measure of compassion for one so cruel and churlish as Hershel Feldman? Oh, she was so mixed up in her heart! Was it possible for her to be in love still with one so draconic, so downright mean? What, in fact, drove Hershel to be so abusive to his wife, yet loving for and doting on his daughter? These questions ran through her mind and heart as she shook two sleeping pills from the plastic bottle and popped them into her mouth, tilting her head back as she did so. Less than an hour later she slept, albeit restlessly.

It seemed to Rose that she was awakened just seconds later by a loud banging noise coming from downstairs. Pulling on her robe, she ran to the stairs and, passing once more by the great clock, she saw that over two hours had passed since she had taken her sleeping pills. The banging was emanating from the front door and was becoming louder and more urgent-sounding. It was as she approached the door that she heard Hershel's muffled and frantic voice; and almost simultaneously, Carmen, Isabelle's nanny, arrived on the scene, replete with nightcap and gown. Waving the poor, frightened woman away and back to her quarters, Rose unlatched the door and opened it to the sight of a drenched and furious Hershel. Though appearing to have been soaked through for some time, he was still falling-down drunk and obstreperous in the extreme. As he lunged over the threshold, Rose instinctively stepped back to avoid the fetid aroma of his breath as well as something else that she did not even care to identify. Hershel stood swaying beside her as the now trembling Rose pushed the door against the jamb and started for the stairway. Before she could take a single step, he grabbed her wrist and swung her around to face him and, as he did so he struck her again with his fist, first in the stomach and then on the side of her face. This time the force of his punches was not limited, as previously by the confinement of the car's cockpit, so Rose was at once doubled over, then knocked to the floor. There she lay for some minutes, stunned but conscious, and then, as she tried to rise to her feet, she called out in a shaky voice, "Oh, dear me! Carmen, come quickly and call nine-one-one! I think I'm going to be sick. No, do not call nine-one-one! I think I'll be all right if I can get to bed. Oh, dear me!" By this time Hershel had staggered to his study and locked the door behind him. Rose crept on hands and knees to the couch and lay there gathering strength before she undertook to walk on her own to her bedroom. Carmen came to her a few minutes later bearing a cool compress for Rose's bruised cheek and temple; and later still she brought Rose a wonderful toddy made from a secret family recipe. Rose slept soundly until late in the morning.

Seven o'clock the next morning found Karen on the job in her tiny office preparing for her meeting with Rose, unaware of the latter's condition. At precisely eight o'clock, she left her office and boarded the elevator for the eighth floor and Rose's office, where she addressed Arielle with a friendly smile. She had grown to admire Arielle's loyalty to Rose, a stance that must have required no little ingenuity due to the fact that she must, on numerous occasions, be obliged to cover for her harried boss. It was not that Rose, under normal circumstances, was apt to be devious, but that her capricious and irresponsible husband frequently forced her into excursions out of the norm. Karen stood in awe of Arielle's ability to anticipate Hershel's errant behavior and to fabricate the necessary excuses in order to cover for canceled appointments and missed meetings and the like. "Is Rose available for our meeting today?" Karen asked the other girl.

When Arielle looked uncomfortable, Karen knew what to expect, but she grew alarmed when the former answered her, "I'm afraid your meeting will have to cancelled, Miss Boschert. Mrs. Mandel-Feldman is at home indisposed. She told me to tell you she'll call you a little later." Karen's concern for Rose grew even greater when Arielle would not meet her gaze, but only looked down nervously at her hands.

"What is it, Arielle?" she asked, "I was with her only last evening and she was quite well. Has she fallen ill?" Karen was certain that Rose had consumed only a small amount of champagne, so she doubted that she could be suffering the effects of excessive alcohol consumption, as she was certain Hershel must be undergoing at that very moment.

It was then that Arielle finally met Karen's gaze and said, "I'm really worried about her, Miss Boschert. Mrs. Mandel-Feldman sounded terribly shaken and I don't think I've ever heard her sound that frightened." The girl began to wring her hands as she continued, "Is there some way we could check on her to see if she's alright? I would go out to her home but I have to stay here for her. She won't answer her cell phone and neither will Hersh... uh, Mr. Feldman. I just don't know what to do. Should we call the police?" Arielle appeared truly distressed.

"Do not worry, Dear, I have nothing much on for today, so I shall go and see to her," Karen answered, "Can you write down her address for me?" Going to see Rose was easier said than done. She first had to take the subway to the

South Ferry terminal; from there she rode the Staten Island Ferry to St. George, Staten Island; and from St. George she hired a cab to take her down Bay Street all the way to Rosebank and to the address Arielle had given her.

Mrs. Bridges, Hershel and Rose's housekeeper, on answering the bell, opened the door to the sight of a shockingly beautiful girl. Even though the rain had long since ceased, a stiff breeze remained, and it tugged relentlessly at Karen's coat and slacks. Mrs. Bridges asked, "May I help you, young lady?"

Karen had almost to shout against the noise of the wind, "I have come to see Mrs. Mandel-Feldman, please. I am Karen Boschert. We are to meet this morning, so I believe she is expecting me."

"I'm sorry, young lady, but Mrs. Mandel-Feldman is not receiving visitors today—she is ill and confined to bed," Mrs. Bridges answered, as she prepared to close the door.

Just then there was a squeal of delight and a toddler with a mop of dark, curly hair slipped through the door and ran to Karen. "Missy Kawen hewe!" she shrieked as she hugged Karen's knees.

Lifting the delighted child up to her face, Karen cooed, "Look how pretty Isabelle is today! I am so glad to see you, Darling! Where is Mummy? Is she feeling poorly?" Smiling at Mrs. Bridges, Karen carried the happy child through the door and into the living room, all the while babbling with Isabelle in baby talk. "Let us go see Mummy, shall we?" she went on as she set the child down, patting her on her ruffled fanny to send her on her way to Rose's bedroom. When Isabelle was out of earshot, Karen addressed Mrs. Bridges, "I know why Rose is indisposed and that is why I am here. Please let me go to her so I can help. Believe me, we have become friends and I have only her best interests at heart. Perhaps she has told you of me, Karen Boschert, *n'est pas?*" For some reason, the French words just slipped out.

Mrs. Bridges, looking a bit dubious, allowed Karen to follow Isabelle down the hall to Rose's bedroom. When the two arrived at the door to Rose's room, Isabelle stopped before the door and, turning to Karen, placed a plump little forefinger to her lips and said, "Shshsh, Ma seeping."

"Well, I suppose we should leave her alone, should we not?" Karen asked. Taking Isabelle by the hand, she added, "I hear you have a room all your own. Will you show it to me, Sweetie?" They met Carmen in Isabelle's room, turning back a quilt with pictures of teddy bears on it, making ready to put Isabelle down for her nap. Isabelle whined a bit and complained but in the end she allowed Carmen to tuck her in. Clearly, she was sleepy and ready for her nap. She would not close her eyes, however, until Karen promised she would still be there when Isabelle awoke.

Turning to Carmen, Karen asked, "Is Mr. Feldman here?"

"No, Miss. A while ago a man come and get him; he take the Mister away in a big, long automovile. The Mister, he is not feel that good, I thin', but he go anyway. The man, he is look very rich and not very friendly, I thin'. The Missus, she does not know the Mister gone. Better not tell her about the rich man, I thin'." Carmen finally took a breath.

Karen thought a moment, and then asked, "Does Mrs. Bridges know about the rich man? Perhaps she knows who he is."

Carmen looked skeptical when she answered, "I don' thin' so, but you aks her, hokay?"

By this time, Carmen had led Karen into the kitchen where Mrs. Bridges was preparing tea, setting out three places at a pine table by the kitchen window that looked out onto a flower garden at the rear of the house. Only pansies were in bloom at the time.

"Will you have tea, Miss Boschert?" Mrs. Bridges asked.

"Thank you, no, Mrs. Bridges, I am really much too concerned about Rose, ah, Mrs. Mandel-Feldman to join you," Karen replied, "but I wonder if you might know the identity of the gentleman who came to pick up Mr. Feldman."

Mrs. Bridges pursed her lips a bit, then replied, "I'm afraid not, Miss Boschert. I don't believe I've ever seen him before. When you arrived I thought you might have some connection with him—I don't know why, though."

Karen smiled reassuringly and continued, "Forgive me, but I feel I must check on Mrs. Mandel-Feldman. Will you excuse me?" An image of Anton Klausman appeared before her eyes; and she shuddered as she walked softly down the hall to Rose's room and tapped gently on the door.

"Is that you, Mrs. Bridges?" a muffled voice asked from within.

"Rose, it is Karen. Please allow me to come in." Karen tested the door and found it unlocked.

"Karen? Oh, dear! What on earth are you doing here? I don't want you to see me. How did you come all this way? Oh, dear." Rose began to cry softly, but did not respond either way to Karen's request.

"Rose, my Dear, I am coming in. I do not want to embarrass you, but I must see if you are all right. Oh, my goodness! That is a terrible bruise! Here, let me look at it. I have had training in nursing, you know. Did Hershel do this?" Karen found the compress on the nightstand and refreshed it in the bathroom sink. As she very gently laid it on the side of Rose's face, she added, "Nothing is broken, I am certain, but it is certainly enflamed. This compress will do the most good, and time will as well, but you should probably rest a few days. After that, your makeup will conceal the discoloring until it goes away. Does it hurt you very much?"

Rose attempted a little smile and replied, "I suppose my feelings and pride are hurt worse than my face, but I can't seem to stop crying. He has just become so cruel and brutal; I don't know how to deal with him anymore. Oh, my, did I hear Isabelle's voice a while ago?"

"She is fine—napping just now," Karen said. "I was getting nowhere with Mrs. Bridges when Isabelle came out and greeted me, saving the day. After that, I seem to have been accepted by the staff." She grinned as she held Rose's hand. She went on, "It has become clear to me that we must come up with some sort of plan. I have a suggestion: If you are able, we should go immediately into the city together, and I will get you settled in your flat at your office; away from Hershel and his ways. After that, when you are up to it, we shall make some very hard decisions about what we shall do about Hershel and his activities at Mandel Family Apparel. But, in the meantime, you need to be out of Hershel's way and out of harm. Carmen tells me you nearly called the police but thought better of it. Fortunately, you had the presence of mind to leave the police out of this. That would have complicated the matter even more than it already is at present." All the while she was addressing Rose, Karen was fussing over her, straightening her blanket, adjusting her pillows and, with lovely fingertips, brushing errant strands of hair away from Rose's eyes.

Less than an hour later, a Mercedes sedan glided noiselessly out of the driveway at the Feldman home and turned northward toward the expressway, heading toward Manhattan. Huddled alongside the very young woman driver was a slightly more mature woman wrapped in a blanket, her head on a pillow against the car window.

Chapter Six

The Hon. Anton Klausman's phone rang far too early on the morning following the grand ball in the hotel ballroom. During the night he had managed only sporadic sleep, assailed by troubling, cryptic dreams and interrupted by periods of wakeful restlessness. Glancing at his bedside clock, he noted the time, 8:43 AM, while he groped for the phone. In a gravely voice, he answered, "Hello, yes?" His head swam and his hand shook, both of these effects from causes unknown to him.

A male voice asked, "Am I speaking with Anton Klausman?"

Klausman endeavored to regain his dignity and his own clear voice before he responded, "To whom am I speaking, may I ask?" He was only partially successful in his endeavor to sound dignified and clear.

"Many pardons, Sir," the same voice rejoined him, "This is Schaeffer, Mr. Lucifer Abaddon's aide speaking. His Excellency wishes for me to speak to Mr. Klausman. Is that he speaking?"

In an irritable voice, Klausman replied, "Why did you not say so at the beginning, man? What is it that Mr. Abaddon wishes at this ungodly hour?"

"His Excellency would have you to meet him at ten o'clock this morning." Schaeffer did an excellent job of concealing his chagrin at Klausman's insolence. "And," he continued, "I will see to it that your driver receives directions to the meeting place and that he is waiting in front of your hotel at precisely nine forty-five. His Excellency will be expecting you." Suddenly there was only a dial tone.

Klausman wondered why he had given his own man the day off as he struggled to dress himself, the task being made doubly difficult by his inability to remain focused on it. Vestiges of the troubling dreams floated in his mind, with visions of Karen and of Abaddon intertwining and tormenting him. Nevertheless, he managed to shower, shave, and to dress in one of his older and shabbier suits: a gesture of defiance toward Abaddon. He hastily boarded the elevator, just in time to meet his driver at the appointed hour. The limousine glided smoothly and noiselessly along the rough and potholed Manhattan streets, finally turning down an alley between two abandoned-looking buildings. The driver brought the machine to a gentle halt alongside a rusted railing that appeared to be guarding a flight of stairs that nearly vanished down into the depths below, next to one of the buildings. After he had opened the rear door for Klausman, the driver said, "The door at the bottom of the stairs is unlocked, Sir and, if you will look to your left on entering, you will find a lighted lamp hanging on the wall. My instructions were to tell you to proceed down the next flight of stairs to the level below, where there will be someone to meet you." With this last, the driver closed the rear door, made his way around to the driver's side, climbed into the car, and drove swiftly away. Klausman was repulsed and disgusted by the filth and rankness of the place he had just entered. The vermin scuttling about him, their frantic squeaking and their febrile scampering here and there set his teeth on edge, and put chills down his spine. What he at first thought to be birds, but later realized were bats, seemed bent on flying right in his face, and caused him to shiver with revulsion. Reluctantly taking the grimy lamp in his hand, he searched about him for another stairway. It was difficult for him to concentrate, so strong was his nausea, but he finally, in the dimness, saw the stone and cement steps leading downward, just ahead of him. Klausman had great difficulty negotiating the stairs, such was their state of decay and disrepair. Many steps were loose and some even missing, so that his progress was gradual at best. Twice he nearly lost his footing and would have toppled to the bottom, but he eventually reached the final step and then stood on the floor at last, looking about him. To his right and slightly in front of him he saw a light. As he walked toward it he perceived movement and scurrying, but saw nothing to support that perception. There was definitely the sound of someone or something shuffling or scampering across the room, but nothing was visible to the eye. At length he heard, or thought he heard, the sound of a voice; or was it several voices? Perhaps he heard nothing. He was unsure. Following the source of the light he discovered, behind a masonry post, an ancient wooden table, littered with animal bones, feathers, various types of excrement, and bits of hairy skin or hide. In the center of the table stood a candle stick in which was a candle of indescribable color, the source of a flickering, wavering luminescence. On either side of the table stood a chair, neither of which appeared to be capable of supporting a person of normal weight. Klausman, on examining both chairs, found himself reluctant to sully even his old, worn suit on either one. Ultimately, he elected to test one chair, the one that appeared to be the least decayed, and after having done so, he sat in it. The place seemed to be alive with something, but there was no discerning what, without his being able to see the evidence. Nevertheless, the invisible scurryings and 'inaudible' voices continued.

Abruptly, without the slightest warning, there was a man standing just beside Klausman. Because he had not heard a sound, nor had he seen the man approach, he jumped with alarm. He shouted, "By Jove! What on earth? Who is it, then?" Klausman found himself trembling with fear.

"It is I, Yong Se, Your Eminence, at your service." As he stepped closer into the candlelight, the man became recognizable as Horace Daemon's servant.

With tremor in his voice, Klausman answered, "For Heaven's sake, man, give a fellow a little warning. What are you doing here? I would have thought that after old Daemon cashed it in you would have gone back to China or Korea or wherever." He wished the trembling would go away.

"China, Sir," Yong Se said. Then he added, "His Excellency will be here directly." With this last, he seemed simply to disappear, and Klausman was alone again.

He had no sense of how long he waited, but Klausman was indignant indeed. He was certainly unaccustomed to being held in waiting, but just as certainly had no qualms about causing others to wait for him—endlessly at times. When, after an indeterminate time had passed, he was awakened from a sort of stupor, and looked across the table at two of the most grotesque and horrifying hands he could ever have imagined. Long, bony fingers terminated in what surely must have been tantamount to talons. The hands themselves were crisscrossed with purple and blood red veins and arteries, and were covered with grime and what appeared to be gore. When he dragged his gaze up to the face of the owner of the hands, he beheld the gigantic hawk nose with the obligatory hairy wart, the snaggle-toothed, lipless mouth, the blotchy cheeks, the fiery eyes, and the greasy strands of dangling and filthy hair; all perched atop the scrawny, sinewy neck with jutting Adam's apple. The monstrous creature was odious in the extreme.

Klausman could hardly hold back a scream of horror. Finally, he exclaimed, "I say! Here now, then! Who, by Jove? Eh?" His hands were shaking violently.

The ghastly ogre gave a phlegmy cackle, its eyes bulging, spittle bubbling from its lipless maw, and its claws scratching on the table with glee. This lasted only a moment, then the creature transformed itself instantly into a most horrendous and terrifying dragon with fire, smoke, and steam spewing from its crocodilian mouth and nostrils, accompanied by a dreadful roar that rattled the ancient building to its timbers. Klausman quaked in even greater trepidation.

The dragon, speaking in a sibilant and vitriolic voice, roared, "Klausman, you spineless idiot, it is I, Lucifer Abaddon! Have you still not discovered my identity? Stop your blubbering and take heed. I am in control of your life, Feldman's life, and was in control of Daemon's as well, until the poor fool outlived his usefulness. But, now you must listen to me, and to me only! We have some lives to destroy and I will require your cooperation, not your defiance. You will do exactly as I say, precisely when I tell you to. Is that clear?" At this last word, the monster, after having first spewed forth fire and smoke, accompanied by a terrifying roar, changed swiftly into the sleekly handsome dance partner who had entranced so many at the ball.

Certainly, Abaddon's appearance as the handsome young gentleman was far more acceptable to Klausman than the dragon or the hideous monster, even though he knew it to be imposture. Despite his intimidation, Klausman mustered a timorous reply, "Quite so, Your Excellency. I am fully and unquestionably at your service. I regret that I was not previously cognizant of your identity. I must say, Excellency, it is rather difficult to converse with you while you are in your, ah, natural manifestation. What is it you wish me to do next?"

In order to relieve himself of the constant effort of maintaining the guise of a young man, as well as to put Klausman in his place, Abaddon resumed the configuration of the dragon. Sounding somewhat like a steam locomotive, he addressed the frightened Klausman, "First you must divest yourself of your own man and take into your employ Mr. Yong Se. You will find him in your rooms when you return to the hotel. He is to be the liaison between us, and you are to confide to him all things relevant to our association. Next, you are to establish a close friendship and business relationship with our Mr. Feldman. After you have accomplished these two things, we will meet again and discuss the situation further. You are **not** to seek further alliances with Miss Boschert—she is off limits to you. Remember, she constitutes such a grave threat to the kingdom that I must deal with her myself. Unless you wish to go the way of our friend Daemon, you will do precisely as I have instructed you." The last phrase or two of Abaddon's discourse were accompanied by copious issuances of fire and steam interspersed with frightful roaring. Suddenly all traces of the dragon vanished, leaving a chilling quietude, after which Klausman rose from his chair and found his way up the crumbling stairs and out onto the alleyway, where he found his driver awaiting him in the limousine. He had no memory of leaving the lamp behind, but it was not to be found in the car, that was certain.

As soon as he was out of Abaddon's proximity, Klausman was able to reclaim a modicum of his former, and characteristic, confidence and self-assurance. Even so, he set out to implement Abaddon's instructions. After having returned to his hotel room, he showered and changed into casual dress, which had been laid out by Yong Se. How in the world had the latter known he would be requiring a change of clothing, and how had he divined precisely the type of attire Klausman preferred under the circumstances? Had Yong Se been in touch with Mr. Abaddon and been told the nature of the impending errand? These questions, and many more, filled Klausman's mind as he sat back in his seat while the limousine glided swiftly along the freeway to Staten Island. He had closed the glass partition between the driver and himself in order that the solitude might allow him to clear his head. Even though Abaddon had commanded him to stay away from Karen, Klausman was determined to circumvent this order and to make Karen his own. How this could be accomplished he, at present, had not the slightest notion. At any rate, first things must come first. He must at least make the appearance of carrying out Abaddon's orders regarding Feldman; and to the Feldman residence he was now headed.

As Hershel Feldman climbed into the backseat of the limousine, he settled himself beside the uncomfortable Anton Klausman, who was nearly overcome by the pungent odor of Hershel's breath. The olfactory effects from the kind of drinking Hershel had been indulging in the evening before take some time to dissipate, so Klausman found it necessary to speak to Hershel while facing straight ahead rather than turning to face him as one normally would do.

It was Hershel, however, who initiated the conversation by asserting, "I hope you realize, Klausman, that I'm meeting you today against my better judgment. Who was that guy that called me a while ago? I could barely make out what he was saying. Where's he come from, anyway, China or someplace?"

"That was Mr. Yong Se, who is, in fact, a native of the Republic of China. He is my aide, and I instructed him to call you so that we could meet together. Since our respective offices are so far distant from your home, we shall conduct our initial meeting at a restaurant nearby. The proprietor is a close friend of mine and we shall not be disturbed. We have some very grave matters to discuss." Klausman had put on his tolerant mien as he, at long last, turned toward Hershel, making a face as he did so to express his disapproval.

In a petulant voice, Hershel said, "I hope you'll be easier to understand than you were last night. We couldn't understand a word you were saying. You must have been drunker than I was, if such a thing is possible. Anyway, what do I have to talk to you about—I mean, just exactly who are you? And, why don't you just back off from Karen? She's too young for the likes of you, you know. Besides, I saw her first."

Drawing himself up to his full height, given the restriction of the roof of the limousine, Klausman exclaimed, "Now you listen to me, Feldman! Whether you know it or not, you are in serious trouble. The reason I know that is because Miss Boschert is in my employ and it is I who have assigned her the task of auditing your accounting department at Mandel Family Apparel. You see, we suspect you of tampering with your company's books and possibly even of embezzling funds from the company. When she has completed her audit, Miss Boschert is to report her findings to me and it will be up to me to take any action that might be necessary. So, you had best keep a civil tongue in your head and cooperate with me."

Operating on the premise that a little bluffing goes a long way, Hershel declared, "You've got Karen all wrong, Klausman; she's gotten really close to my wife and me and I don't think even you could get her to turn against me. Anyway, what proof have you got that I've done anything wrong? If, as you say, Karen answers to you and, if she had found anything bogus going on, you would know about it by now, wouldn't you? So, don't try to pull that one on me, okay?"

"You are partially correct," Klausman chuckled, "Miss Boschert has indeed become quite close to your wife, and that very fact probably explains why she has not yet reported her findings to me. But, do not deceive yourself, Feldman; the facts will eventually come out, and then even your wife will be unable to protect you from justice, Miss Boschert notwithstanding. In the final analysis, her allegiance lies with me and with Klausman, Walther, und Hahn, GmbH. Eventually, the truth will out; so you see, as you Americans are wont to say: 'The jig is up'."

Hershel remained truculent, saying, "Your argument has holes in it, Klausman. If the jig really is up, why then are we meeting like this? If what you are saying is true, why aren't the cops knocking at my door already?" He smiled with satisfaction, believing that Klausman was the one who was bluffing.

"You are correct," Klausman resumed, "The police have not been informed, but not for the reason you think. It is my belief that there is a possibility that we can salvage something from this impending disaster."

"Oh, okay, here we go with the blackmail!" Hershel put on his outraged look.

"You would do well to hear me out at least," Klausman said calmly, "before you accuse me of blackmail. I happen to know why you married your wife, but I have an entirely different proposal to make to you. If you do not wish to spend a large part of the rest of your life behind bars, you will take heed to what I have to say."

"You don't think I'd be interested in marrying you, do you?" Hershel quipped.

This time, despite Hershel's disagreeable aroma, Klausman turned to face him in order to address him in a grave voice, "Your flippant attitude is inappropriate in this or any other situation. Furthermore, neither Miss Boschert nor I have been deceived by your pretence at buffoonery. I happen to know that you are quite intelligent, but that you have a propensity toward calumny. This is not the time for that either; it has come to the point where you will do well to drop all of your deception and trickery, and deal with me with complete candor. I am in control of this situation and I am quite serious. If you persist with your antics, I will simply allow this audit to proceed to its logical conclusion. The choice is yours, as far as I am concerned." With this, Klausman carefully placed an Egyptian cigarette in his holder and lighted it with an elegant gold lighter, blowing acrid smoke at the car's ceiling.

The transformation in Hershel was instantaneous. He asked, "Very well, Mr. Klausman, what is it that you wish to tell me?"

For a moment Klausman was too astonished to reply; then he did, "What I wish to disclose to you is the fact that I may be in a position to connect you with one who is in incomparable authority; one who may be your only possible path of deliverance from the consequences of your errant behavior. If you should be willing to commit yourself to my care, I shall take you to him, where you and he can discuss your fate. I must caution you, however; unless you are willing, ultimately, to surrender your allegiance to him, you will be wasting his time as well as your own. Ah, here we are at the restaurant. Let us suspend our discussion until we are seated in a private booth."

At four in the afternoon the restaurant, which was owned and operated by the elegant woman with whom Klausman had passed an evening when he first arrived in the U.S., was far off the beaten path and appeared to cater to extremely restricted clientele. The table to which they were shown by the proprietor herself was indeed private, being situated all by itself in a small alcove. After having taken their order and having delivered to them a light lunch, the waiter pulled a curtain across the opening of the alcove, leaving Hershel and Klausman in complete seclusion.

Hershel broke the silence that had prevailed while they were being seated and were being delivered their meal. "So, what if I should decide, after hearing his pitch, not to give my allegiance to this person?" he asked while he rearranged the food on his plate. "What then? Will this be one of those cases where I'll never be able to get free from him? I mean, what's to keep him from learning all about me and then using that information to blackmail me?"

Klausman paused with his fork halfway to his mouth, answering, "As far as that goes, he already knows enough about you to put you away for a very long time. However, he is not the kind who would betray someone without first having given him a chance to take advantage of his friendship. But, I must leave that to the two of you. Asking me such questions is a duplication of effort. You must address those things to him. Let us enjoy our meal, and I will arrange for you to meet him, if that is your desire. If not, we shall simply drop the matter and let the situation run its course, eh what?" With this last, Klausman completed the process of taking his bite, and consumed the rest of his meal with gusto. Hershel hardly touched his food, simply toying with it until Klausman had finished his to the last morsel.

Lucifer Abaddon, utilizing his comprehensive authority, had commandeered the sitting room in Klausman's hotel suite for the purpose of meeting with Hershel Feldman. He had also selected from his repertoire of personalities, the visage of a dignified gentleman of noble station, a dashingly handsome man in his apparent sixties with wavy silver hair and a ruddy complexion. Even though the maintenance of one so attractive and agreeable was difficult for him in the extreme, Abaddon believed it important enough to his proper image that he was willing to go to the effort on this occasion. He was sitting erect in Klausman's favorite chair when the latter showed Hershel into the room.

Indicating Hershel with a flourish, Klausman announced, "Your Excellency, may I present Mr. Hershel Feldman?" Turning to Hershel, he further stated, "Mr. Feldman, let me introduce you to His Excellency, Prince Lucifer Abaddon." With this, Klausman stepped back a pace or two behind Hershel.

Looking a bit puzzled, Hershel said, "I've already met a Lucifer Abaddon—at the ball night before last. Could there possibly be two Lucifer Abaddons in the world? And, of what monarchy are you prince, may I ask?" He finished the question with a chuckle, but suppressed it when he saw Abaddon's expression of slight annoyance.

With a wave of his cigarette holder, Abaddon replied, "Ah, I see you have met my son. He did, I believe, attend the ball earlier in the week, but I do not recall his mentioning a Hershel Feldman. Nevertheless, we are pleased to meet you, Mr. Feldman. Perhaps you will be kind enough to take a seat in that chair opposite. We are told by Herr Klausman that you may possibly be in need of our assistance. He has previously apprised us of your predicament of which, I must say, we find ourselves in full empathy. Klausman, perhaps you would be kind enough to bring Mr. Feldman a drink, there's a good fellow. Hershel—may I call you by your given name? What is your pleasure? We have, I believe, some fine scotch whiskey as well as an excellent cognac. Name your poison! Aha, ha, ha!"

It seemed to Hershel that he might have seen a tiny flame accompanied by a miniscule puff of smoke flicker about Abaddon's mouth; but no, this could not be. He respectfully replied, "Nothing for me just now, Sir; and my first name will be fine." Why was he being respectful of this obvious fop, he wondered. Was not this entire performance truly bogus? In spite of his doubts, Hershel could not prevent himself from bowing slightly at the waist. He was totally and utterly bewildered and intimidated, completely drawn in. Without his realizing it, he was beginning to surrender himself to this Prince Abaddon. Hershel was gravely disturbed but knew not why it was so.

"Well, tell us then," Abaddon went on, drawing deeply on his cigarette holder, "in what manner could we possibly be of assistance?" It escaped Hershel's notice that, although Abaddon had not lighted his cigarette, his puffing produced a prodigious amount of smoke.

Hershel squirmed in discomfort, but replied, "Mr. Klausman, here, seems to be convinced that I am guilty of altering the books of the company where I am employed; and even embezzling, I suppose. Unfortunately for me, he has one of his employees auditing my work and feels that she will uncover some criminal activity on my part. Also unfortunately for me, I have no control over this person so, for all I know, she could be fabricating these things in preparation to bringing charges against me. And, to make matters even worse for me, I think my wife is in on the whole scheme. For some reason she's jealous of me—has been ever since we got married. It wouldn't surprise me if she had hired Mr. Klausman to take me down. You've heard the old saying: 'Hell hath no fury like a woman scorned,' haven't you?" Hershel ignored Klausman's huff of disdain.

"In view of your suspicion of Mr. Klausman's complicity, I am afraid we fail to see how we could possibly fit into the picture. Perhaps you would be so kind as to explain." Removing the cigarette holder from his lips, Abaddon placed it, along with the still unlit cigarette, on a huge ashtray and exhaled a cloud of smoke. Hershel took no notice of this.

"Well, for one thing, this whole idea of my meeting with you was his idea. If he's not involved with trying to frame me, why would he have any interest in me at all? What have I ever done for him? What would either of you have to gain from helping me? I don't know if you would call that an explanation, except to say that this is what I have come to suspect." All the while Hershel was speaking, he gazed not at Mr. Abaddon, nor even at Mr. Klausman, but he merely looked down at his hands. If he had indeed met Abaddon's glance, he would have seen the tiny flame issue from the latter's mouth.

Abaddon sighed, then answered, "You make a good point, Mr. Feldman. At first glance, one would not perceive our motives in offering you our aid. And, of course, we will not attempt to deceive you; if indeed we were to help you, we would most certainly ask something of you in return. Still, we believe, once you have heard us out, you will find our offer to be most attractive, and beneficial, as well." By this time Hershel had lifted his gaze to meet that of Mr. Abaddon, thereby missing the interesting spectacle of the cigarette in the holder lighting itself. Abaddon went on, "If you find this of interest, we shall continue."

Hershel perked up visibly. He said, "I'm all ears, Your Excellency."

Turning to Klausman, Mr. Abaddon said, "Leave us, Anton, there's a good fellow." Then, ignoring Klausman, he turned his attention back to Hershel, addressing him,

"Suppose, dropping all pretence, we candidly assess your present situation. Then you will be in a better position to apprehend the benefits of our mutual positions. We are informed that, although she is in a position to wreak destruction on your life and career, you have definite designs on Herr Klausman's employee, Karen Boschert. This is so, is it not?" Abaddon raised his eyebrows in inquiry.

Hershel put on his hurt look, and blurted, "Well, if my wife wasn't so…"

"When we proposed we drop all pretence," Abaddon interrupted, "we had supposed that included yourself as well as us. Do try to keep your side of the bargain."

"Okay, I'll admit I'm very attracted to Karen, but I happen to know your son is just as gaga over her as I am. And, who could blame us? And, why does that make me the bad guy?" Hershel hadn't totally abandoned his hurt look at this point.

Abaddon smiled indulgently and replied, "The difference is, of course, our son is unmarried." He picked up the cigarette holder and took a puff or two, and then set it back on the ashtray. He continued, "Putting all that aside for the moment, let us consider the rest of your plight, continuing to eschew all attempts at pretence, of course. We are informed, on excellent authority, that Miss Boschert's findings on your behalf are profoundly condemning; that you have indeed been altering the books of your wife's company and that there are considerable funds unaccounted for. All of your denials, Mr. Feldman, are to no avail. Herr Klausman would need simply to press Miss Boschert for the submission of her report and there would be no recourse but to file criminal charges against you. We hardly think a court in this nation would acquit you. So, as we see your situation, and correct us if we are in error, you are doubly confounded: You are headed for certain incarceration, and you are in love with someone other than your wife. We ask you: how do you propose to extricate yourself apart from availing yourself of some sort of succor?"

Giving Abaddon a sour look, Hershel replied, "If I thought I could get myself out of this mess, I wouldn't have met with Mr. Klausman in the first place. So, I admit I need help. But, I still don't see what you would have to gain by helping me. It looks to me that you have all you could ever need, so why even bother with a poor sucker like me?"

All the while he was speaking this last, Hershel reverted once more to looking down at his hands. Hearing strange sounds coming from Abaddon's direction, he shifted his gaze in that direction and, leaping to his feet, he exclaimed, "Oh, my god! What th'? What is this? Jeez, who, or what, are you?"

Opposite Hershel, writhing on the couch, a horrid dragon hissed and spouted flame and smoke in Hershel's direction. Instantly, the atmosphere became fetid with the dragon's rank issuances. The creature's scales and plates scraped and rattled as it squirmed and swished its tail about. Finally, in Abaddon's voice, it spoke, "You needn't be alarmed, Feldman, I am not going to harm you. Sit back down and listen to me." It belched more flames and smoke before it settled down to talk, saying, "Sooner or later you will have to learn my identity, and it is tiring for me to remain in the configuration of that royal gentleman, especially when I am nothing at all like him. Heed now what I am about to say."

Hershel could utter not a sound, but cowered in his chair, afraid to move.

Dropping the royal personal pronoun 'we', the dragon went on, "I must say, you *are* in rather a predicament, aren't you? Fortunately, you have come to the right party for assistance. Here is what I propose: In exchange for your unconditional surrender, and for your solemn promise to abandon your pursuit of Miss Boschert, I hereby offer you the following: I shall arrange for Mr. Klausman to remove Miss Boschert from your case, and to assign someone else over whom he has absolute control. You will therefore be absolved of all misdeeds and restored to good favor in your position at Mandel Family Apparel. In addition, I shall see to it that your wife will no longer constitute an impediment to your progress in the world of business and accounting. You will find yourself elevated to a position far loftier than your wildest expectations. And finally, I shall see to it that Mrs. Petersen, or perhaps another such beauty of your own choice, will find her way into your arms. In short, I shall provide for your complete rejuvenation, without any complications whatsoever. What do you say to that?" The chuffing and spewing increased accordingly as the monster concluded its discourse. Fire, smoke, and steam pervaded the entire room, scorching the couch and its throw pillows.

Before he made to reply, Hershel mused on the matter a moment. Although he was entirely convinced that without some sort of rescue he was doomed to incarceration, he was also confident that he should be able to negotiate better terms than Abaddon had offered him. It galled him to think that someone, even one such as a dragon, should be able to deprive him of the girl he had dreamed of all his adult life. In fact, he resolved not to agree to anything that would prohibit him from attempting to win Karen for himself. However, after having meditated on this for a full minute, he made his decision: He would agree to Abaddon's terms but would continue to pursue Karen anyway. After all, if one is dealing with the devil, why not behave much as the devil would do? He saw no justification for his being loyal to Abaddon when he knew for certain that Abaddon would betray him without giving it a moment's thought. Turning to Abaddon, who had by then transfigured himself into the snaggle-toothed monster with the claw-like hands, he said with a resigned voice, "Okay, it looks like you've got me up against the wall. I have no possible defense, so I guess I'll have to accept your terms. It's hands off little Miss Karen for me and from now on I'm a player on your team. When you put it like that: that if I don't swear allegiance to you, and if I don't stay away from Karen Boschert, then I go to jail, I guess you win. But, I have one question before I seal the deal." It struck him as irony that now Abaddon's stench was worse than his own.

"What makes you think you deserve any answers to questions at this point?" the monster asked.

Hershel sighed and answered, "I didn't say I deserved an answer, I simply stated that I had a question. If you don't choose to answer it, so be it."

Abaddon took a second to exhale a horrid-smelling gas before replying, "Very well, what is your question?"

"What about my wife? I mean, it strikes me that she has the power to wreck this whole deal if she chooses to. She's no fool, you know. As a matter of fact, I can't think of anyone else I'd rather not cross than Rose. So, what would you propose to do about her, if I may be so bold as to, ask?" Hershel was beginning to see the entire scheme falling apart right before his eyes.

For a split second, Abaddon was the dragon, then he returned to the ogre, as he replied, "Don't you worry about Rose Mandel. I will see to her. If you will do exactly as I tell you, there will be nothing for you to worry about. That is all I will say. Do you agree to my terms or not?"

Hershel sighed once again, then replied, "What choice do I have? Yes, of course, I agree."

There was a tremendous sound as if a jet aircraft had passed the window, and the dragon, to which persona Abaddon had returned, vanished from the room. Hershel sat alone for some time before Klausman finally slipped back into his sitting room, looking as if he had swallowed a canary.

Chapter Seven

A fierce pain in his neck woke Hershel from a drugged sleep. Dragging himself to a sitting position, he looked about him, attempting to get oriented. The recliner he was struggling to sit up in was the fine brown leather one that Rose had given him and he discovered he had gotten sick in the night and the fruits of his sickness had run down into the crevice between the seat cushion and the backrest. The smell was causing resurgence of his sickness. He must get up out of this mess and go to work. What time was it? What *day* was it? The pain that had started in his neck from sleeping in a twisted position began to work its way to his head; only it was intensifying. He called out, "Rose! Where are you?" There was no answer. Where was that woman when he needed her? "Mrs. Bridges!" he yelled. "Get in here, will you? And bring me a Bromo!" He felt like he was going to be sick again. Sitting on the edge of his chair, head in his hands, he reasoned: he wouldn't have had to get soused again if it hadn't been for that disgusting dragon or whatever it was messing with his life and threatening him. A half hour in the presence of that awful thing would make a lifelong drunk out of anyone. He shuddered, got up, and staggered into the bathroom. Mrs. Bridges placed the effervescent anodyne on his dresser and quietly left the bedroom.

As he entered the garage, Hershel noticed Rose's Mercedes was missing, giving him to assume she had not returned the previous day from her office in the city. This piqued him for two reasons: First of all, why did Rose have to make such a big deal of his knocking her around a little? She knew how he got when He'd had too much to drink. And second, she knew how he hated to drive his BMW into New York City. If it wasn't the pigeons crapping all over it, it was the potholes and the mud puddles. Maybe he would just take the limo service and save his car from the city's hazards. It was only fifty bucks each way. So what if he was a little late for work. Kevin could take care of things until he got there.

When he did arrive at his office, Hershel took one look at Kevin and knew something was up. Rather than his usual cheerful self, Kevin was forlorn and listless. He did not even smile at his boss as the latter hung his coat on the rack in his office and trotted to the elevators. In keeping with his usual behavior, Hershel simply burst into Karen's office without knocking or announcing himself in any way. To his surprise, he was confronted by a middle aged, balding man in a white shirt, narrow tie, and suit vest. He held in one hand a sheaf of papers and in the other a cell phone over which he shouted obscenities. Glancing at Hershel, the man simply stopped talking on the phone and flipped it shut and then, turning to Hershel, he shouted, "Ah, Feldman, you're here. Give me a minute." With this he turned to an ageless woman in a tweed business suit and barked some orders at her. She, in turn, grabbed the papers he was holding and sat down at Karen's desk and set to work.

"Who are you," asked Hershel, "and where is Karen?" He looked as worried as he was.

"Ginsberg," the man answered, "Aaron Ginsberg. His Eminence, the honorable Anton Klausman sent me here to get things straightened out. It shouldn't take us more than a day or two. He—Mr. Klausman, that is—sent Miss Boschert back to Switzerland last evening. I wouldn't want to be in her shoes. This is the biggest mess I've seen in all my days. Clara and I will have a favorable report in Mr. Klausman's hands in short order. With this last remark, Ginsberg gave Hershel what he believed to be a wink, but what amounted more to an extreme facial distortion.

Hershel was aghast. "What did you say about Karen? Where did she go? Did Klausman do this? I'll have his hide for this!" He turned on his heel and headed for the elevator and his own office where he dialed the number Mr. Abaddon had given him for direct contact.

A voice Hershel recognized as that of Schaeffer answered after only two rings. As if he thought shouting would impress Schaeffer, Hershel exploded, "This is Hershel Feldman and I want to talk to Abaddon right now!"

In a tone calculated to put Hershel in his place, which it did not do, Schaeffer replied, "I will ask His Excellency if he would be disposed to speak to you, Feldman. Hold the line."

After at least five long minutes, Mr. Abaddon finally picked up and asked, "To what do I owe this rude interruption, Feldman? I have many matters to attend to other than your petty disappointments, you must know."

Hershel, not to be put off, rejoined, "What do you mean by sending Karen back to Switzerland? There was nothing in our agreement about that!" He was flushed with anger and frustration.

"Well, first of all," Abaddon said smoothly, "who do you think you are speaking to? I will tolerate no insubordination from you or anyone else. Second, I have given no instructions whatsoever regarding Miss Boschert's disposal, *ergo,* she should be found in any of her usual locations. They would be her flat in the West Village, her office at Klausman, Walther, und Hahn, GmbH, or in her temporary office at Mandel Family Apparel, if that could possibly be any of your business. What causes you to believe she has been sent back to Switzerland?" Abaddon had become testy sounding as he added, "And why, might I ask, do you presume to demand anything concerning one to whom you have been, by virtue of our mutual agreement, denied access?"

His anger increasing, Hershel yelled, "Our 'agreement' as you call it is beside the point. The girl is missing and I want to know why you allowed it. I didn't agree to her being abducted or otherwise abused. Where is she? And, if you don't know, why not?"

Very softly and evenly, Abaddon declared, "This conversation is concluded." He hung up. What Hershel could not possibly have seen were the flames coming from the ogre's cruel mouth and the smoke curling from his hawk nose.

While Karen drove the Mercedes, Rose huddled in the passenger's seat and gave directions. Karen drove swiftly but carefully, taking advantage of the car's ample power and excellent balance, but exercising caution as well so as not to attract the attention of police. Neither spoke much; Karen needing to concentrate on driving in a country foreign to her upbringing, and Rose finding it all she could handle giving directions to Karen, given her fragile physical and mental states.

"Please go on home and get some rest. You've been taking care of me all day." Rose, though she felt a bit guilty keeping Karen to herself for the entire day, scarcely sounded convincing as she pleaded with the girl from her comfortable bed in the tiny apartment adjacent to her eighth floor office. "I'll be all right after I've rested through the night," she added.

Karen looked at Rose tenderly before she replied, "I am not so much concerned about your recovery from Hershel's beating as I am about your vulnerability to another attack. He would certainly have no difficulty finding you here, would he?"

"Oh, he knows were to find me, of course, but I don't believe he will be a threat to me again so soon." Rose said, "If I know Hershel, he'll be oh so sorry for what he did to me, but only for a while, then he'll want to discuss it, and finally he'll revert back to his hostile ways; but this will take some time. In the meantime I'm supposed to forgive and forget, and to be grateful I have such a wonderful husband."

She dabbed at her eyes and nose with a tissue, sighing as she watched Karen fuss about the room. When the latter gathered up a teacup, plate and some silverware and headed for the kitchenette for the purpose of washing up, Rose exclaimed, "Please, Karen, don't bother with those things. I have a woman who comes in tomorrow to clean up. She'll take care of all that. You've done far more than I could have asked for. I feel terrible about your taking up your whole day." She began to cry softly, wiping her eyes some more and, after a bit, blowing her nose gently.

Dragging the dressing table chair over, Karen sat beside the bed and said sternly to Rose, "It is not right! You are so good to him and you tolerate so much. Why must you put up with this? Have you spoken to anyone about it—perhaps a counselor or a priest? Oh, I forget—a rabbi, then? You must not try to carry this burden alone. I would be happy to help if I knew what to do. I have already been praying for you; did you know that?"

Not wanting to deal with the question yet, Rose answered, "I know I shouldn't let Hershel do me this way, but I'm torn between loving him and hating him." She wept louder but continued through her tears, "I appreciate your praying for me but I don't see what good it will do. Hershel wouldn't respond to God's reprimand, would he? I'm so tired and confused and, and afraid, I guess. I keep wondering if he, Hershel I mean, will try to kill me next time."

"Do not even say that!" Karen said sharply, "Just say the word and I shall call the authorities and we shall have him arrested. Surely there are laws to protect you. Why not make use of them? Perhaps you will allow me to ask Herr Klausman for assistance. He is, I am certain, well versed in legalities, even in the U.S. I could merely ask his advice. What do you say?"

Rose, having ceased her crying, looked skeptically at Karen and said, "Somehow I doubt if your 'Herr' Klausman would find it in his heart to give me much thought. Now you—that's a different matter." In spite of her agitated condition, Rose chuckled a little at the thought of Klausman tearing his attention away from Karen in order to give aid to someone such as herself.

Karen appeared confused. "Pardon? I do not catch your meaning. Are you intimating that Herr Klausman has an interest in me? That is absurd."

"No, you're absurd. Since you arrived here in New York, I have seen not one man who caught even a glimpse of you who did not have an interest in you." Rose gave Karen an almost pitying look. "It took me a while to see that, although you're highly educated and practically a genius about business and numbers and such, you're extremely naïve about men. I'm afraid Hershel is up against some pretty serious competition for your favor. There are Mr. Klausman and Mr. Abaddon to start with, and there's no telling whom you left behind in Switzerland, panting with passion. Are you going to tell me you're not even aware of all this attention men give you?"

For the first time since Rose had met her, Karen flushed a bit. "Well, I am aware of Mr. Abaddon's interest because he has been so aggressive, but Mr. Klausman has said nothing to me." Karen had finally realized the address "Herr" sounded a bit strange in America. She continued, "And, I suppose I have been too busy in my life so far to make note of the men at home and any possible interest on their part. But, we are straying from the point. All right, let us forget about Mr. Klausman for the moment. Is there no one else to whom you could go for help? How about your father or your mother? Surely they would come to your aid, or they would know of someone to call upon."

Rose sighed again and said, "I've given up on both. My mother lives in her own little world and sees nothing wrong about the way Hershel treats me; at least I believe that's what she thinks. When I complained to her about him she said, "Well, we women just have to put up with the terrible things men do. If you don't like him, divorce him." That's what she did with her first husband and also my father who, by the way, is totally useless. Since he retired and moved to Florida, he has just faded away into senility. So, they're both useless, I'm afraid." Throwing off the blanket Karen had tucked under her chin, Rose went on, "Neither of my parents understands about my relationship with Hershel. They both think he pursued me and that he thinks he got a great catch. When I try to explain that I tricked Hershel into marrying me, they both turn off their brains and go into denial. They're crazy! They wonder why *their* wonderful baby would have to trick anyone into marriage. They're definitely the ones who're crazy." She had to struggle with her emotions to keep from crying again.

Shifting in the uncomfortable little chair, Karen began, "I recall when I was fourteen years old and my parents were beginning to drift apart, how my mother wept and wept because she believed she was alone with no one to help her. My father was a very troubled man, but a good one. They both were still in love, I think, but their interests had changed; my father wishing to go into Christian ministry and my mother was intent on raising four daughters, of which I was the oldest. Neither seemed to be able to understand the other. Also, I believe my mother was much concerned about my education because my father had removed himself from the lucrative business world and had begun training for the priesthood, where there is little or no monetary compensation. Mama (accent on the second syllable) had a dream one night in which she saw Jesus, and He told her she must not worry, that He would take care of her needs, and that she need only trust Him completely for all things. When she told Papa (second syllable again) of this, they prayed all the night through—I heard them in their room—and from that night onward our lives began to improve. It took some time for us all to understand what had happened, especially for Enid because she had only five years at the time, but I do remember that we prayed often to Jesus." She had been looking directly at Rose the entire time she had been speaking, but she then seemed to gaze into another place as she continued, "I, too, had a visit from Jesus, but He came to me one afternoon as I sat by a lake when we were on holiday. It seemed as though I could reach out and touch Him; as though He were sitting next to me on the sand. I do not recall whether or not He actually spoke audibly to me but I understood Him nevertheless. From that moment onward I have known that I would live the rest of my life following Him. Jesus is all that I will ever need. He fulfills my every wish and desire and He watches over me. I never seem anymore to be afraid or in want. Oh, I wish I knew better my English."

Rose sat silently for so long that Karen thought she might not have heard then, clearing her throat, she said, "I'm a little confused here, Karen. What are you saying? I'm not even interested in God, let alone Jesus. My father has always wanted me to believe in God like he does, but I really have never pursued that sort of thing. It all sounds so phony, especially when my father and his cronies get to chanting and singing and putting on their shawls. Can you imagine what he would say if I told him I believe Jesus is the Messiah? He'd have a funeral for me and never again acknowledge my existence. If I were to tell him I'm a follower of Jesus he would be even less helpful to me than he is now. No, no, I have no interest in Jesus, if that's what you're working up to."

"I was not attempting to evangelize or even to start a discussion with you, I do not believe. I was—how do you say it—simply thinking out loud. But, I did want you to know why I am like I am, you see, because Jesus is in my life and in my heart. I was illustrating to you how Jesus lifted me out of despair and, at the same time, put happiness in my heart. Oh, I am saying this so badly. You do not happen to speak German or French, do you? We could communicate better, I should think." Karen, because she had been caught off guard, was flustered and a bit embarrassed. She continued, "I merely meant to point out that Jesus has the capacity to lift us out of our misery if we should ask Him to. But, Rose dear, I would not advise anyone, especially one such as you, to commit to anything that is life-changing without their first having examined it."

Rose interrupted, "Wait, I thought you said this Jesus came to you without your first having gotten to know him, at least that's how it sounded to me. Why would he not do the same to me?" She knew this question was contentious, but at the same time, she was truly curious about Karen's claim to be so closely connected with an ancient prophet. Feeling as if she had scored a point, Rose set her mouth in a little straight line across her face and awaited Karen's reply.

It was a while in coming. Karen shifted her gaze from space to Rose's eyes, then answered, "I have no doubt whatsoever that He would, Rose, if you should ask Him to do so. It is a matter of opening one's heart to Him and confessing one's sins to Him. But, of course, one must recognize her sinfulness to herself before she could confess anything of the sort to God. I know that, in my case I had to reach a point of complete desperation and despair before I could admit such a thing to myself. Up until that point at the lakeside I had convinced myself that I needed no help from anyone at all; but the condition of my life continued to worsen until I arrived at the conclusion that all I could possibly do on my own would never in a thousand years serve to rescue me from my despair. Does this make any sense to you, Dear?"

"But, I still don't see why a person like you, with so many things going for her, would be in despair." With her attention now shifted to Karen, Rose had ceased her crying completely, and she continued, "You're so beautiful, so intelligent, so sweet; why on earth were you in despair?"

"You know, I wondered about that for some time afterward," Karen said, "but then I realized that all my education, my plans, my beauty, as you call it, and even the mending of my family's situation did not seem to fulfill my life. Is 'fulfill' the correct word? I do not know so well. At any rate, I knew that there was something altogether significant that was missing from my life, something or someone without whom I could not go on living. I had no real purpose in my life, you see, no reason to be educated or to be attractive or to be 'sweet', as you put it. In short, I did not know where I had come from, why I had been born, nor did I know where I would go when I should die. My life did not seem to have any significance at all. Do you see now why I despaired?"

"Sort of," Rose answered, "but I still don't see where Jesus comes in. Wasn't he just some sort of prophet or teacher? I can see why you would want God to help you, but Jesus; I don't understand." She appeared to be completely confused.

Karen looked astonished: "But, they are one and the same, Rose, did you not know that? I am sorry, I do not know what the Jews teach now."

Rose almost giggled as she responded, "I don't really know what the Jews teach, either. I've made it my business to avoid anyone who tried to brainwash me with all that religious nonsense. I love my father but I never listen to him. The only reason I agreed to get married in a Jewish ceremony was because my mother would have cried forever and my father would have had a heart attack if I had not. I learned the rituals by rote but my heart was not in it." She thought a moment and then asked, "What do you mean by saying they, God and Jesus, are the same? That's ridiculous!"

Without a hint of impatience in her voice, Karen answered, "It is the Christian teaching that God exists in three persons: Father, Son, and Holy Spirit. The Father is the

One your people call Yahweh, the Son is Y'shua, and the Spirit is—oh dear—I do not know what you call the Holy Spirit. In any case, they are all One, that is, the Trinity or Triune God. Often, when we say "God", we mean the Father, when we say "Jesus" we mean the Son, and sometimes we call the Holy Spirit the "Holy Ghost". But, that does not change things. The fact remains that we can hear from any or all of the Three."

Rose went from giddy to befuddled as she remarked, "That's just too confusing for me. I thought my father's religion was perplexing, but Christianity is worse."

"It is really quite simple." Karen explained patiently, "I will try to put it to you as simply as I can with my limited English. Are you certain you do not have any French or German?" Her broad smile as she asked this helped to put Rose at ease. She went on, "When Adam and Eve sinned by eating of the forbidden fruit of the tree of the knowledge of good and evil, that act caused the undoing of much of the good and innocence that God had created when He made the universe. It put into the hearts and minds of all future mankind a nature that was and is completely sinful. We are all therefore born totally bad and must learn to be good. Some learn well and live good lives and some others do not learn so well and live horrid lives, but all retain their evil, sinful *nature*; even those who live relatively good lives. Nevertheless, all are sinners, every single one. Even though it is written that God created us all in His image, we spoiled it with sin. Because of our sinful nature, we shall all go to hell when we die. The reason for that is that God will allow no sin to be in His heaven because, you see, God will only accept into heaven, then, those who are perfect. Oh, to be sure, God loves us—those whom He has created—but He hates sin and evil. If you or I wish to go to heaven when we die we must be perfect. But, the problem here is that; if we commit just one single sin, perhaps have an unkind thought, or steal some trifling thing, we cannot be perfect in God's eyes and we are going to hell. Of course, God did not create us in order that we should go to hell. He created us in order that we should live with Him forever in heaven; but only if we are heavenly, that is, perfect. How might we make ourselves perfect? That is impossible, simply because we are evil by our nature." She paused a moment to let Rose digest these notions.

Rose was astonished and she declared, "If that's true, what can possibly be done for us? I mean, if we're bad to begin with and it only takes one little thing to keep us that way, how can we possibly get into heaven? And, why would we even want to go there if God is going to be so exclusive about it? It's all so useless, how can you be so happy and confident yourself?" Rose was devastated.

Karen patted Rose's hand and continued, "God is no happier about this than you or I. After all, He made us perfect—we are the ones who fell from *His* favor by sinning. But, all is not lost! God had planned for just such a possibility before He had even created the universe. You see, He loves us and does not wish to punish us, but He hates our sin and must punish it. As humans we would have no idea how to solve this problem; but God is not like us. He must have decided before time began that He would take upon Himself the punishment for our sins so that we should be perfect and therefore able to go to heaven. So it was that He sent His only Son to be the Man Jesus Christ who would die upon a crucifixion cross in order to take the punishment we deserve for our sins. You have heard, of course, the name 'Messiah'? That is what Jesus is—the Messiah—or perhaps we could say the 'Saviour'. So, when Jesus died on the cross He took upon Himself the blame for all of the evil things that will have been done by mankind throughout history, and he paid the price that we should have paid ourselves for all the terrible things we have done, and all the good things we have failed to do. Now, because of what Jesus did for us on the cross, we have taken on His righteousness so that we can be perfect and go to heaven. That is why I am so happy and why I am so confident that Jesus has already done for me all I need in order to be eligible for heaven."

Rose was more confused than ever as she asked, "Even if this is all true, which I doubt, and even if he did that for you, why on earth would he do such a thing for a Jewish girl who doesn't even believe in him? It sounds completely hopeless to me." She looked as if she were going to cry again. "I mean," she continued, "you were a Christian as a young girl and God, or Jesus, already knew you, I guess. Oh, I don't know what to think. I'm so confused. God doesn't even know I exist!" Her lips trembled with emotion.

Karen was horrified: "He most certainly does know you! He created you, did He not? And, He loves you without conditions. He wants so much for you to trust Him and to believe in Him. After all, why would He have died for you if He did not know you and care about you? He has told us that *anyone* who will believe in Him and put their trust in His Son will be saved from their awful state of hopelessness and will be with Him in heaven forever." Karen was flushed with excitement as she spoke these things.

"How do *you* know what God has said?" Rose was brimming with anger—or perhaps frustration.

Karen smiled and said, "I am no different from anyone else who wishes to know about Jesus so she can know Him personally. I began some years ago reading about Him in the Bible. My parents gave me a Bible when I was quite young, but I rather ignored it until I had that encounter with the Lord Himself. After that I could not—how do you say—acquire enough about Him to satisfy myself. Is 'acquire' the correct word?"

"I suppose it is; I think I know what you mean." Rose was beginning to apprehend Karen's meaning. "So," she asked, "must I read the entire Bible before I understand who God and Jesus and the Ghost are?"

Karen chuckled a bit before she answered, "You Americans have the quaintest way of putting things sometimes. No, reading the Bible is not at all necessary for you to know God personally. There must be many, many people who cannot read at all, but they know God more closely than some of those who are good readers. I am simply saying that the Bible is an excellent way for someone who reads to acquaint herself with God. I found it much easier to understand by purchasing on my own a modern translation in German. But, of course, you should not purchase a German Bible; you should find a modern translation into English. I believe there is even an American version of the Bible. I would suggest that, if you are interested, you should speak to Kevin, Hershel's assistant, for the best information about the Bible. Because your family and many of your friends are Jews, they will not be good sources of information about the Bible. But, we are straying from the point of our discussion. I know what God says because the Bible *is* the words of God. He is quoted many, many times throughout the entire book, and He has spoken to many, many men and women for many centuries. Some of those to whom He has spoken have been inspired to write what He has told them, and these writings are the Bible. Some are from as long ago as Moses, and others as recently as Saint Paul. But, the one thing they all had in common was that they were inspired by God to write what they heard Him say. You do understand, do you not that, when I say they heard God I do not mean that it was necessarily an audible voice. Many people hear Him in their hearts or their minds."

"Hold on," Rose interrupted, "this is getting to be just too weird, and I'm getting more confused by the minute. I'd almost rather hear my father try to explain his religion to me. I know you mean well, Karen, but we are not getting anywhere. If I should decide I want to know more about God the way you know about Him, what should I do? Should I go out and buy the kind of Bible Kevin suggests? And, then what? Just start reading? Where should I start? Isn't it rather a long book? If I start at the beginning it will take me a long time to finish. I'm sorry, Sweetie, but I just don't know what to do."

Karen fixed her gaze on Rose's eyes for a long moment before saying, "All I know for certain to tell you is that which worked for me. I simply went to the bookstore and bought a modern translation of the Bible, and then I took it home and sat in the chair in my room and began to read it from the very first page. After a few months I had finished reading it and I started over from the beginning and read it once more. Since that time I have not been able to stop reading it; not necessarily from the beginning to the end, but I find that I am prompted—is that the correct word—to start in different places at different times. Surely this is not the way with all who read the Bible, but it is the way it happened for me. But, you must remember, Dear, that none of this is really necessary for you to find Him. All that is required is for you to submit to Him and to place your trust in Him. I believe you and I are alike in that we are reticent merely to step out in faith without first educating ourselves. In that respect, I believe, we are at a disadvantage compared to those whose minds are not so—how do you say—cluttered. Let us go tomorrow to Kevin and ask him to help you find the right Bible. What do you say?"

Rose was silent for a long moment; then she nodded solemnly her assent.

Chapter Eight

The Hon. Anton Klausman was distressed, so much so that he paced about his rooms at the Ritz-Astoria, smoking one Turkish cigarette after another. Unaccustomed to being denied anything he desired, he fretted and fumed. How was it possible, mused the pompous statesman and business tycoon, that the likes of His Excellency Abaddon should be able to deny him, Klausman, access to Karen Boschert? This was unacceptable. Klausman had set his sights on Karen the moment he had first encountered her. This obsession with the girl transcended even his usual avarice. Perhaps it was because she seemed so unattainable that he was absolutely possessed with the desire to have her. Whatever the actual reason was for his distress, he was nevertheless frantic to take her from Abaddon, Feldman, or whoever else might purport to have a claim on her. As a consequence, he was feverishly plotting his next move. How to snatch her from the jaws of the monstrous serpent? How to trick her away from the feckless Jewish clown? Sooner or later, he resolved, he would find a way to make the delectable Karen his own. He put his not inconsiderable intellect to work.

Karen was herself somewhat anxious, but it had nothing to do with Herr Klausman. She was concerned for Rose Mandel-Feldman's soul. She felt that she had bungled terribly her first, and perhaps only, opportunity to lead Rose into the presence of Jesus. If only she knew better how to express herself in English—but now, perhaps it was too late. The only recollections she had of her discussion with Rose were the searching for the correct English words and the difficulties she had putting her thoughts in the proper order so that they might make some sense to Rose. In this respect, she considered herself an utter failure. The one comfortable upholstered chair in her West Village flat squatted by a window that looked out onto an asphalt playground that sported a basketball hoop. Sitting sideways in the chair and idly watching a motley assortment of boys, along with one lanky girl, shoot basketballs at the net-less hoop, Karen allowed her conscious mind to go quiet and her subliminal mind to awaken, an ability she had possessed since her childhood. Before her subconscious eyes there appeared a sort of tapestry on which was inscribed, in Greek, a brief text: But, whatever is given you in that hour, speak that, for it is not you who speak, but the Holy Spirit. Almost immediately the tapestry was supplanted by the image of a peasant girl with long black hair walking slowly along the furrows of a field, sowing seed that she took from a pouch hung about her waist, outside her apron. Dense clouds gathered in the sky beyond her, promising rain to irrigate the seed.

It may have been an hour or more later that Karen awoke, because the sun was definitely lower in the sky and a slight chill had thinned out the group of boys who were shooting hoops outside her open window. Had she really slept all that time, or was she in some sort of trance? It really was of no consequence to her; she was now possessed by a great calm—a peace that could only have come from one source—Jesus. Had His Holy Spirit actually put into her heart the words Rose needed to hear? Doubt had now left her and she smiled comfortably at the boys' antics as they dodged and feinted, stretching their arms in front of their opponents, giving no quarter to the girl, who remained in action. Even though she understood nothing of the game the boys and girl were playing, she watched contentedly for a while, until her mobile phone peeled like church bells, coming from the vicinity of her nightstand. "Hello, yes?" For some reason, she answered without so much as a glance at the phone's display.

A slightly slurred voice on the other end came back, "Is this the beautiful Karen Bosch...Bosch...ugh...B-Boschert speaking?" Hershel wondered why foreigners always had to have names that were hard to pronounce. What, after all, was wrong with just plain Bosley or Bosnic? He hiccupped into the phone.

Karen nearly hung up until she recognized Hershel's voice, but she asked nevertheless, "Who is this speaking?"

"It's Hershel Feldman, your most ardent admirer, of course." Even though he wished to come across as confident, he laughed nervously.

"What is it you wish, Mr. Feldman?" Why did she not hang up, she wondered? She certainly had no desire to entangle herself with this devilish man.

Hershel cleared his throat and went on, "Well, for starters, I want to have a word with the most beautiful girl I've ever seen. Can I come in?"

"You most certainly may not come in, Mr. Feldman. It is quite late and I am most tired from working all day. Surely this can wait until a more opportune time, can it not?"

"No, wait! You don't understand. This is very important. I need to talk to you now. I'm in a parking lot right down the street and I can be there in a jiffy. Come on, let me come over and talk just a few minutes. I won't stay very long."

"What is it that you wish to talk to me about that is so urgent that it cannot wait until another time? I have not yet even dined."

"I need to talk to you about—about, ugh, my wife, Rose—yes, that's it, Rosie, my wife. What about it, Gorgeous, just for a few minutes, okay?"

"Mr. Feldman, I am not properly dressed and I am very tired. Another time, perhaps, would be better for us both. I shall be dressed and rested and you, you will be, ah, in better condition, I should think." She thought a moment and then asked, "Is Rose all right? I spent most of yesterday with her and she seemed to be recovering from her, ah, mishap. You have not struck her again, have you?"

Hershel sounded aghast, "No, no, of course not. That was just an accident, and it's what I need to talk to you about. Please let me come over, okay?"

Karen waited a moment before answering, "Very well, give me five minutes, and then press the button below my mailbox. I am in two-bee." She touched END on her phone.

It could not possibly have been five minutes before Karen heard the buzzer sound in her kitchen. She walked slowly to the door still tucking her blouse into her slacks. Because she cared only about propriety, not necessarily about her appearance, she didn't check her hair nor was she wearing any makeup at all. Opening the door slowly until it was arrested by the chain, she peered through the opening straight into the leering face of Hershel Feldman. It was another minute or two before she could force herself to release the chain and open the door fully and allow his entry. She did so with quite some reluctance. "Enter, Mr. Feldman," she said, "have a seat on the couch, if you wish." He sat, and she in turn sat across from him on an upholstered chair, eying Hershel far too long to suit him. "What is it you wish to say?" she asked at last.

He didn't answer at first, but simply stared at her. For the first time in his life he could think of nothing to say. One single thought scrolled endlessly through his mind: *"I must have this girl for my own; she is the one I've been waiting for all my life."* Finally, he spoke, "I, ugh, I just wanted to tell you how much I....I mean, I think you are the most, ugh, beautiful, I mean, you are *really* something, you know that?" He seemed to be having trouble breathing, and lapsed into silence, resuming his staring.

Pursing her lips and twisting a simple silver ring around her finger, Karen regarded the pitiful creature squirming in the chair across the coffee table from her. Finally, she asked,

"What has this to do with Rose, whom you have treated so abominably? Is she not the one about whom you wished to talk? It would seem to me that you have gained entry to my flat on false pretenses. You must leave immediately!"

"No, no, please don't make me go! I didn't really mean anything by that. It's just that I have trouble thinking of anyone else when I'm with you. I feel like I've been searching for you all my life and I can't think straight; my thoughts get all jumbled up and I say things that offend people. I don't mean any harm, really. Could we please just start over? I did come to talk to you about Rose, I promise." Hershel discovered that he was perspiring profusely.

Karen looked at him sternly before replying, "You are not helping your cause by saying those things about your feelings for me. Having experienced your recent antics, I must warn you that you have thus far given me no reason to find you credible. In addition, you have treated a lovely person very brutally, both physically and emotionally. Why should I be willing to listen to you, even for a moment; which is, by the way, all the time you have left to make your case for why I should not throw you out immediately."

This last remark from such a young and beautiful girl set Hershel off: "Oh, going to throw me out, are you? I'd like to see you try it, Sweetheart!" He squared his shoulders and stared at the girl menacingly. In the next five seconds he found himself first screaming in pain as his right thumb was twisted against his wrist, then he was ejected through the apartment door by means of a kick in the small of his back, finally sprawling on his face on the hard tile floor of the hallway. As he writhed in agony from the pain in both his thumb, and his cheek where it struck the floor, he was still barely able to hear the door slam behind him.

For her part, Karen found herself ashamed even before she had hurled the door shut behind Hershel. Why had she allowed herself to be brought down to his level? Was she, a Christian, not supposed to be in better control of her own behavior? Even though she tried to justify her actions by virtue of Hershel's cruelty to Rose, she knew in her heart that her returning Hershel's malice upon himself was not the answer to dealing with him. She was nearly to the point of looking out into the hallway in order to see if he was still in sight when there was a tentative tap on the door. Opening the door cautiously, she beheld an even more pitiful sight: Hershel, his cheek blazing from the contact with the tile floor, cradling his right hand in his left and wincing with pain.

"Okay, I see your point; I'm an arrogant fool. Where did you learn to do that? I'm ready to talk the truth, now. May I come in, please?" He even sounded miserable.

If Karen weren't so perceptive, she would easily have been deceived by his apparent sincerity. At the risk of sounding convinced, she answered, "The brother of my mother instructed me in the art of Wushu—you may know it as kung fu. I am sorry if I injured you, but you must know you had it coming. I would prefer it if you did not come in just now."

"Please, please, just for a few minutes. I'll behave myself. I really need to talk to you a minute. Anyway, I don't think you need to worry about your personal safety. Ouch! I won't be able to write for a month; and how am I going to explain the shiner that's going to develop under my eye?" He made himself look even more pitiful.

"Pardon? What is this shiner you are developing?"

Hershel sighed, "I'm talking a black eye here. You ought to be ashamed of yourself practicing dangerous martial arts on a perfect novice."

"If you must know, I *am* a bit ashamed. You may come in, but only for a few minutes; then you must leave. Sit on the couch and I will get you a cool cloth for your cheek." She padded softly toward the rear of her apartment, her Chinese house shoes making practically no sound at all.

As he watched her go, Hershel's heart pounded in his chest. Restraint was not one of his strengths, nor was common sense. Rising from the couch, he followed Karen into her bedroom where he heard her running water in the adjoining bathroom. He firmly believed that surprise would give him the advantage so, standing to the side, he waited until she started out from the bathroom and then he made his move. Wrapping both arms around her, pinning her arms against her sides, he figured to render her helpless. This, of course, did not work at all. As he attempted to kiss her, he felt almost immediately the impact of a sharp fist as she drove it into his solar plexus, just under the heart. He subsequently discovered that he could no longer breathe and collapsed to the floor, gasping for breath. She resisted the trained follow-up kick to the ribs, and sat on the edge of her bed watching while he attempted to recover his breathing. At this point she should have lost completely any compassion she might have held for Hershel Feldman. But, much to her surprise, this was not the case. She regarded the now sitting Hershel with a solemn look but said nothing.

It was Hershel who next spoke, "Well, I guess I had that coming, too. You don't seem to have any tolerance for my confused state of mind." Cradling his sore hand, he struggled to his feet and sat on the chair to Karen's dressing table, adding, "I don't suppose you would be willing to give me another chance to speak to you. I wouldn't blame you for throwing me out instead; but please, if you do, just do it verbally. I don't think I can endure much more physical abuse today." He made himself appear as pathetic as he possibly could.

Karen felt as if she were losing her grip on this situation. Should she eject this miscreant one last time? Was there some minute vestige of worth in one who appeared to be a complete hedonist? How was she, who knew so little of Hershel, to be able to perceive whether he was actually plagued with confusion, as he had asserted, or possessed with an inscrutable sagacity? Finally, she said, "Your purpose in coming here is quite transparent, you know. Even if you were not married to a lovely woman whom I hold in the highest regard, I would have absolutely no interest in you whatsoever. But since you are Rose's husband, I find your advances even more reprehensible. I cannot see how any conversation we might have at this point could possibly be productive. Perhaps, if you will give some consideration to sincerity, we could speak together about Rose on some future occasion, but not this evening. Please leave immediately." Leading him out of her bedroom, through her miniscule living room, and to the door, she bade him, "Good evening."

The vision of Karen, devoid of makeup, dressed casually in slacks and mannish blouse, and in her own personal environment, remained in his mind's eye as he made for the parking lot where he had left his BMW. This picture had total possession of him and, rounding the corner of Karen's building, he nearly ran the Hon. Anton Klausman down. "What are you up to, Klausman?" he laughed, "Don't you know Miss Karen Boschert is off limits to a fusty old codger such as yourself? Besides, I would have thought old Abaddon would have you cowering in the corner for fear he would stomp you like a cockroach. Where did you come up with the audacity to darken the lovely Karen's door?"

Klausman was livid as he asked, "Who do you think you are addressing, Feldman? Such insolence in my country could easily get you killed. I can only hope that you are intelligent enough to retract those impertinent remarks lest you reap the consequences." He held in his right hand an over-under barreled Derringer pistol, waving it menacingly in Hershel's direction.

Hershel was brought up short. He was not so much afraid of Klausman himself, but he was very concerned about the man's stability. He exclaimed, "Whoa, put that thing down, Klausman. Somebody could get hurt and, if you're not careful, it might be me. If you were to pull the trigger on that toy, you wouldn't get fifty feet before all the hippies in the neighborhood would be all over you, and drag you off to the nearest precinct office. Come on, put it away, you idiot, before someone sees you waving it around. You can't get away with having a gun on you in this country—I don't care what goes on in Switzerland, or wherever. Hide it quick, you moron, before a cop wanders by! Gee, what a bonehead!" He reached out toward Klausman and attempted to wrest the weapon from his hand. It discharged with a sharp **CRACK!**, the projectile ricocheting off a metal grate in the sidewalk; whereupon Klausman dropped the pistol and turned to search behind him for Yong Se, who was not far behind. The altercation ended with Klausman proceeding to Karen's apartment, Yong Se returning to Klausman's Mercedes, and Hershel lying semiconscious in the gutter. When the police officer finally arrived, Hershel explained that he had seen a man brandishing a pistol, tried to persuade him to put it away, and was rewarded for his good citizenship by a thorough beating by the man and his companion. He gave the officer full and accurate descriptions of Klausman and Yong Se for the police report, adding that he would be glad to testify against them if asked to do so. Then, he limped the rest of the way to his car and drove home, cautiously, lest he become involved in yet another act of violence. Dusk was just beginning to shroud the city.

Karen placed the little skillet on her stove and set the heat at medium, warming the pan slightly before she added the small amount of oil needed to sauté a modest filet of sea perch she had just that afternoon brought home from the market around the corner. The sound of the door buzzer startled her so much that she nearly forgot to turn off the burner before she spoke into the intercom, "Yes, who is it?"

In halting English, Yong Se said, "Missy Karen, this Yong Se speaking. His Eminence wish you to come with him to rest'rant for talk. When you be ready? We wait outside, you come soon."

Karen, in her housecoat and slippers, asked, "Right now? Immediately? Tonight? Oh, dear, I do not know. Let me see. Oh, all right, I shall be a few minutes, though." Leaving the filet on the counter and the couscous to cool on the table, she made for her room to dress as quickly as she could. In ten minutes, she let herself out of her flat and descended the stairs where she was met by Yong Se who escorted her to Klausman's limousine, which was parked illegally in front of the nearest convenient fire hydrant. When Klausman saw Karen approaching, he was stunned by her loveliness. She had on shimmering black slacks that went down to her black low-healed pumps, showing only a hint of shapely ankles, over a white silk blouse she had on a red cotton vest with gold embroidery, and in her hair a gold ribbon gathered the black masses into a long pony tail. Somehow she had managed to apply a modicum of makeup and a slight amount of lipstick. She did not take the time for eye makeup, but there was no need for it anyway. Klausman's breathing became irregular.

Klausman made the tactical error of taking Karen to the restaurant owned by his elegant female friend, the same restaurant to which he had previously taken Hershel. The woman, whose name was Ramona, was not particularly pleased to see the likes of Karen in her restaurant. A truly vain person, she viewed one as beautiful as Karen a threat to her relationship with Klausman. She was certainly not far off the mark. Even though Klausman had consumed the greater part of their journey to the restaurant in praise of the establishment and its owner, all of the positive attributes failed to materialize, as did the proprietress herself. Klausman and Karen (Yong Se remained in the car.) were treated rather shabbily, in the opinion of the former, and their order was a long time in arriving. There was no private alcove offered, nor was their table placed so as to give them any privacy whatsoever. Apparently Ramona had instructed her staff to treat the middle aged roué and his beautiful comrade as rudely as they could without being too obvious about it. As a consequence, their conversation was of necessity conducted in hushed tones and lacked any sort of conviction, particularly on Klausman's part. His arguments seemed tentative at best and Karen felt slighted and confused. The party at an adjacent table were inclined toward outbursts of laughter and loud exclamations, resulting in the obscuring of much of what Klausman had to say. Karen gathered that he seemed to be offering her a way out of some sort of scandal by means of matrimony— presumably with Klausman himself. At length, she requested they adjourn to his car so that she could hear clearly what it was he was proposing to her.

In the limo, with the glass divider closed for what he presumed to be privacy, Klausman recounted that which he had endeavored to put before Karen in the restaurant, "My Dear, it is unfortunate indeed that your audit of Mandel Family Apparel turned out as it did. I was convinced all along that you knew exactly what you were about, but I am afraid that was not the case. Mr. Ginsberg has found numerous anomalies in your work and is now diligently at work attempting to salvage the entire audit. It appears, according to Ginsberg's analysis, that all is well with the books at the aforementioned company, and his revised audit will be submitted to my office tomorrow. It would seem that our suspicions about Mr. Feldman were completely unfounded. When you return to your office in Zurich you will find your separation papers awaiting you. You cannot possibly be more disappointed than I, my dear, but there it is, I am afraid. I do not consider your shortcomings in business and accounting of significant concern and am therefore happy to repeat my previous offer, in the horrible din of that detestable restaurant, that of your giving me the honor of becoming my bride. Now that you have heard me clearly, may I expect a reply to be forthcoming?"

Karen was aghast and horrified, and she replied accordingly (in German), "You shall have an immediate reply, Herr Klausman! I would not, under *any* circumstances, consider becoming your wife! This sudden turn of events smacks of the worst kind of calumny, an act of which I would not have suspected you were capable. It is transparent in the extreme that you have conjured up this ploy in order to implement some sort of self-gratifying purpose and I have no intention of becoming party to it. You will have the decency to instruct your driver to allow me egress at the earliest possible opportunity! I shall make my way back to my flat on my own."

Klausman had not the vaguest suspicion that Karen would react in this fashion. At worst, he had anticipated that she would weep prettily and then concede, perhaps with a respectable amount of reluctance. But, this eruption of outright defiance, accompanied as it was with such courage, completely stymied him, leaving him temporarily at a loss for words. At length he said (also in German), "Well, My Dear, I did not intend for my proposal to sound like an ultimatum; I offered it in the greatest sincerity. I surmised that you would be greatly distressed by the loss of your position at Klausman, Walther, und Hahn, GmbH, and I wished to convey to you my promise that your loss would not be the end of the world. I was not to know my offer would anger you so, was I?"

"Obviously you were not to know also," she said in a perfectly level voice, "that I would discern the hidden motive behind your proposal of marriage. Such detestable sophistry! How could you be so devious, so debasing?"

It was Klausman's turn to be incredulous: "To what are you alluding, young lady?"

Karen's anger was beginning to affect her tone: "You cannot win my favor by means of earnest declaration of affection, so you resort to connivance, the fabrication of a flawed audit and the threat of dismissal from your employ in order to force me into your camp and that of Abaddon. I would far rather perish than to yield to the likes of you and that monster; surely you must realize that, if nothing else." Her voice trembled more from passion than from fear.

"My Dear, you are quite mistaken, I assure you." His attempt at conciliation went unnoticed.

"Do not, I pray, refer to me as your dear—I am anything but. Now, if you will be so kind as to instruct your driver, I wish to be allowed to exit this automobile immediately!" With this last she began to tug at her door handle. It was to no avail, however, since the lock must be released electrically from the driver's door.

In an effort to sound concerned Klausman said, "Miss Boschert, we are on Staten Island, far from your flat. How will you, in such unfamiliar surroundings, make your way to Manhattan and thence to your home base? If you will just be patient, Yong Se will drive us there directly."

"What does that matter to you? I demand to be let out instantly!" Karen had finally raised her voice.

Klausman sighed and replied, "Very well, My D...ah, Miss Boschert." Sliding the glass partition aside, he commanded, "Yong Se, pull over at the next intersection."

Yong Se had, of course, heard every word, all of which would soon reach the ears of Mr. Abaddon. He pulled the car smoothly over at a busy intersection and unlocked Karen's door from his control panel, making a mental note as he did so of the intersecting street names. Karen stepped swiftly from the limo and almost immediately managed to hail a cab. Klausman studied the diminishing image, as it receded into the distance, of her shapely form entering a dingy taxi. Yong Se drove quickly away from the scene, bound for the Ritz-Astoria Hotel. In spite of himself, the Hon. Anton Klausman felt a pang of regret. Perhaps he could have handled this situation more effectively and not risked allowing Karen to slip from his grasp.

Chapter Nine

Lee Min-jun raked slender fingers through his straight black hair in a gesture of frustration and distress. He stood before the only window in his tiny loft apartment situated on an upper floor of a warehouse in the garment district of Manhattan. The only view afforded him was of the cluttered street below and of another similar warehouse building across the street, not thirty feet from his window. So, this was his reward for four and a half years of faithful service to the Hon. Anton Klausman. Apparently that phony Chinaman with the made-up name, Yong Se, had replaced him, and now he was left out of the picture. It was as if he had vanished from the earth; there was no contact, no communication from Klausman or any of his associates. Who was protecting Herr Klausman? Certainly not that fop, Yong Se, who did not even carry a weapon, let alone take pride in his own family name. Mr. Lee began to pace the floor, frustrated and bitter. All the grandiose promises Klausman had made to him had come to nothing; now he was trapped in America without any means of survival and without so much as an acquaintance. If he had known Klausman would betray him thus, he would have taken advantage of his cousin's offer to partner with him as a drug smuggler. The more he contemplated his present predicament, the more angry and petulant he became. Abruptly, he fell into a stance of Tae Kwon Do, lashing out with his feet and fists, felling an imaginary foe. Breathing heavily, he completed the form he knew so well; then went through a series of moves from Chung Do. The extreme exertion seemed to calm his spirit. At this point, the telephone rang. Lee listened a moment and then said in broken German, "Very well, I shall be ready."

When the 'grosser' Mercedes slid silently to the curb in front of Mr. Lee's building, Lee was gratified to see Klausman's regular driver, Rolf, seated behind the wheel. Opening the passenger's front door, he climbed in beside the driver, who accelerated away in a swirl of trash and debris. They parked in the parking garage at the Ritz-Astoria Hotel. Klausman was doing a bit of pacing of his own, but with the difference that he was smoking Egyptian cigarettes in a cigarette holder of some eight inches in length, and he was swearing in German. Dismissing Rolf, he beckoned Mr. Lee to enter and to have a seat in an uncomfortable straight chair. Lee didn't mind at all; he was just glad to be back in the game, whatever it might offer.

While he gazed reflectively at the ash on his cigarette, Klausman asked, "What, pray tell me, Mr. Lee, is your attitude regarding an assignment of some considerable risk and personal danger?" He stubbed out his cigarette in a gold ashtray that resembled a rose bloom.

Summoning his best approximation of German, Lee responded, "At a sufficient price, Master, I shall consider anything. Fear is not in me." Regarding Klausman with suspicion he considered justifiable, Lee attempted a smile, revealing several gold teeth. Although he sounded at ease, he was nonetheless quite tense, and his twitching hands revealed this.

"Perhaps you could be persuaded to take your mind off money long enough to give genuine consideration to a proposal," Klausman remarked wryly.

Refusing to be intimidated, Lee retorted, "You will forgive me, Master, for having in my thoughts a commodity of which I at present have virtually none. I have received no compensation since we departed from Zurich; therefore I have depleted my resources to nil. Consequently, I am understandably sensitive to the matter of money." There were the gold teeth again.

"I see, I see," Klausman said, "There has been some sort of clerical error to be sure, but it will be rectified at once. May I assume, then, that you are prepared to give audience to a proposal that, I might add, could prove to be quite profitable to you, if you should agree to undertake it?"

Mr. Lee said nothing for some minutes, only nodded slowly with an introspective expression on his face. At length, he spoke, "I shall listen intently, Your Eminence."

"Ah well, then," Klausman sighed, "Here it is: I wish you to go this very night to Miss Boschert's West Village flat and abduct her, taking her by force, if necessary, to MacArthur Airport on Long Island, where our aircraft will be awaiting to take you both back to Switzerland. I shall arrange there to have someone collect you and Miss Boschert and to deliver her to an undisclosed destination. At that point your responsibilities will come to an end and I shall have arranged the second half of your fee be given you. What do you say?"

"I say: How much?" Lee's gaze was piercing.

It was with some difficulty that the two arrived at a suitable amount due, no doubt, to the fact that, while Herr Klausman made his offer in deutsche marks, Mr. Lee insisted on it's being given in dollars, and Klausman was uncertain of the current rate of exchange. At length, they settled on a figure and Klausman paid him half the amount in cash. The die was cast. It never occurred to Lee to wonder how Klausman was able to come up with so many dollars when he had initially made his proposal in deutsche marks. Such was Klausman's perfidy.

As Mr. Lee prepared to leave, Klausman blocked his way and exclaimed, "You are aware, I am certain, that the girl is trained in Wushu. You would do well to be on your guard; I am informed that she is quite proficient in the art. Perhaps you should disable her by means of some sort of drugs, but do not, under any circumstances, cause her bodily injury. Do you understand me?"

With a smug expression, Lee replied, "I hear your words but I do not understand you. Did you not offer me remuneration to deliver the girl to Switzerland? Why, then, do you proceed to instruct me on how to go about it? If I did not know myself how to accomplish the mission, I should not have accepted your terms nor your payment. Now, if you would be so kind as to allow me to pass, I shall be on my way." It was no accident that Lee brushed roughly by Klausman on his way out the door.

The taxi that Karen (and Klausman) had perceived as dingy proved to be merely a bit scruffy from wear and tear, but by no means unsanitary. It was, in fact, scrubbed and polished clean inside and out, rendered so by a fastidious, dark chocolate-skinned man who kept up a continuous chatter, not one syllable of which Karen could comprehend. He did, however, manage to locate Rose's home without much fuss, and even insisted on waiting in the driveway until he was satisfied that Karen was safely admitted into the house. On entering the Feldman home, Karen was instantly captured around the knees by an ebullient Isabelle who squealed with delight and excitement at the sudden appearance of her new friend, 'Missy Kawen'. To embrace Karen, Rose was required to lean over her daughter, who was loath to release Karen so quickly. Finally, they walked back to Rose's sitting room, albeit awkwardly at times, due to the persistent clinging of the happy child. Once the two women were seated, Isabelle bounced back and forth between Karen's and Rose's knees, attempting to entice one or both of the women to give her a 'howsebacky wide'. After a few minutes of this, Rose called to Carmen to come and fetch the child to her nursery where Isabelle almost immediately fell asleep on the floor with her head on her giant stuffed tiger.

Rose asked, "Why did you take a cab? I would have sent someone to get you, you know." Following this, Karen gave her a brief account of her abysmal encounter with Herr Klausman, along with the details of his betrayal and the ensuing offer of matrimony. Rose was stunned, to say the least, adding, "I don't understand why you have to put up with that sort of thing. Aren't there some sorts of rules of etiquette, even in Switzerland, governing that kind of behavior? I mean, even though he is your boss, that doesn't give him the right to make up a big lie about you so he can proposition you into marriage. That is detestable and slanderous!"

"That is true," Karen answered, "but I do not believe you have seen the entire implication of what he has done. The override of my audit has exonerated your husband from any wrongdoing; but worse, it has pointed a light of suspicion on you, Dear Rose. Why did you suspect your own husband, they will ask, of tampering with the books of your own company? Are you therefore attempting, by virtue of your accusations against Hershel, to cover up something in your own life that you do not wish to be noticed? Do you not see? Hershel will emerge from this the injured party, and you and I know that he is guilty of the most cunning thievery; and you are seen as the villain. Oh, my, what a scandal he could make of this if he were to wish to discredit you!" Karen got up from the chair where she was sitting and went and sat next to Rose on her maroon velveteen couch. She took Rose's hand in hers. "The question we must ask ourselves is," she went on, "what has motivated the wicked and devious Herr Klausman to do such a thing?"

Brushing her forehead with a shaking hand, Rose said, "I would think that is an easy one to answer: Klausman wants you for his own and will go to any lengths to get you; even criminal acts, although I don't believe he's in any danger of arrest in the States because our laws are too vague when it comes to foreigners. In any case, you are in grave danger,

Karen! I believe Klausman will stop at nothing in order to get his way, and I mean *nothing!* With all his wealth and influence, he is a dangerous man. I think you had better stay here until we can figure this thing out."

Karen, her eyes blazing with emotion, said, "No, no, that will not do. You must distance yourself from me as much as possible. And, do not be concerned for me; I am able to defend myself. I simply came here to warn you and to give you as much information as I have. I plan to make my way back to Switzerland as quickly and silently as possible where my parents will probably send me to be with relatives in China. Herr Klausman would never be able to locate me there." She turned to face Rose directly and took her other hand, saying, "You are the one about whom I am concerned. You must immediately hire a first-rate barrister, ah, attorney to protect you. As much as I hate to say it, you must also inform Hershel that you know all about Herr Klausman's plan. It is not implausible that he is complicit with Klausman. Yes, you must find a very, very good attorney to protect you."

Rose, her eyes brimming with tears, pleaded, "Karen, please, stay here with me! I wouldn't be surprised if Klausman is in your apartment right now, waiting to grab you and carry you off to his lair. All that charm and oozing politeness—ugh, such a sickening and deceptive put-on—it makes me sick to my stomach. You can stay in the guestroom until we can make a plan for you. And, besides, I don't trust that Abaddon character either. Speaking of oily and slick characters, he's the worst of all; too handsome to be true, and all that mystery, too. Where do you find all these sinister characters?"

"I do not find them," Karen answered, "they seem to find me. Why, I do not know. In the case of Herr Klausman, it was simply a matter of postgraduate employment; but, as far as the mysterious Herr Abaddon is concerned, I do not even know how he came to know of me. Perhaps Herr Klausman told him; but why, if what you believe about him is true, would he introduce me to a competitor? There is a part of me that is in agreement with you entirely: that these men are both extremely dangerous and to be avoided at all costs. The other part of me, while still agreeing, wishes to distance myself from them both without delay, no matter what. Still another part finds herself loath to remain near you for fear of attracting these evil men to you, my wonderful new friend." Karen searched Rose's eyes intently for she knew not what. Continuing, she asked, "What do you say to this? I shall go at once to my flat and retrieve all my belongings and leave a note with a cheque for the landlord. Then I shall return here for a time while we plan our next tactic. If we tell no one at all, perhaps they will not know where to search for me, thinking that you and I could not have formed a positive relationship under the prevailing circumstances. Then, I shall exploit your sweet nature by using your telephone rather than my own mobile one to purchase my airline tickets to Switzerland. Oh, but where is your husband? Would he not betray us?"

Rose quickly said, "Whatever you do, don't leave a note for the landlord. That would tip off even Klausman about what you're up to. You can pay your rent by mail and I'll mail it at a Manhattan post office, so they can't trace your whereabouts. Anyone else but a sweet person like you, under these circumstances, couldn't care less about the landlord. You're amazing! And, you don't have to worry about my domestic staff, such as they are. Both Carmen and Mrs. Bridges have fallen in love with you at first sight. You don't have to worry one bit about their loyalty; they'll keep a secret if I tell them to. I think you'll be safe here until you can make proper plans for your escape. Let me call a taxi for you. I know the driver and I'll pay him to keep his mouth shut, and to wait for you to get your things together. He'll bring you back here quickly and no one will be the wiser. And, as for Hershel, he's so mad about you he wouldn't dream of harming you in any way." As she reached for her phone to call the cab, Rose cast a glance at the porcelain lady, posing on the dressing table, harboring a tiny clock in her poor belly. It was nearly two in the morning.

Rose and Karen sat together on the huge leather couch in the living room, watching through the bay window for the arrival of the taxi. Almost simultaneously they sensed the presence of someone else in the room; and almost in unison they turned their heads in time to witness Hershel's entrance in a burgundy satin robe and house slippers. Rose, leaping to her feet, exclaimed, "Don't come near me!"

Laughing sardonically, Hershel said, "Don't worry, I see you have expert protection. What are you two up to?"

Before Rose could answer, Karen did it for her, "We are awaiting a taxi to take me home. I had no intention of staying so late, but we were talking and forgot the time."

Rose added her own answer, "Yes, that's right. What are you doing up so late, Hershel? Did we wake you? I'm sorry." As Hershel approached her, she backed away from him, holding her hands before her as if to fend him off.

"Yes, but what are you doing here in the first place, Karen?" As he turned to Karen, Hershel appeared slightly tipsy but perhaps not totally drunk.

Karen's reply sounded perfectly natural and plausible: "Well, you see, I had a bit of a disagreement with Herr Klausman at a restaurant here on Staten Island and I, ah, rather leapt out of the car, perhaps you would say and, since I was close by, I came to pay Rose a visit. As I explained, I did not intend to stay long at all but, as women often do, because we had so much to say we lost all notion of the passage of time. I am sorry to have awakened you." Her smile was friendly but, by design, not suggestive in the least. She saw no reason, either, to burden Rose with the revelation of her husband's antics earlier that evening.

Hershel did not appear entirely convinced but, glancing out the window, announced, "Here's your cab now. I'll walk you out."

Rose acted horrified and exclaimed, "Hershel! You're not dressed! And, anyway, look; he's driving right up to the porch. I'll turn on the porch light and Karen'll be perfectly safe." She added, "G'night Karen, Dear. Be careful and run right into your apartment. Make the driver wait to be sure you're safely inside." She gave Karen a peck on the cheek and a hug while Hershel burned with envy.

Feigning chivalry and attempting not to stare, Hershel held the door for Karen as she moved swiftly out the door. He tried not to be too obvious about it but, try as he may, he simply *had* to watch her walk across the porch, down the steps, and slide gracefully into the backseat of the taxi. His torment was consumptive. When he turned back to look, he met Rose's eye as she slipped by him and made her way to the taxi, where she had a word with the driver. Hershel had had enough and repaired to his room.

For Lee Min-jun this was a swan song. He would deliver on his promise to Herr Klausman and then return to hearth and home in South Korea. Having turned over the neat little package of Karen Boschert to Klausman's party in Zurich, he would then collect the remaining half of his generous fee and grab the first flight to Seoul. Klausman will never see him again and, with the kind of money he will take home, he will be able to retire to an easy life without the need to pair up with his cousin in the smuggling business. He was fed up with danger and risk—it was time to find a woman and settle down. Instructing Klausman's driver, Rolf, to pull over to the curb across the street from Karen's apartment building, he told the man to wait for him to return, however long that may be. This simple task was difficult enough given the fact that he spoke precious little German while Rolf spoke no Korean at all. In addition, neither trusted nor respected the other. When Rolf grunted some sort of assent, Mr. Lee slipped from the limousine and strode briskly across the street, blending himself into the shadows of a narrow alleyway. He passed the next half hour in intense meditation, practicing his silent breathing and keeping an eye on Klausman's limo and driver on the other side of the street. When the time was ripe to go into action, he would know it. Ten minutes later he reached into an inner pocket of his all black jumpsuit and produced a scrap of paper Klausman had given him bearing the combination to Karen's security lock, along with the key to her door. Once in the apartment, he went straight to the small utility room—more a porch really—where he prepared himself for a lengthy wait. Myriad thoughts flitted through his mind, giving him cause for great anxiety. At length, the realization came to him that Klausman had no intention of letting him complete his mission, that Rolf was no doubt armed and set to kill him when he emerged from the apartment with the girl. Knowing he had ample time to carry them out, he made his plans accordingly.

In the faint light of a streetlight Rolf checked his Walther P38K, short-barreled automatic pistol. One round in the chamber and eight more in the magazine. Satisfied, he slid the piece back into his side coat pocket but did not release it from his grip, leaving his hand in the pocket while holding the pistol loosely. Why in the world did Herr Klausman have to hire these crazy Asian nitwits to do a real man's work? This one could hardly weigh sixty kilos and he was sure to mess up the whole assignment. Rolf knew he could easily go inside himself, grab the girl by brute force, throw her in the back of the car, and deliver her to the boss in a fraction of the time this character was taking, with all his slinking around and hiding. If you were big enough and scary enough, like Rolf himself was, you could get away with almost anything. And besides, he had his Walther just in case there was trouble. He made up his mind; he would go inside, take the little guy apart, and then sit and wait for the girl to return.

Maybe he would even keep her for himself. Klausman was far too old for her, but Rolf was only thirty-eight—just about right. These Asian girls are crazy about men with blonde hair, and she was sure to be impressed by his imposing physique and physical strength.

After exiting the car, Rolf closed the door softly and locked it, then walked leisurely across the street, maintaining a natural and calm appearance. No one seemed to notice him as he pressed the button on Karen's security box and waited. When, after a long delay, he heard Lee Min-jun whisper in English, "Yes?"

Rolf whispered back, "Quick, let me in!" but, in German. Recognizing the voice, Mr. Lee touched the button to allow entry to the apartment. It was practically dark in Karen's apartment, illuminated only by a yellowish streetlight across on the opposite side of the street. Where was that sneaky Asian elf anyway? Rolf asked himself.

Even as Rolf reached to turn on a table lamp, Min-jun hissed, "No turn on light! Miss Karen see from street."

As the two stood warily apart, Rolf waited for his eyes to adjust to the dimness. He fondled the weapon in his pocket and breathed heavily, waiting for his chance to move. Neither thought to re-lock the door or to reset the security lock. Without so much as a change in the rhythm of his breathing, Min-jun went into his combative mode, tensing his muscles and heightening his reflexes. He withdrew a slender, razor-sharp knife from a compact holster located in the small of his back, out of Rolf's sight, and slipped it up into his sleeve. As Rolf's eyes began to adjust, he focused on Min-jun, hoping to catch him unaware and, as a result, he himself was oblivious to the slight scratching sound as Karen attempted to turn her key in an already unlocked bolt. Min-jun heard the sound, however, and turned toward it, trying to make out the cause. In that short moment in time, while Karen opened the door and switched on her overhead light, Rolf drew the Walther from his pocket and pointed it toward

Min-jun, who was himself attempting to persuade his slender knife to slide down his arm and into his palm. Just as Rolf fired at Min-jun, Karen passed through the space separating the two men and the bullet struck her in her right side, causing her to first grunt sharply and then let out a long, whistling breath. She made no other sound but crumpled to the floor in a sitting position, her torso against the wall to her left and her head tilted to one side. Rolf fired again as Min-jun's knife passed so close to his cheek that it left a vivid red mark. The bullet entered Lee Min-jun's neck just at the base of his throat, shattering his spine and killing the poor fellow instantly. Rolf stood still for only a second or two, then, leaving the scene at a run, he flew down the flight of stairs and out into the street, gaining the Mercedes and fumbling with his keys before remembering to open the car with the remote he held in his shaking hand. The powerful car left two wavy black stripes on the pavement as it accelerated between the parked cars along the narrow street.

Much against his better judgment, Hershel parked his BMW in the same small, unattended parking lot he had used previously, locking it and setting the alarm. As he hurried toward Karen's apartment, he heard a gunshot, and then another and, following a delay of perhaps twenty seconds, he caught sight of a familiar figure running hell-bent toward a Mercedes limousine, a vehicle that he recognized as the one owned, or used by, Anton Klausman. It was then that he realized that the running man was Rolf, Klausman's driver. The big car was out of sight almost before Hershel could react to the scene he had just witnessed. He yelled, "Hey!" but it was much after the fact. Instantly, it was as if a cold hand had grabbed his heart, and he ran as fast as he could to Karen's apartment, where he found the door ajar and the overhead light casting an illuminating wedge into the hallway. He was terrified to enter the lighted room, but finally forced himself to do it, and was sorry he had. The first image that struck him was that of Karen against a wall, her hand clutching her side and blood seeping through her fingers. Her mouth was working as she tried to speak to him, but no sound came from her lips. Her eyes were glassy and distant. As he knelt down to her, he caught a glimpse of Lee Min-jun, lying on his side with a giant, bleeding, angry-looking opening at the base of his neck, and his legs twitching in odd, rotating spasms. Finally, while Hershel watched in fascination, the twitching stopped. Gore began to pool up beneath the back of Min-jun's neck. Hershel heard Karen gasp and try to speak, but it was German and he couldn't understand any of it. He whispered hoarsely to her, "Can you speak in English, Karen?" He had taken his handkerchief out of his pocket and was attempting to staunch the flow of blood from her side. There did not appear to be a great deal of it. Karen attempted to say no more.

He had to call an ambulance, but where was his phone? He must have left it in his car. Looking around the room for a phone, he remembered that Karen usually seemed to use a mobile phone, so he rummaged in her purse for one. At that precise moment, a New York City police officer stormed into the room and discovered a disheveled young man rifling a woman's purse, along with a beautiful young Asian woman, wounded and bleeding, lying against the wall, and an apparently wounded or dead Asian man in a pool of his own blood, sprawled on the floor just opposite the woman. The man that was pawing through the woman's purse was sobbing and cursing, and there was blood on his shirt and one arm. He looked startled when he spotted the officer but continued to search frantically in the purse.

In the interrogation room it must have been ninety degrees, the wooden chair he sat on felt like it was made of iron, and the cuffs were chafing his wrists something awful. Hershel was sweating freely and he needed desperately to visit the bathroom, but neither the heavy-set man nor the calloused-looking woman in the room with him seemed to care in the least. The man was saying, "Okay, Hershel, let's go over this all again. I mean, none of what you have told us makes much sense. And, you still haven't told us what you did with the weapon. Now, come on, let's have it! Where's the gun and why did you do it? If you're so crazy about the girl, and by the looks of her I can see why, why in hell did you shoot her? Who is the poor goon that you shot, and what did he do to deserve being shot? You gotta lot of answers to cough up, buddy." By the time he had finished his tirade, the man had pushed his face so close to Hershel's that the stink of garlic and stale beer was oppressive.

"Sit down, Sean, and let me talk to Romeo here." The woman, who seemed to outrank Sean, turned to Hershel and, blowing a lungful of tobacco smoke in his face continued the interrogation, "Look, lover boy, we've seen, Sean and me, a thousand cases like yours and we ain't been fooled yet. This is so clear a case it could be used in a textbook. You walk in on your sweetie makin' out with this Asian character and you go nuts and try to off 'em both; then you try to make it look like robbery by goin' through the dish's purse. So, why don't you just save us all a load of time and tell us what we need to know? Who's the girl, who's the dead guy, and where's the murder weapon? The sooner you unload, the sooner we'll all get to bed and catch some winks."

Sighing heavily, Hershel asked, "If I go through it all for you one more time will you please let me go to the restroom? If you don't pretty soon, someone's going to have a big mess to clean up, and it's not going to be me."

Sean and the woman, rolling their eyes in unison, breathed, "One more time!"

"Okay, here's exactly what I saw and did," Hershel resumed, "First of all, the girl is not my sweetheart; she's a good friend of my wife's and my daughter's. I won't lie to you, I think she's gorgeous, but she won't give me the time of day. Her name's Karen Boschert, and she works for a foreign company called Klausman, Walter, und Hahn. She's been auditing my wife's company; you know, Mandel

Family Apparel, and her boss is actually Anton Klausman, who I'm sure has the hots for her big time. She won't give him the time of day either. The dead guy is, believe it or not, this guy Klausman's bodyguard. I know who killed him, and the same guy shot Karen, probably by mistake. His name is Rolf somebody and he's Klausman's chauffeur. Call him, Klausman I mean, and see. He's a big shot staying at the Ritz-Astoria while Karen—uh—Miss Boschert does all the work auditing my wife's company. Go ahead; call him, Anton Klausman, at the Ritz-Astoria. You'll see; ask him about Rolf and his bodyguard. Hey, I think the dead guy's name is Lee something. I heard Klausman talking to him one time. It's Mr. Lee something. That's all I know, I swear. So, like I said before, I went over to Karen's apartment to check on her because my wife was worried about her—you can check with Rose on that—and when I was walking toward her place, I heard two gunshots; and then I saw this big guy Rolf running out of Karen's place and he tore off in Klausman's big Mercedes limo. I ran into her apartment and found her lying on the floor bleeding. She couldn't talk. Then I saw Mr. Lee on the floor sort of wiggling and bleeding all over the place, and then I looked in Karen's purse for her phone 'cause I left mine in my car. That's it! I don't even own a gun—never have." Hershel was wringing wet from perspiration and his face was a vivid red. He added, "Can't I please go to the restroom now? And, can't you tell me anything about how Karen is? If anything bad happens to her, my wife and baby will go crazy!" He began to sob pitifully.

Hours later Hershel sat on a hard bunk in a cell that was otherwise devoid of furniture or any other amenities. It was like being in a cage at the zoo. No privacy, no means of escape, no hope. Presently, a guard came and opened his cell door, admitting a uniformed officer who appeared to be in his fifties. He spoke to Hershel, "Mr. Feldman, I'm Lieutenant Casey and I have a little information for you: The contents of the young woman's purse verify what you have told us about her; that she is identified as Miss Nhung Karen Boschert of Zurich, Switzerland; employed by Klausman, Walter, und Hahn, GmbH, also of Zurich, Switzerland; and that she is based temporarily in New York City in order to conduct an audit at Mandel Family Apparel, which is also verified as the company of your wife, Rose Mandel-Feldman. Miss Boschert is in critical condition at Metropolitan Hospital and is presently in an induced coma. As yet we have not been able to interrogate her, but we will when she wakes up; you can bet on it. With regard to the two men you have identified by only their first or last names, we have a call in to one Anton Klausman at the Ritz-Astoria Hotel, but no callback as yet. The desk clerk confirms he is registered there at the Ritz. We can't verify the information you gave us about the deceased and the one you claim to be the perpetrator until we reach this Klausman guy. I guarantee you are not going anywhere until we both verify what you've told us and until we reach your wife. We left her a message but there's been no reply. So far, this is not looking too good for you. Just identifying the girl, and even the deceased man, does not necessarily clear you of guilt. We still haven't found the murder weapon and, until we do, this is an open investigation, and you are the prime suspect for murder. Just hope that this Klausman fellow can shed some light that will help to clear you. It's quarter to nine in the morning and in a few minutes we will administer the paraffin test to see if you have fired a gun recently, and then you'll be moved to a permanent cell where you will have a cellmate you had better make friends with. Things can be pretty hard in this place, so mind your Ps and Qs. Good luck; you're going to need it."

The Hon. Anton Klausman could not answer his phone because he was not in his room at the Ritz-Astoria Hotel. He had been summoned once again to Lucifer Abaddon's 'office' in the basement of the abandoned warehouse two blocks from the riverfront. The table, filthy and disgusting as before, was no place to rest his elbows, even though he was dressed as casually as possible, given his elegant wardrobe. He detested this place, and was certain that Abaddon knew it. If the man was as powerful as he had suggested, why could they not meet in a decent office or, at the very least, in Klausman's hotel suite? The skittering about of the phantom 'beings', along with the whisperings and dreadful laughing sounds gave him horrible chills and left him a wreck. Why did he not just ignore these summonses from the redoubtable Abaddon? After all, was not he himself a personage of world renown, the *Honorable* Anton Klausman? And who, after all, was this Lucifer Abaddon person? To be sure, Horace Daemon had sworn that Abaddon was a royal prince; but, prince of what or where? Moeshe Weiss' identification of Abaddon as the prince of darkness was utter nonsense. Why should he, Klausman, have to kowtow to a man who would not even condescend to properly identify himself? After having sat in waiting for half an hour or so, Klausman decided he should leave.

The moment Klausman stood to his feet, the entire building reverberated with the most frightening sound, a voice of explosive quality, one that made Klausman's skin crawl, **"Sit down, Klausman! You have not been dismissed! Where do you think you are going?"** Almost worse than the quality of the voice was the fact that it seemed to emanate from all around the entire room. Klausman sat. Then he waited. At length, his nostrils were assailed with a foul stench: the putrid smell of decomposing flesh, burning hair and nails, raw offal, and other fetid elements that Klausman could not, and did not, care to identify. With a suddenness that made him leap from his chair, a considerable fire broke out on, and finally consumed, the chair opposite Klausman, across the table. Out of this minor conflagration emerged the dragon that he dreaded and despised so much; and it was from it that the horrible voice was stemming.

Recoiling in fright, Klausman shrieked "Away, away! What the deuce?" then, more calmly, "Oh, it is you, Your Excellency! Goodness, what a fright! If only you would appear to me as Mr. Abaddon, I should be ever so grateful. Your appearing as the dragon is needless, is it not? Spare me of it, I pray, for I shall attend you assiduously." (All of this was in German.)

"Silence, Dolt!" the dragon rejoined, but then relented and morphed into Mr. Abaddon. He continued, flames still occasionally flickering from his lips, "I have a mind to snuff you out because of your disobedience. Have you so quickly forgotten poor Mr. Daemon? If you suppose that I killed him outright, you are mistaken. I originally discovered him as a cadaver and it was I who held him together during his ersatz 'life'. He disappointed me gravely and where do you suppose he is now? That's right, in Sheol, his condign fate. I simply allowed him to perish for the second time. Such is my power. Perhaps you wish to join him? And, for heaven's sake, speak English; German is so laborious."

Stiffening with offense, Klausman replied, "Certainly, Your Excellency. Would that I had a better command of the language; but I shall try my best."

Abaddon emitted a puff of what appeared to be pent-up smoke, then replied, "Enough of your false deference, Klausman; what do you have to say for yourself?"

"I cannot imagine to what you are referring, Excellency," Klausman's reply, though strident, was strangely put.

"Your cryptic language is intolerable, Fool! You had best pay close attention, or you will rue the day you did not." Abaddon was livid. "If you wish to live out the day, you will shut your mouth and attend me closely."

In a meek voice Klausman said, "I am your suppliant, Excellency."

Abaddon's voice, accompanied by sparks and smoke, was orotund itself as he continued, "I have been informed that your idiotic attempt at chicanery designed to thwart my specific command against any attempts on your part to acquire for yourself the delectable Miss Boschert has itself been foiled. Now you are without a bodyguard *and* a chauffeur; and Miss Boschert has been wounded, mortally for all we know. How is it that you are able to surround yourself with such morons? Well, I suppose morons will attract morons. Now, what do you propose to do about your dead bodyguard and your missing driver? You do realize, do you not, that you will be the subject of a murder investigation? If I were you I should expect presently a call from the New York Police Department."

Klausman was incredulous. "To what are you referring, Excellency?" he asked. "I know of no murder or anything of the sort. Did you say that Lee Min-jun has been killed? By whom, I must ask you? And, what is this about Rolf being missing? I do not understand." Having risen from his chair, he began to pace back and forth, the cobwebs that became entangled in his hair going unnoticed.

For perhaps ten seconds Abaddon became the dragon, then resumed the part of Abaddon once more. He seemed to relax a little, and explained, "Yong Se has reported to me that both of your employees converged on Miss Boschert's flat simultaneously and, to no one's surprise, they apparently entered into some sort of altercation between themselves. It seems that just at the crucial moment, the girl entered and was caught in the crossfire. Pity. You had better hope that she survives, for I have my own plans for her."

"What? An altercation? Do you mean with firearms and the like? Oh, my goodness! But, who would wish to kill such a lovely girl?" Klausman was truly distraught.

The flames and smoke intensified as Abaddon became more impatient. He shouted, "How can you be so stupid? The two did not set out to murder the young woman; they set out to slay each other and both were trapped by their own incompetence. It was Miss Boschert who was the unintended victim. I surmise that your Rolf must have distracted Mr. Lee long enough to get off two shots; and then, of course, he bolted. Perhaps you are better off without a bodyguard who can be that easily caught off his guard."

"Oh, dear, oh dear, what shall I do?" Klausman asked in despair.

With a leer Abaddon answered, "I will tell you what you *must* say and do. When the New York police contact you, you will say to them…."

Klausman was so stunned by his predicament that he hardly heard Abaddon's instructions.

Chapter Ten

Rose Mandel-Feldman sat in a chromium-framed, plastic-upholstered chair facing her doctor, her face drained of color and her eyes welling up with tears. "But I'm only thirty-seven," she said in a tremulous voice, "how can this be?"

Dr. Franz looked at Rose with a sort of frigid concern and replied, "This really has very little to do with age, Rose; I suspect it is genetic. Have your mother or grandmother ever suffered from breast cancer?"

"My mother, no, not yet anyway; my grandmother, I don't know. She was gone really before I was born and my mother never mentioned what she died of," she answered. "Do you think that could be it?" Before Dr. Franz could reply, Rose burst into tears and, through her sobs asked, "Why does this have to happen to me? All this trouble with Hershel and now this ugly thing. Oh, God, why this?" She dabbed at her eyes with a soggy tissue.

By way of an answer, Dr. Franz handed her a prescription on which were written the name and phone number of a cousin of his who was an oncologist. "Here is the name and number of a good oncologist, Rose," he said, "Give his office a call and try to get in to see him as soon as possible. The pain you are having in your armpits and groin is significant, too. Time is of the essence with this type of cancer. I'm sorry, Rose." He rose from his chair as a gesture of dismissal.

Dr. Franz's cousin was not the least bit encouraging, but instead directed one of his staff to immediately make an appointment for Rose with a surgical practice. She was to report to a rather distant hospital in two day's time for

137

surgery. Meanwhile, she was to go through some distasteful preparations. Driving back home proved problematical because she was nearly blinded by her tears and distracted by fear and trepidation. When she arrived home, her trembling hand nearly prevented her from inserting her key in the door lock. When Isabelle came running to her she could not possibly stem her tears and the child was alarmed.

"Why Ma cwying?" the little one asked in a tiny voice.

Rose had to gulp back sobs before answering, "Mommy is sad today, Darling. Where is Mrs. Bridges, my Sweet?"

Isabelle ran toward the kitchen howling, "Missy Bwitches, Missy Bwitches, Ma want you!"

They sat at the kitchen table, Rose and Mrs. Bridges, after Carmen had taken the inquisitive Isabelle out into the yard to play with Puffy the poodle. "Why must you go to the hospital so soon?" Mrs. Bridges asked.

"The doctors seem to think I'll die if they don't hurry up and operate," she answered tearfully. "Oh, Mrs. Bridges— Mary—I'm so frightened. I can't imagine what Hershel is going to say; nothing supportive I wouldn't think. Where is he, by the way?"

"Oh, the mister was out and gone in the wee hours of the morning," Mrs. Bridges sniffed. "I declare, I cannot understand the man. He's not returned, either; but he did call twice, once very early in the morning and then again just a while ago. Mad he was, too. I told him you were out to an appointment and I didn't know when you'd be back and he got madder still. He cursed me, he did." She nodded as she spoke, her eyes getting wider and wider.

Rose looked anxious and asked, "Oh, dear, what did he want, did he say?"

Mrs. Bridges nodded some more and answered, "No Ma'am, he just said you'd better call, and sooner better than later." She handed Rose a scrap of paper with a number on it written in the hand of the barely educated.

When Rose called the number, she got the desk sergeant at a police precinct in Manhattan. When she identified herself and asked to speak to Mr. Feldman, the sergeant informed her that Hershel had used all of his phone calls and that she had better come to the precinct anyway, as quickly as possible. The drive from Staten Island to Manhattan in the middle of the day was madness and, given her present condition, Rose was hardly up to it. What it was that had Hershel confined in a police station, she could not imagine. He was so shifty and given to drunkenness, Rose presumed it must be something related to those. She finally arrived at the precinct office only to find the parking lot filled to capacity. She burst into tears once again and simply sat in her car parked on the street right in front of the police station. Of course, what with all the blaring of horns and shouted expletives, it hardly took long at all for the officers inside the station to discover her out there. Two came out to investigate, one directing traffic around her and the other tapping on her window with a rolled up newspaper. "Whatsa matta wit' you, lady; you nuts or sump'n? Get outta heah!" He looked at Rose carefully and called to his partner, "Hey, Al, get ova heah an' look at dis lady, OK?"

Al abandoned his traffic control and strolled over to Rose's car and looked in at the poor creature hunched over the wheel, sobbing uncontrollably, her face contorted in anguish. In no more than five minutes Rose was seated in a comfortable chair in the waiting area under the care of a policewoman, who had thoughtfully brought her a cup of tepid tea. The woman kept handing her tissues even after Rose had quieted down somewhat. At last, she said to Rose, "Come on, Honey, let's go talk to your husband, OK?"

A guard brought Hershel in, disheveled and in spotted slacks and shirt, to a counter that was separated from the similar counter at which Rose sat, by a heavy wire grille. Looking savagely at her he screamed, "What the hell has taken you so long to get here?" He sat in a steel chair and gripped the vertical bars in the grille with dirty hands. "These people in here are absolutely crazy!" he raved, "They're trying to pin a *murder* on me, for gosh sakes, even after I told them I didn't do it. I even told them who did, and they still won't believe me! Come on, Rosie, tell these jerks I wouldn't hurt a flea." He shook the bars as if he could break them loose. He paid no mind to Rose's flushed face and shaky voice.

Dabbing at her eyes some more, Rose said, "I'm sorry, Honey, but I've got a horrible problem. I've been at the doctor's office nearly all day and I'm scared!" She coughed into the poor, overwhelmed tissue.

Hershel seemed to become even angrier, shouting, "What could possibly be so important that you couldn't even return my call for an entire day? I tell you, I've had about all I can take of this place and these jerks—and you too, for that matter. Bail me out or whatever and let's go home." He got up and started pacing back and forth behind the grille.

"That's what I've been trying to tell you, Darling; They, the doctors, they told me I have bad, bad cancer and, if they don't operate on me in a few days, I might die. I have to go into surgery day after tomorrow and I'll probably have to have a mastectomy! Oh, Hershel, I'm so afraid!" She pulled another tissue out of her purse, causing eight or ten of them to spill out onto the counter where she sat.

"What?" he exclaimed, "Did you say cancer? Well, of all th…" He was livid. "First you can't take the time to come and get me out of here and then you come up with this phony cancer thing—trying to make me feel sorry for you, I guess. I know, you just don't want to spend your precious money on my bail, that's it. So don't, I don't care! I'll find somebody who'll help me. Maybe Karen—yeah, Karen, she'll help! So get the hell out of here; I don't need you!" He turned away and yelled, **"GUARD!"** Then, he was gone.

Rose staggered out into the office area, wailing and crying her heart out in fear, grief, and frustration. She found the policewoman who had helped her and, calming a little, asked, "Can I have my car now, please?" She rummaged in her purse, through all the tissues, and found her keys.

The woman answered, "Honey, I don't think you should be driving, not in your condition. Let me get you a cab."

Rose flew at her without meaning to, "I can drive fine! I have to, don't I? No one else, especially not my husband, is going to do it for me! What do I need his support for? I'm not beautiful or sexy or built like she is!" Putting her hand over her mouth, she said, "Oh dear, I'm so sorry. It's just that..." She turned and looked back toward the cell where Hershel had been and said, "It's just that I love him so much." Rose touched the matron's forearm and asked softly, "My car, please?"

The drive back out to Staten Island was hell. Rose's mind was a tempest of random images and thoughts, all jumbled up into fearful 'if onlys' and 'why-oh-whys'. She finally pulled her car into the garage and noticed that Hershel's BMW was not in its usual spot. She hoped the police would impound it forever! "Mrs. Bridges, Mary!" she called out from the entrance hall.

Mrs. Bridges brought her tea and a hug and Rose settled into her little chaise lounge and picked up her phone. She dialed her attorney's office. His secretary answered and got her right in to the attorney himself. Rose's voice was still trembling as she said, "Bruce, I have a couple of jobs I want you to do; I hope you don't mind."

"Not a problem, Rose, that's what you retain me for. What's up?" He had always liked Rose and thought the way Hershel treated her was abominable.

"Okay, first you need to know that Hershel is being held in jail in a precinct in Manhattan. I'll give you the Lieutenant's number in a second, but here's what I want you to do: Go down there and represent me and see if you can get Hershel out on bond or something. I'm sorry, but I can't do it—I just can't face him, Bruce." She began to weep softly, but added, "Whatever it takes, please get him out of there, but don't volunteer the name of who is responsible for his release, OK? Next, I want you to see if you can call a state audit on my company." When Bruce tried to dissuade her, Rose added, "Yeah, I know, it could cost me a bundle, but I don't care. There's this Klausman character who I think is trying to cover up all of Hershel's shenanigans, in the name of what or who I don't know. But, he's trying to undo all of the work Karen Boschert has done to get my accounting department all straightened out, and Klausman's trying to cover all that up. It's a dreadful mess and it needs a big spotlight shown on it." She paused to blow her nose and then went on, "I'm really very sick, Bruce, and I won't be able to help you out—I'm sorry. Please just do the best you can. Oh, also, I have a question for you: Did you complete the changes in my will? You know, the part where Hershel can't touch my business and all of that goes to Isabelle? I want Karen to run it for me, but I don't know if that can be done."

Bruce sounded shocked as he asked, "What sick, Rose, what's wrong? You don't need to worry about your will; I took care of that a week ago. Don't you remember signing the documents? I'm still working on that part about Karen but it's not looking too promising. She's not a citizen, you know. I'll keep you apprised on that." He sounded worried, too.

When she hung up talking to her attorney, Rose looked satisfied and relieved, her mouth set in a little straight line across her face.

The police lieutenant seemed awfully close-mouthed about the release and the bond, Hershel thought. It couldn't have been Rose who had had him released—not after the way she looked when she came to visit him. Well, she ought not to have come up with that cancer thing. What a lousy, stupid trick, pretending to have cancer! The boneheaded cops wouldn't let him have his car back, so he went and booked into a nice hotel downtown, but not until he had bought himself a bunch of nice clothes. He charged everything to Rose's account and then checked into his room and took a hot shower. The hotel bed was a big improvement over the bunk in his cell.

The following day Hershel attempted again to get his car from the police impound but they wouldn't take charge cards. Stupid cops! He took a taxi over to the hospital where Karen was admitted and approached the information desk. Addressing the middle aged woman seated behind it, he said, "Hi, Snooks, I need to see Karen Boschert. What's her room number?" He gave her a broad wink and his most winsome smile.

The woman leveled a glance at him and replied, "Just have a seat, Sir, and I'll check." She dialed a number, waited a few seconds, and then asked, "Are you inquiring about Miss Nhung Boschert? We have no Karen."

Hershel sighed impatiently and said, "Yes, yes, that's her: Nhung. I need to see her."

Smiling gently, the woman answered, "I'm sorry, Sir, Miss Boschert can't have any visitors. She's in Intensive Care. Are you related to her?"

"Well, I'm her first cousin, ugh, H-Harold. How about it, Tootsie?" He gave the woman everything he had in the way of smiles and winks.

The woman asked wryly, "What happened to Snooks? I'm sorry, Sir, I'll have to check again. Please sit over there and wait. It shouldn't be too long."

When, after a good ten minutes had passed and the woman did not call him back to her desk, Hershel approached her and asked testily, "What's the big holdup, Lady? I need to talk to Miss Boschert, and right away, you hear?"

Looking directly into Hershel's eyes, the woman replied, "I'm told there are to be no visitors. Family members are expected in from Europe tomorrow. Why don't you come back then and they will probably give you the information you want. I'm sorry."

Trying to stem his anger, Hershel said evenly, "No, you don't understand. I must see Kar—ugh—Miss Boschert this minute! It's a matter of life and death!" He pounded the heal of his fist on the information desk, alarming the woman.

"Sir, I must ask you to lower your voice; this is a hospital! I've already told you; Miss Boschert can have *no* visitors. That's final! I'm sorry." The poor woman was flushed with stress.

Hershel was adamant: "That's not acceptable! I want to see your supervisor immediately!"

"I'll get him," she said, "but you're wasting your time. No one but her attending physician can allow her visitors, and Dr. Rae has made it perfectly clear there are to be **NO** visitors."

Hershel had no better results from the woman's supervisor and, of course, he was not allowed to talk to Dr. Rae. Finally, he gave up in disgust and headed to the men's room that was situated part way down a long hall. As he approached the men's room, he spotted a man about his size and build, wearing green scrubs, about to enter a room marked **'STORAGE'**. He followed him into the room. In a few minutes Hershel emerged from the room, wearing the man's scrubs, and headed for the elevators. The elevator control panel was very helpful in identifying the floor on which he would find ICU.

His initial plan was to spin some tale to the nurses in the nurses' station, hoping he could gain entry to Karen's room. Spotting a lone nurse working behind a counter, he strode jauntily up to her and said, "Hi, Toots, how're you doin'?"

Looking up at him suspiciously, the nurse asked, "What do you want?" Letting her gaze fall to the identification tag hanging from Hershel's belt, her eyes widened in alarm and she yelled, "Milton, come here quickly!"

Hershel froze in panic and just stood in place. Perhaps he could use his old charm and work his way out of this fix. Unfortunately, Milton, as he approached at a trot, proved to be huge black man with an angry look on his face. Before Hershel could take two steps, Milton had him by the arm. "What's goin' on here, Beth?" the man asked.

"Look at this guy, Milt, he's got on Dr. Sanchez's scrubs, name tag and all!" The nurse glared at Hershel and poked her finger in his chest.

Milton was none too pleased either, asking, "What you done wit' Dr. Sanchez, man?"

It turned out that virtually no one at the hospital was pleased with Hershel, least of all Dr. Sanchez. The hospital security wasted no time in calling the New York police who showed up in short order. In a matter of an hour Hershel was back in his interrogation room at the same precinct office as before, seated at his favorite table, and looking at the perspiring face of a detective Horne. Horne spoke first, "You don't seem to think too good, Feldman. What made you think you could break into a room in ICU at the hospital? Those people are a lot sharper than you are, Genius; and that big guy, Milton, he don't like you a whole lot either. I'd stay away from him if I was you. He could squash you like a grape." Horne chuckled at his own humor.

'Yeah, well I didn't mean any harm," Hershel said, "I just wanted to check on Miss Boschert and see if she's all right. Why's that such a big deal?"

"Why don't you ask that Dr. Sanchez?" the detective replied, "I don't think he liked the way you swapped clothes with him. You'd better be glad he decided not to press charges. Boy, you're really some kind of a jerk; you know that? I'd like nothing more than to hold you here until you finally get smart and tell us the truth. So far I haven't believed a word you've said. Yeah, whatta jerk! Oh, by the way, we finally got ahold of a guy named Anton Klausman—some big shot from Europe—says he knows you and your wife. You know what else this guy says?" The lieutenant drummed big, meaty fingers on the table.

Attempting to appear bored, Hershel asked, "No, what?"

The detective sat grinning at Hershel for a while, letting him stew a bit, and then answered, "He says he never heard of no Rolf. He says that when he comes to New York he just hires a limo and a driver and he don't need to have a chauffeur of his own. Ain't that a kick? Heh, heh—never heard of Rolf! You know what else he said?"

It was clear that Horne was enjoying himself. He added, "Talkin' about that Korean guy that got killed he, that Klausman, he says he canned the skinny little guy a couple a' months ago, right after they got to New York and he found out that the hotel security was, as he put it, 'adequate', and so he sent the little guy—Lee is his name—supposedly back to Korea or someplace. Turns out this Lee didn't go back home but stayed in New York and got hisself a little hole-in-the-wall apartment in the garment district. Who'd a' thought?"

Hershel stretched elaborately and asked, "So, what has all this to do with me?"

"You really wanna know, Feldman?" Horne asked, with eyebrows raised, "I'll tell you what I think really happened: There really ain't any Rolf, but you, you got the hots for this little dish Boschert and you go to her apartment an' try to put some moves on her and the little skinny guy Lee walks in on you and you plug him then and there. Then you turn an' pop the girl so's she can't put the finger on you! That's what I think, Feldman. Do you also know that we found that her door was not locked and the security system was unarmed, so Mr. Lee could just walk right in? Let's say the girl was expecting the little guy and left her place unprotected; so you din't hear him come in. Holy mackerel, what a scene that must have been for him! The both of them come from the same country, don't they? So, it could be that they were close, or even married. We're still checking on that."

146

"That's preposterous!" Hershel shouted, "That's nothing at all like the way it happened! And, they are *not* from the same country! Lee Min-jun was from Korea and Miss Boschert is Swiss-Chinese, and she was born in Germany, I think. Anyway, they're not from the same place. And, what difference would it make if they were? I still didn't kill Mr. Lee! Rolf did! I saw him running away, like I already told you." Hershel was screaming and sweating profusely.

Horne leaned back in his squeaky chair, clasped his hands behind his bald head, and remarked, "Well, it ain't the way that Klausman fella tells it, and it don't really matter, does it, Feldman. Sooner or later the chic is goin' to wake up an' spill her guts an' finger you. An', you can be sure we're not goin' to stop lookin' until we find your weapon, and then it's in the fryin' pan for you, Pal; it'll be all over for ol' Romeo Feldman—heh, heh." He slipped a cigar out of its cellophane wrapper and bit off one end, spitting the end piece in Hershel's direction. Fortunately for Hershel, it fell short and landed on the table.

The hair on the back of Hershel's neck bristled as he said, "Yeah, well you guys don't have a thing on me—this is all guesswork. When Miss Boschert wakes up, you'll find out the truth and I'll turn right around and sue for defamation of character!"

Horne chuckled, then quipped, "What character?"

"Go ahead and laugh," Hershel said, "but you don't have a thing on me and you can't hold me."

"You're wrong, Feldman," answered Horne, improving his grammar somewhat, "Until the girl wakes up and proves otherwise, you're our prime suspect for the murder of Lee Min-jun, and the attempted murder of Nhung Karen Boschert. The only reason we're not holding you now is because someone has paid a whopping bail to get you out. I can't imagine why anyone would want to bail out a guy like you out, but go figure. Now, get out of here! I'm sick of the sight of you." He spat at Hershel's feet in disgust.

Hershel paid the cabbie with the last of his cash. The idiot refused to take credit cards, too. The un-tipped cab driver left Hershel with some colorful new vocabulary to contemplate. The house appeared different somehow as he entered into the garage through a small back door. Rose's Mercedes, parked in its usual spot, looked strangely unused; as if it hadn't been driven for a month. He discovered his key to the back door would not fit the lock. He tried another, but even though he could insert it, it would not turn in the lock. What was going on? In a fit of rage he hit the doorbell button about fifty times and then turned to leave. The door to the kitchen opened slightly and Yetsye stuck her head out and yelled, "Stop that!"

"Aunt Yetsye!" Hershel appeared confused. Yetsye was supposed to be in Miami where she belonged. "What are you doing here?" He asked, "Where's Rosie? I need to see her."

Yetsye spat the words at Hershel in disgust, "If you want to see my daughter you'll have to wait for visiting hours at the hospital. Good luck getting in; she goes into surgery early in the morning. I might ask you the same thing: Where do you get the nerve coming here? You belong in jail like any other murderer! And, I'm not your aunt!"

"That's crazy, I'm not a murderer," Hershel answered, "Where did you hear that nonsense? And, what's Rose doing in the hospital? I never laid a hand on her."

Yetsye screamed back, "She has cancer, you fool! What's it going to take to get that through your thick skull? I'm taking care of my daughter and my granddaughter like you should be doing, you worthless lout. Now, get away from here!" As she was about to close the door, Isabelle crept up behind her, clung to her skirt, and peered out through the closing gap between the door and the doorframe. Her face contorted with terror, the child shrieked the piercing, nearly ultrasonic scream of a three-year-old girl and bolted. Yetsye slammed the door and followed Isabelle to her room. The child had dived under her bed and pulled her stuffed tiger under with her, using the lifeless beast as a shield. Yetsye cooed, "That's all right, Baby, Abi's not going to hurt you. Gram's right here to take care of you. Don't worry, Baby Doll." After coaxing the little one out from under the bed, she cradled her in her arms and carried her to the kitchen for a treat, Yetsye's cure-all.

Hershel discovered the door was still locked and he beat on it repeatedly yelling, "Open up, open up!" No one did. He took to ringing the bell again and that produced results, some for which he was not prepared.

Yanking the door open once more, Yetsye hissed, "If you don't leave here right away, I'm going to call the police, and they'll put you where you belong. Now **GET!**"

Before she could shut the door, Hershel blocked it with his foot and countered, "I told you, I didn't kill anyone, and I have a right to see my own daughter; now let me in my own house!" He was, by this time, livid.

"Over my dead body!" Yetsye screamed, "You no longer have any rights around here, the way you've treated your wife and everything. Now, I'm not fooling; I'm going to call the police and they'll set you straight. You'd better get out of here because Mrs. Bridges is already dialing and they won't take long to get here—they've been on the lookout for you. Here, take this; go away and don't come back!" She thrust an envelope at him and slammed the door in his face. No amount of doorbell ringing would bring her back.

Hershel walked around to the front of the house and tried the front doorbell, without result. Circling the house, he searched for some means of entry but could find none, a tribute to Rose's cleverness and diligence. Finally, he walked back to the rear of the house and sat on a low brick wall that separated the driveway from the backyard. At that point he became aware of the envelope he was holding and he regarded it with nothing more than curiosity, attempting finally to open it by tearing off one end. Extracting a couple of pages of printed text, he read:

Dear Hershel,

By the time you read this I might already be dead. The doctors say I have about an even chance of surviving this. Oh, how I hate that it all may end this way. I had hoped we could somehow grow old together, but I guess that's not to be. I do love you so much, you know.

I don't believe that you killed Lee Min-jun and I don't believe you shot Karen but, unless she pulls through, it looks like you will be indicted for that poor man's murder and for Karen's too. Oh, how awful for you to be caught up in this mess. I believe it is all the fault of that awful Mr. Klausman, but I can't prove it.

It seems there is no helping you, but I have done my best. I have given Bruce some instructions that should keep you going until your innocence has somehow been proven. He has paid the impound fees for your car so you can get it whenever it is convenient. You have a one-bedroom apartment in Manhattan for which the rent is paid for the next thirty days and to where your clothes and other of your belongings have been moved. You will find the address at the end of this letter. All of your frozen credit cards have been paid up, along with the interest and late fees, so you can begin to use them again. Your bail is paid and in effect until such time that you are either indicted or released.

Some other things have happened that I have no control over. The Board of Directors at Mandel Family Apparel have taken the following actions: You have been terminated without any severance package, and a new Comptroller has been put in place. The on again—off again audit by Klausman, Walther, und Hahn, GmbH has been superceded by a state audit and Mr. Klausman has been extradited to Switzerland in disgrace. I'm afraid there will be no way of concealing your activities prior to the audits when this last one is completed. I'm so sorry. Also, do you remember the ketubah we signed in our marriage ceremony? Well, it is an iron-clad, legally binding document that states that, if I should die, basically the ownership of Mandel Family Apparel goes to my father or, if he is deceased, it goes to our offspring, if we should have any. So, since my father died last month, the company will actually belong to Isabelle. I'm sorry, Hershel, but I'm afraid I didn't pay all that much attention to the details of the ketubah at the time. Bruce says there is nothing that can be done about it because you and I both signed it and it was witnessed. Finally, a restraining order has been issued against you to keep you from contact with Isabelle, Yetsye, and me. The judge issued it based on numerous police reports of your abuse of Carmen, Mrs. Bridges and me. I'm sorry about that too, but at the time we just didn't know what else to do about you. For obvious reasons, there is another order in effect preventing you from trying to contact Karen too. No matter how mad you get, please try to obey these restraining orders. If you don't it will make it even harder on you.

One last thing: There is a way out of this and all of your other troubles, something that Karen told me about and that I have found to be the truth. If you will get down on your knees and tell Jesus that you realize that you are a sinner, and if you will ask Him to forgive you for all your sins, and if you will place all your trust in Him and surrender your life to Him; then you can just throw away all your worries and cares and just rest in Him, knowing He will take care of everything. I have done this and I'm ready for anything that might happen to me in this world because I know He will take me to Heaven when I die. I know I can't say this very well so, when all of this terrible mess is over and Karen gets healed, you must go and talk to her about Jesus.

Please don't tell Yetsye I said all this. She'll hate me for it, but it's the truth; I know that now, for certain.

I love you, Honey,

Rose

Hershel looked up from his reading just in time to see the patrol car swing into the driveway. He walked over to the car and, much to the dismay of the two officers in front, he opened the back door, got in, and sat down. "Goin' my way?" he asked, his eyebrows arched almost up to his hairline. When neither officer spoke a word, Hershel added, "And, since I'm not allowed near my own daughter, my wife, my mother in law, or my own house, maybe you guys wouldn't mind taking me to the nearest ATM machine so I can get some cash to get me as far away from Staten Island as you want me to be. How 'bout it?"

The first night in his apartment Hershel found to be almost intolerable. Accustomed to the relative peace and quiet of Staten Island, he was wrenched relentlessly from slumber by the all night traffic and pedestrian noises. If it wasn't a fire engine screaming beneath his window, it was some jerk yelling at a cabbie or, worse yet, a shot fired. Finally, dawn arrived and he rose from his bed and took a shower. That always seemed to help calm him. After preparing himself a lavish breakfast, he sat down to read the paper. Bruce had had the decency to have his favorite chair brought over from the house. He simply could not concentrate on even the sports section, so he stood up, stretched, and began to pace the floor. His eyes came to rest on Rose's letter lying on the dinette table. Picking it up with the intention of re-reading it, he instead rolled it into a ball and threw it into the kitchen trashcan. What a bunch of bull! Maybe a little walk would calm him. He spent most of the rest of the day walking aimlessly about Manhattan, stopping only at an Orange Julius for a stand-up lunch. It was nearly dark when he arrived home, a little drunk by then due to a few subsequent stops along the way home.

On entering his apartment, Hershel was struck by a most offensive odor; a morass of smells really, that made him at once curious and sick to his stomach. Had he left something on the stove to burn? He didn't think so. Had something gotten into the wall and died? That must be it. The stench seemed to get stronger as he approached his sitting room; and there was a strange sound as well—a sort of hissing or panting sound. He was unprepared for what he discovered. Reclining on his couch was a repulsive dragon, its tail draped over the backrest and its strange, clawed forelegs splayed over an armrest. Steam and flames issued from its great, fanged maw, and between its scales it seemed to be oozing some sort of gross effluvium. It cackled at Hershel's arrival, "Ah, there you are, Feldman. Where have you been keeping yourself? I was just about to fix myself a drink."

Oddly, Hershel was neither afraid nor taken aback, but answered, "Who, or what, are you?" Perhaps if he had been sober, he would have been frightened at least; but, being just comfortably drunk, he added, "Get out of my apartment, whoever you are. I'm going to fix myself a drink and you're not invited."

"Come, come, now," the dragon replied, "That's no way to treat a guest. Let's have that drink." With that, it transformed itself into Mr. Abaddon, the sleek, handsome, younger Abaddon. It, or he, took a pack of cigarettes from his pocket and offered one to Hershel. When Hershel nodded the affirmative, Abaddon took two cigarettes from the pack and proceeded to light them both without the benefit of a match or a lighter, handing one matter-of-factly to Hershel. Both took a deep drag before either spoke. Finally, Abaddon did, "How about that drink now, Feldman?"

As he returned from the kitchen carrying two straight-up whiskies, Hershel asked, "To what do I owe the pleasure?"

Studying Hershel a moment before he spoke, Abaddon finally said, "Unless you do not care to live out the rest of this day, we have an issue or two to discuss."

"What issues are those?" Hershel asked.

For just a second or two, Abaddon was the dragon, then he reverted back to Abaddon and continued to study Hershel for another second or more. At length, he answered, "I was given to suppose we had a bargain, you and I. But, it seems you are determined to break trust with me and to do everything you had agreed not to do."

Hershel crossed his legs and blew cigarette smoke toward the ceiling. Regarding Abaddon as coolly as he possibly could, he asked, "By what authority do you claim to be able to hold me to anything? I don't owe you allegiance and I'm not obligated to you in any way that I know of. I agree, you seemed to have some sort of hold on, or authority over, that character Klausman, but I don't see what that has to do with me. By the way, what do you hear from old Klausman these days?"

Abaddon laughed sardonically for an instant and then, just as suddenly, he was deadly serious as he replied, "I do not hear from Herr Klausman at all anymore. Much as you are now doing, he betrayed me and he is, for all intents and purposes, no longer. You will doubtless read about his demise in the press in the near future. But, forget about Klausman; let us examine all the wonderful events that have taken place in your life since we last spoke and, I might add, you vowed to cease pursuing the lovely Miss Boschert." He took a last drink of his whiskey and then regarded the glass appreciatively. While holding his glass aloft, he asked, "Another perhaps?"

Giving Abaddon a sour look, Hershel sauntered into the kitchen to refresh both of their drinks. He was glad he had mixed the drinks in distinctly different-looking glasses; he would hate to have gotten them reversed and drunk from

Abaddon's. Just the thought made his skin crawl. "Enjoy," he said, as he extended the glass to Abaddon.

Abaddon took a long pull from his drink before he went on, "Very well, let us take a good look at all of the shining events that have transpired in Hershel Feldman's life since he had the temerity to defy me and to go after the delectable and charming Karen Boschert. Perhaps you misunderstood me, Feldman, when I admonished you to stay away from the girl. I did not mean for you to take a shot at her instead. I had in mind that you not be in pistol range of her either. But, this does not explain, of course, why you chose also to off the poor Mr. Lee. But, be that as it may, you are now the prime suspect in a murder case and an attempted murder case, possibly two murder cases. You have lost your job, your wife, your daughter, and most of your possessions. You haven't a prayer of claiming the slightest interest in Mandel Family Apparel. In addition, you are now the subject of an investigation into your possible felonious activities as the accounting manager of the same company. One wonders what other terrible deeds cloud your life; assault on one poor, unsuspecting physician along with theft of his clothing, perhaps. Or, let us say, accumulation of staggering credit card balances, which you are unable to pay. It boggles the mind." He paused to let these things seep into Hershel's mind, and then continued, "Is it possible, even for a mind such as yours, Feldman, to apprehend a connection between all of these unfortunate events in your life and the fact that you betrayed me and turned against me? I daresay a preschooler could have doped it out by now. All of the above notwithstanding, however, the one redeeming and reprehensible act that you committed, an act that has practically restored my confidence in, and admiration for, you has surfaced; and from this single, reprehensible gesture you have rescued yourself from annihilation. The totally self-absorbed way in which you have mistreated and abandoned your wife has caused me to have some hope for you after all.

Perhaps I can work with you even so." Abaddon sighed with pleasure as he said this last.

"What on earth do you mean?" Hershel asked.

"What I mean is this:" Abaddon replied, "That, if you can pull off just one simple chore for me, I might be disposed to let you off the hook and spare your life."

Hershel not only took the bait, he swallowed it, asking, "And what chore is that, may I ask?"

Abaddon threw back his head and laughed as he answered, "All you have to do, my friend, is restore an old friendship of yours, and bring the subject of that alliance back to me so that I can establish a relationship with him, you see."

Hershel was suspicious, but he asked anyway, "Who is it that I have to befriend again, and why can't I just introduce you two to each other?"

Abaddon finished off his drink before answering, "Why, it is the Reverend Ellis Keaton that I wish to meet. After all, I have admired the gentleman ever since he became a famous evangelist. So, tell me, do we have a deal?"

"What do I have to do?" Hershel asked again.

Abaddon sighed, "All you have to do is find the Reverend Ellis Keaton, relive old times, and then bring him to me so I can enjoy him too. That's all there is to it."

"Deal," said Hershel. Abaddon's hand was a clammy fish.

PART TWO

Chapter Eleven

As I sat, uttering not a single word but simply listening, Hershel talked incessantly up to and including the point at which Luigi finally ordered us to leave Giordano's Ristorante. He continued to talk without interruption even as we walked the half-block to a coffee shop situated on a busy Manhattan street. The name of the street and that of the shop escape me now, but I do remember that we were finally turned out of that establishment promptly at midnight; and Hershel was still talking. He kept it up as he drove me to my apartment on the second floor of a brownstone house in the Upper East Side of Manhattan. My apartment, in fact, occupied the entire second floor of the house, the main floor of which was jammed full of the furniture and belongings of a diminutive Polish lady who spoke practically no English at all. For this reason alone, if for no other, we got along famously. We rarely encountered each other and therefore caused each other little or no bother.

Hershel let up in his narrative only long enough to nod his assent to a cup of coffee; then he regaled me with his exploits for another half hour before finally falling silent after over five hours of nonstop talking. Following a moment of rest, during which he regarded me with a somber expression, he said, "So, after I said, "Deal," I shook his hand and it felt like a cold, dead fish."

I remember thinking at the time that all during his discourse Hershel seemed to evolve from the arrogant, rude, and obstreperous profligate I had cringed under in my youth to a quiet, calm, and sentient young man, full of worries and anxieties to be sure, but speaking now in my living room almost timorously and with due respect for his listener (me). What had changed him, and what had changed *in him,* I wondered? So, I asked him, "What happened to you, Hershel? I've never known you to act this way; and it seems to have come upon you as you related the particulars of the last six or eight years of your life. In the last five hours you've become a totally different person from the one I had to endure in high school."

"Yeah, I know," he replied. Looking down at his hands, he continued, "As I was relating all of these events to you, Ellis, I felt something strange coming over me—a feeling I have never experienced before in my life. It was as if..."

"Wait just a minute!" I exclaimed, "Did you hear what you called me just now?"

Hershel, raising his eyes from his hands to my eyes, replied, "Yeah, I can't explain it, though. But, as I was saying, something has come over me and I don't know what it is. I remember when I first walked into the restaurant I felt just as sure and cocky as I always have; but then, as I went along, I began to see the absurdity of it all. How could I continue to be so confident and sure of myself in the face of the terrible mess I've made of my life? I guess when I had the opportunity to relate the entire grisly mess to an outside party; I could see how ridiculous the whole thing has been. I mean, who the *hell* do I think I am?"

I interrupted him long enough to ask, "Yes, who in the hell *do* you think you are?"

He chuckled and said, "Yeah, really. But, here's the odd part, Ellis: After I'd been talking an hour or so, it seemed as if there was someone else there besides you and me—and good old Luigi, of course. Remember that letter I told you about that Rose wrote to me? Well, the last part of it—you know, the part about Jesus—kept coming back to me; and I realized then that I'm not alone in this. I felt—no, I knew—

that there was, and is, someone in this with me; and now I know who it is. For the first time in my life I prayed, Ellis, and I really meant it, and I felt Him there with me. Seriously, I felt like I was having to answer to someone much, much bigger and smarter than either you or me; someone who already knew all the answers to my questions, and answers to questions I didn't even know how to ask. Know what I mean?"

"As a matter of fact, I do," I answered.

"Well then, give," Hershel came back. "Are we talking about God or somebody here? If it was him, I don't get it. I figure he was through with the likes of me long ago. After the way I've been my whole life, why would God care one way or the other about me?" He looked a little frightened.

I held his gaze and replied, "Why would He not care, Hershel; He created you, didn't He? You're one of His children; one, I might add, that He may not be too thrilled with at present, but one of His at any rate."

"So, what are you saying? Was God sitting there with us like a ghost, overhearing everything I said and making me feel guilty for being such a jerk all my life?" He looked even more frightened.

I put my hand on his shoulder to calm him and said, "It's not like that at all, Hershel. God was already there; He didn't come sneaking up to the table to eavesdrop on our conversation. He's everywhere—omnipresent, we call it. That's just His nature because he's God who is everywhere present. That's the beauty of having a relationship with Him; you don't have to call Him and ask permission to talk to Him because he's always with you anyhow and all you have to do is address Him and start talking. And, I figure He was there with us at the tables in the restaurant and the coffee shop, and in the car on the way over here, and he's here with us now; and He wants you to know that He does care about Hershel Feldman. He cares because He made you with His own hands and He loves you no matter what you do or say.

Of course, He would be more pleased with you if you would acknowledge and obey Him, but we'll get to that later." I squeezed his shoulder to emphasize my point, then continued, "But, back to your original question—and you're either not going to believe me or you will think I'm an idiot—I firmly believe you are under conviction by the Spirit of God!"

"I don't need a sermon, Ellis; I would just like to know whether or not I have to worry about God listening in on what I say. If God is suddenly interested in me, where has he been all the rest of my life? And, besides, don't *you* think you're going to convert me over to your religion or anything; I was born a Jew and a Jew I'll die." Hershel sounded truly resolute as he spoke.

For the entire afternoon and evening, I had been picking Hershel's brain for details about his plight in order that I might attempt to address his issues and perhaps give him some assistance. After all, that was his ostensible purpose in ringing me up in the wee hours of the morning. So far, however, the present conversation was leading us elsewhere and I was not quite ready for that. By way of redirecting our thoughts, I asked, "Just what is it you really want from me, Hershel?"

Hershel laughed nervously, but answered, "Well, when I called you yesterday morning I thought I had it straight in my mind what I wanted you to do; but now, I don't seem to have a clue. Of course, I know that I'm a prime suspect in a murder case; I'm suspected of having fiddled with the books of my wife's company and possibly embezzled a bunch of money; I've treated my wife abominably since the day we met; I've so terrorized my own daughter to the point that she won't get near me; I have put moves on a girl little more than half my age with the intention of having an affair with her; I have abused almost everyone I've ever met so that nobody can stand me; and, to top it all off, I have made a deal with a man who I think could quite possibly be the devil, and he has promised to kill me if I don't do what he says. The strangest part of all this is that, until I related all of this to you, I really didn't care at all what happened to me. So, I guess what I'm saying is, what I want from you is for you to tell me what has happened to me in the last five hours; because, Ellis, I swear I just don't know what is going on. And, besides that, I'm scared to death! Now, all of a sudden, I really do care, not only about what happens to me, but also I care about how Rose—who's probably dead by now—feels about me, about how Isabelle feels about her Abi, about how I have offended a lovely young woman who is probably at the point of death. But the scariest part of all is the fact that I don't really *want* to get away with all of the rotten things I've done—I want to make them right somehow. Please, Ellis, what is going on here?"

I could scarcely believe my eyes; Hershel Feldman was close to tears! I said gently, "Let's take it a little at a time, Hershel. First of all, Abaddon *is* the Hebrew name for Satan, but I have no idea how you could actually have seen or talked to him. I do know that, because he has tremendous control in this world, he could find a way to cause your death. But, let's set that aside for a moment and let me ask you some questions: Are you expecting me to somehow get Rose and Isabelle to not be afraid of you? Are you hoping I can intercede for you with the police and the courts and get them to drop the murder case against you? And, the same about your criminal embezzlement case? And, are you hoping I can somehow clear you with Karen about the way you have treated her—assuming, by the way, that she is still alive? Now, getting back to the devil, I do believe you are wrong about there being two individuals going by the name of 'Abaddon'. I'm thinking there is just one and he is able to materialize as either a fatherly figure or his son. Now, what is it you want me to do about him?" I tried not to sound cruel, but I also felt he ought to realize the magnitude of his expectations for me.

Hershel was silent for so long that I feared he might have become too discouraged to continue our conversation. Nevertheless, he did finally answer, "I see your point, I think. Okay, I guess I really didn't think through how you could possibly help me, but I suppose I thought you might have some supernatural powers that you could bring to bear on all my problems. So, as you say, let's take them one at a time. I did see a Mr. Lucifer Abaddon, and his son of the same name. The father type could turn himself at will from a terrifying dragon, to a monstrous ogre, to a slick-looking prince; all in the space of a second or two. As far as I know, the son could become all of those too, as well as a very handsome and polished gent of thirty-some years old. He's the one who seemed to have it really bad for Karen, and he's the one who came to my apartment and sucked me into the deal I told you about—the deal where I introduce him to you. I guess I didn't think he was Satan because I never really have believed such a person exists. Now, I'm not so sure, because I get afraid every time I think of him. Now that I'm beginning to see what an ass I've always been, I don't want to die. Go figure! Now, all I want to do is tell everyone how sorry I am and try to get my wife and baby back. I hope Karen makes it and that she recovers and goes back to Switzerland to her parents. I hope they find out how crooked Klausman is and they put him away for good, or maybe extradite the old fool. I hope they find Rolf and pin the murder of Lee Min-jun on him like they should, and that they nail him for shooting Karen, too. See, I *know* this is the way it all should turn out, but I have absolutely no credibility, so no one believes me; and why should they?"

"You're wrong, you know," I said, "I believe you and I'm going to do everything I can to help you. But, it's going to be insanely difficult, I warn you, and I don't know whether or not we can accomplish anything at all. In fact, I can promise you that you and I will fail at this unless we can get divine help. Do you understand what I'm saying?"

"I'm not sure I follow," he answered, "Do you mean I need to go and see a rabbi or a priest?"

"No, I mean *we* must cry out to *the* Great High Priest, The Messiah, Y'shua, Jesus, God The Son," I said, "however you wish to address Him. He is your *only* hope! I can assure you of His grace, His undeserved favor, only if you have surrendered your life to Him."

"Do you mean I have to become a Christian before Jesus will help me?" he asked, "I thought you said he loves me even though I'm rotten to the core."

"This is interesting," I said. "When did you decide I was talking about Jesus when I said God loves you?"

Hershel looked nonplussed as he said, "You said just moments ago that God made me with His own hands and that He loves me! What are you asking?"

"I did say that," I replied, "But I never mentioned the name Jesus. How do you know Jesus is the same as God?"

Looking even more agitated, he replied, "No, you said…I mean, didn't you say that Jesus…no, you said that God…Oh, I'm not sure what you said, Ellis. You've got me all mixed up. Are you saying Jesus is God? Are you saying that I have to surrender my life to Jesus before he'll help me?"

"No, that is not what I said. I said that I can *assure* you of God's grace—His help—only if you believe in His Son. He may be disposed to help you without your becoming a Christian, but I cannot assure you of that. That's what I said. He often does help those who do not believe in His Son and we call that prevenient grace, but I can't assure you of it. That's up to God." I held eye contact with him as I spoke.

Hershel was stricken. He said, "But I'm a Jew! There's no way God, or Jesus, is going to listen to me. I can't be both a Jew and a Christian, can I?"

"Why not?" I answered, "Jesus was a Jew; and He was and still is God!"

Without taking his eyes from mine, Hershel said, "I'm going to have to think about this for a while. Could you do me a big favor, Ellis?"

"Of course," I replied, "I'll help anyway I can. What do you want me to do?"

Still holding my gaze, he said levelly, "Come with me to meet Satan."

The instant Hershel uttered these words there came upon me the most awful feeling of fear and dread, to the extent that I felt an icy hand clutch my heart and my breath begin to come in gasps. Never had I imagined that I would be required to confront the old devil face-to-face. Frantically I searched for some argument to use to dissuade him from holding me to my promise of unconditional help. Finally I said, "First things first, Hershel. Before we actually get to the point of meeting Abaddon, we need to determine the condition of two very important people in your life. Tomorrow we'll go together to the hospital where Rose had her surgery and let's see how she's doing. Then, we'll go, also together because I'm sure *you* would not be so gladly received there, to the hospital where Karen was taken after the shooting, and we'll try to find out if she has survived and, if so, what her condition is. We have a lot of other places to go but they'll have to wait until we check on Rose and Karen."

"I don't mean to sound callous," Hershel said, "but what difference does it make to me how Rose and Karen are if I'm dead? Shouldn't we first go to Mr. Abaddon and use your offices to try to change his mind about putting me to death? If we do that this afternoon, we could still go tomorrow and see about the girls, assuming you are successful in placating the devil with your presence. After all, that was the deal he offered me: that I bring you to him to meet him. He just said he wanted to meet you—I believe he put it that he wanted to enjoy you, nothing else."

"I doubt that most of us share the same meaning for the word 'enjoy' that Abaddon uses," I responded. "It's pretty plain to me that Abaddon means to bring me down to his level—to corrupt me to the point that I renounce God and pay homage to him. This, of course, I would never do, but it's bound to be an excruciating test of my faith and resolve. I can't even imagine what a horrible and terrifying scene it will be for both of us! But, as I said before, we need to address some other things first. The devil will keep. After all, until you demonstrate the fact that you refuse to uphold your end of the bargain, he has nothing to act upon. Please just be patient. Believe me, there's no reason to hurry into that showdown."

Hershel appeared truly fearful, exclaiming, "I'm telling you, Ellis, this guy knows everything! I don't know how he knows, but he just does. He'll know about us going to the hospitals and checking on the girls and he'll know that I'm welshing on the deal, I'm sure. You don't have to worry— you're not the one he has promised to snuff out; but me, I'm the one he's watching to see what I'll do. Please, let's get this thing over with!"

Grasping both of his shoulders, I said gently, "I don't wish to be harsh with you, my friend, but you're back to thinking of old Hershel first and everyone else second. Let's find out first about the welfare of two people that you love and then we'll see what we can do about Mr. Abaddon. If you can't find it in your heart to have faith in God, just hang onto me and maybe you'll see Him in action. We're both going to have to put our faith in God here, and I have just as much at stake as you do. It won't be easy for either of us when we do meet up with the old dragon."

Chapter Twelve

Inasmuch as he was a resident hospital physician, Nestor Sanchez was required to work endless hours with very little rest. This did not prevent him, however, from taking a profound interest in the patients whose care fell under his responsibility. One patient in particular held his interest firmly, and that was one Nhung Karen Boschert. To be sure, Dr. Sanchez was quite conscientious and caring, but he had also fallen head over heels in love with this particular patient; this being due not only to her considerable beauty, but also to her incredible courage. In his short career, Dr. Sanchez had seldom witnessed such patience and endurance in the face of relentless pain and discomfort. Karen just never complained, but simply complied with the instructions of all the nurses, technicians, and doctors who were in attendance. This she did without fuss and with the best humor she could summon, given the condition she found herself in as a result of having been in the line of fire when Rolf took his first shot at Lee Min-jun. Incredibly, she took advantage of her confinement in the hospital to brush up on her Spanish when she communicated with Dr. Sanchez. They rarely spoke English together. On the other hand, since he spoke neither Mandarin nor German, the good doctor was no more help than any other of the hospital staff in conveying to Karen's parents, when they arrived from Switzerland, the particulars of their daughter's condition at any given time. Still, Dr. Sanchez had become bonded very closely with the Boschert family in general, and with their daughter in particular. The two young people viewed their bonding in distinctly different ways; Karen's view being that of deep friendship while Nestor's was heartfelt romantic love. Somehow, however, these two diverse approaches to the couple's relationship did not seem to be at all contentious, but were based on solid affection.

Supervising nurse Beth Feeney approached Dr. Sanchez, a carefully controlled smile playing across her lips, and announced, "Dr. Sanchez, you won't believe who is in the lobby asking permission to visit your favorite patient."

Sanchez looked up from his laptop and asked, "Who might that be, Beth?"

Beth tried her best not to giggle but only partially succeeded as she replied, "It's that freak that stole your clothes and tried to get in to see Karen when she was in ICU the day after she was admitted. You remember, Milt had to rescue you and get your clothes back for you while you waited in the store room." She just could not restrain her laughter as she concluded her announcement, but she was an incurably cheerful woman in any case.

"What? Of all the nerve! Who does that creep think he is?" Sanchez was incredulous.

Beth was having a terrible time controlling her mirth and only barely managed to add, "And, you'll never guess who is with him, vouching for his harmlessness and swearing to keep him under control."

"Who's that?" Sanchez asked.

Pausing a few seconds for effect, Beth said, "None other than the Reverend Ellis Keaton of TV fame!"

"Who?" The doctor had no time to watch TV.

Beth sighed impatiently and replied, "Oh, you know, that TV evangelist with the gray hair and kind of silly smile, the one who's on the religious channel early Sunday morning. He has a huge following among Christians all over the city. You *must* have seen him on TV!"

Returning to his laptop only to turn it off, and then looking up at Beth again, Dr. Sanchez replied, "No, I've never seen the man. Is there something really special about him—something I should know before I ask Karen if she wants to see them?"

Beth seemed a little disappointed, but answered, "Well, no, I guess not. Are you really going to bother Karen about that jerk, or are you going to send Milton down to deal with him?"

"The reverend is a jerk?"

"No, no, Ellis Keaton isn't a jerk, but that Feldman character definitely is! You're really, seriously going to bother Karen about the nut that robbed you of your scrubs?"

Nestor was properly serious as he said, "Oh, I don't know. Maybe your evangelist sees something in Mr. Feldman that we don't. I need to ask Karen in any case."

In exasperation Beth remarked, "Sometimes I just can't figure you out, Sanchez." Before she could say another word, Dr. Sanchez was headed down the hall toward Karen's room.

In ten minute's time, Beth was on the phone to the information desk clerk saying, "You're not going to believe this, Betty, but not only did Dr. Rae approve Miss Boschert's having visitors, but the patient herself has agreed to see that creep. Can you believe that?"

Betty looked shocked and exclaimed, "Ellis Keaton is no creep! I watch him every Sunday and I love him. You'd do well to watch him yourself."

Hershel Feldman had probably not been as nervous at his wedding as he was in the elevator as he and I made our way up to Karen's room. Trying to calm him a bit, I assured him by reminding him that we were on our way to visit with a *living* witness to Rolf's alleged murder of Lee Min-jun and of his near murder of said living witness. Hershel was not to be much composed, but continued to pant and appear flushed and at loose ends. In a trembling voice he said, "Ellis, you're going to have to do all the talking. I don't think I'm going to make it; I'm such a nervous wreck. What if she screams bloody murder and calls security or something?"

"Come on, take it easy," I said, "She's already agreed to see you, hasn't she? She must have forgiven you, at least enough to allow you in her room. Anyway, you're going to have to introduce me to her; and then I'll do all of the talking if you can't find your tongue."

Fortunately, after we had been in Karen's room a few minutes, Hershel had come out of his shell long enough for introductions and some truly profound apologies, after which Karen, with much grace, chatted with us without a trace of malice or reluctance. I had to admit, I could not blame Hershel one minute for his attraction to this lovely creature. Even under the worst possible conditions: having been shot and come near to death, suffered significant loss of blood and body weight, had few if any opportunities to attend to her appearance, and endured tremendous physical and emotional trauma; Karen Boschert remained incredibly beautiful and desirable. True, she was pale and fragile looking, but this somehow added to her appeal, especially with her gorgeous black hair spilled over the white pillow, its radiance unable to belie the utter blackness of it; and her graceful arms and hands, sheer elegance hiding their thinness, still lovely and animated as she spoke to us in her soft, musical voice: "Thank you for coming to visit me, Hershel. Won't you introduce me to your friend?"

Hershel's tremulous answer: "Oh, of course; Karen, this is my close friend Reverend Ellis Keaton—Ellis, let me present Miss Karen Boschert. If it hadn't been for Ellis, here, I'd still be waiting downstairs for the law to show up and drag me off for questioning." Having said this, he began to regain his composure and sense of humor.

As Karen smiled and extended her hand to me, she volunteered, "What a pleasure to meet you, Reverend. Oh, dear, is that the proper way to address you, Sir?"

Her hand was velvet-soft and a little cool and I hated to release it to its owner, but found I must do so. I answered her, saying, "How about just 'Ellis'? I really dislike standing on formality. And, after all, I'm just a common preacher, a servant of Jesus Christ."

With a tiny sparkle in her eye, Karen responded, "Well hello, just Ellis. I am still very pleased to meet you in person. I have had the pleasure several times before, but you were confined to a box with the picture on the front. You are much more pleasant to see in person and at close range."

It was my turn to be a bit nervous as I said, "Oh, oh, I take it you've had the dubious experience of seeing me on the tube. I have to admit that I'm never so clever as when I have a script in front of me. But, in my defense, I must claim to be sincere, if nothing else."

Karen smiled and, turning to Hershel, said with a chuckle, "I hope you will not fail to acknowledge Dr. Sanchez when you give credit for your positive reception here. I understand that he could quite well have an issue with you if he were not such a forgiving person."

Hershel, looking very uncomfortable, said nothing in his defense, but said to Karen, "K-Karen, how are you feeling? Are you in a lot of pain?"

"I am improving daily, so they say, and am much encouraged since Thursday when my parents arrived from Zurich." She cared not to discuss the pain, apparently. "If you will linger—Oh, is that the right word?—you shall meet my parents in but a half hour. They are having an early lunch. Stay and meet them, will you please?"

I piped up, "Miss Boschert, we shouldn't tire you out. We only came to see that you were being well cared for and I, personally, to offer my very best wishes for your speedy recovery. I'm sure Hershel is profoundly relieved to see that you are conscious and alert, ready to reveal the truth about who attacked you and Mr. Lee."

"He certainly appears to be happier than the last time I saw him," she said, adding, "And please, if I am to address you 'Ellis', then you must call me Karen. Hershel, your appearance is vastly different from the last time we saw each other. What has transpired in the last few days that has changed you so?"

Hershel squirmed uncomfortably as he replied, "I-I really don't know, Karen. I asked Ellis and he won't give me a straight answer; all he will do is preach to me."

Again I interjected, "We mustn't take too long, Hershel, because Karen needs to save her strength. Just tell her quickly, please, how you feel and why."

Karen seemed to awaken to something important and declared, "But, wait, we are going too quickly! I must know about Rose before we speak of anything else. Is she in hospital still? I must telephone her wherever she is!"

Once again I answered for Hershel, "We called her home yesterday and got a very poor reception. Hershel's aunt Yetsye, Rose's mother, wouldn't speak to Hershel and she even hung up on me once before I could get her to listen to me a moment. Finally, after several tries I was able to gather that Rose is at home in bed following surgery, but will be returning to the doctor's office in a few days for follow-up and, at that time they are to discuss her further treatment— probably radiation and chemotherapy. Yetsye finally, very reluctantly, agreed to my coming to visit Rose this afternoon, but she will not hear of Hershel's presence in that house. It would seem that the title 'Pastor' carries precious little weight in that household. I'm surprised at that because I was given to understand that that title is used quite often in Jewish culture. At any rate, Yetsye has promised me only a half hour in that house and then I'm out of there. I'll call you, Karen, with any news I can get about Rose's condition."

Before Karen could utter a single word, there came a knock on the door and a pleasant looking man wearing green scrubs entered the room and strode directly to Karen's bedside, where he immediately began to test her pulse rate, examine her eyes and skin tone, as well as several additional unidentifiable procedures, before he exclaimed, "Gentlemen, you have to leave immediately! Miss Boschert must be allowed to rest." His eyes then shifted to Hershel, who bore a most troubled countenance.

"We were just leaving, Dr. Sanchez," Hershel hastened to point out. Then, catching Karen's eye, he added, "Karen, I can't tell you how grateful I am that you allowed me to come here, given my behavior in the past. If you'll permit me, I'll wait a few days and then call and ask permission to call on you again. By then we should have some news of Rose's condition for you." Touching Nestor's sleeve, he remarked, "Dr. Sanchez, you are most gracious for allowing me here. You're quite a guy. Thanks."

As I followed Hershel to the elevators, I clapped him on the back, saying, "Well, the new Hershel Feldman did all right in there. I think you're getting somewhere. If you'll run me out to the Staten Island cabstand, I'll keep my appointment with your Aunt Yetsye." When he protested my taking a cab, saying that he could deliver me to his home himself, I reminded him: "I don't think that would be a great idea, your showing up at home in defiance of your aunt's warning. No, I'll take a cab out there and then I'll meet you back at the cabstand in about an hour. Got your phone with you?"

Yetsye Goldman was beginning to have second thoughts about allowing some *goy* preacher fellow come and talk to her on behalf of Hershel. What in the world could he possibly have to say that would change her mind about letting that crazy half-nephew of hers come back and wreak havoc in her daughter's household? Hadn't he done enough damage already? Hoping the man would be late and give her grounds for refusing him entry, she paced in front of the living room window, glancing out into the bright afternoon just in time to see a taxi turn into the drive. A rather non-descript man of medium height emerged from the cab and mounted the porch steps. He certainly did not match the description Mrs. Bridges had given her of a locally famous

TV evangelist, one who had been instrumental in changing the housekeeper's life, or so she had claimed.

Before I could find the doorbell button, the door swung open and in the doorway stood an imposing woman of perhaps sixty, with a mass of dyed red hair and garishly made-up face, presuming to stare me down. In a baritone voice she asked, "Who are you, already? If you're the preacher, I thought you'd be tall and good-looking."

"Sorry, Mrs. Mandel, I'm neither tall nor good-looking, but I am a preacher, and a Gentile at that," I answered, then added, "My name's Ellis Keaton. I called and made an appointment to speak to you. You are Mrs. Mandel, aren't you? May I come in?"

"Huh," She snorted, "I used to be Mrs. Mandel, but when I divorced my husband I resumed using my maiden name of Goldman. I'm Yetsye Goldman. Come in if you have to."

"Sorry to bother you, Ms. Goldman, and I won't take any more of your time than necessary, I promise." As I spoke I examined the room into which I had been admitted. It proved to be furnished and decorated in truly excellent taste. I gave all the credit for this to Rose Mandel-Feldman.

Yetsye merely stated, "You have thirty minutes." She motioned to a long couch tastefully upholstered in gold, and sat in a matching chair across from me, giving me tacit permission to talk by raising her grossly exaggerated black eyebrows. Her entire visage looked as if someone had defaced a poster of a middle-aged woman. "So, how do you happen to know the likes of Hershel Feldman?" she asked, exhibiting her distaste of the man by the turning down of her mouth.

"We attended the same high school together in Atlanta, and he was, well, sort of my tormentor," I said, "until we both graduated and went our separate ways. I hadn't heard a word out of him for years until he called me a few days ago and asked for my help—said he was in deep trouble and no one else seemed to be able to get him out of it. Up to this point, all I've done is just listen to his story of the last several years of his life. To tell you the truth, it didn't sound like he had changed a bit since we were in school together; you know, still overconfident and arrogant, abusive and rude. But, much to my surprise, as he was relating his story to me, he seemed to change completely. I wish you could talk to him now—he's actually very polite and considerate—almost timid sometimes."

"Wait a minute! Are we talking about the same Hershel Feldman?" Yetsye sounded skeptical.

"I know," I said, "I feel the same way. If I hadn't been with him the whole time, I wouldn't have known who he was. At any rate, I just came to tell you that, wonder of wonders, he is very concerned about Rose's condition and asked me to find out from you and pass the information back to him. He is truly worried about her, Ms. Goldman."

"You've been taken in, mister preacher man. Hershel never had a compassionate bone in his body. You'll see—he'll get what he wants out of you and then turn on you and stick a knife in your ribs—I know. He's no good and never will be. All men are no good. Nothing personal, of course." Behind all that makeup she flushed with anger. She added, "I suppose you'll be wanting to see Rose."

I looked at her as evenly as I could and said, "I would like that very much, if it wouldn't be imposing on her."

Sighing as she stood, Yetsye said, "I'll go ask. You look harmless to me." She shuffled down a hall that led off from the living room, only to return in about two minutes, saying, "Rose says she'll talk to you for a few minutes, but I don't want you tiring her out, you hear me? Don't say anything to get her excited either, got it?"

"You have my word," I said, as I followed her down the hall, trying not to breathe in the dreadfully overpowering aroma of some cologne or perfume she wore.

"Huh!" she exclaimed, as she opened the door to Rose's room. Much to my surprise, she left us alone.

Rose Mandel-Feldman turned out to be a surprisingly pleasant-looking woman of perhaps thirty-eight. She wore no makeup and her hair was not 'done', but she had what I would have called a good face, expressive and open, without any appearance of guile or theatrics. Smiling gently, she said, "Dr. Keaton? I'm very pleased to meet you. You may not believe this, but Hershel has spoken of you often, and with his best approximation of affection. Please, won't you sit? Try that chair over there—it's not as unaccommodating as that absurdity you're trying to sit in." She was referring to the chair for her makeup table that I was sizing up as a place to sit.

"Thanks," I said, "I would be grateful if you could call me Ellis. I never could actually believe I had somehow earned a doctorate, so I just never use the 'Doctor' thing." I pulled the better chair a little closer to her bed as she lifted herself into more of a sitting position. When she only nodded, I went on, "I would like to begin by assuring you that I have nothing whatsoever to gain, or lose, by using falsehood, exaggeration, or any other type of deception with you. I came here with the truth and I intend to utter nothing else. I say that because I daresay you won't be inclined to believe me otherwise. Other than the fact that I hope I am an honorable and truthful man, I have no other allegiance to Hershel than to be who I am. After all, I too have suffered his abuse for quite a while, although it was in the distant past, I admit. But still, I find that I have no little difficulty believing what has happened in the last two days. I respectfully ask you to bear with me and just let me get it all out; then I'll try to answer any questions you might have. Will you please do that?"

Rose looked at me for a long moment, and then replied, "I almost said, "Why should I?" but you have a way about you, Ellis, that is most engaging. Somehow you seem to have disarmed me. Please go ahead."

Without going into too much detail regarding the retelling of Hershel's story, I tried to fill Rose in on the process whereby Hershel had been transformed from his former imperious, inimical, vitriolic, and obstreperous self; into the seemingly contrite and reasonable person he had never been previously, but had, in my view, become while in the process of relating to me the events of the preterit few years of his life. As I spoke, I observed the expression on her face change and contort, manifesting her struggle for and against disbelief in what I was saying. Clearly, she wanted desperately to believe me but was terrified to give herself over to doing so. I had scarcely finished relating this when Yetsye stuck her head through the door and announced, "Time's up, Father."

Rose was much prettier when she laughed. Somehow, we both found Yetsye's dubbing me "Father" hilarious. Through her laughter Rose said, "That's okay, Ma, Ellis's just getting started, and I'm perfectly all right. You can throw him out in a little while." When Yetsye, with an odd gesture, withdrew, Rose said, "Please continue, Padre."

Her gentle teasing made the whole thing much easier on both of us; allowing me to continue from the point where I had left off before Yetsye's interruption. Still, she struggled with herself, wanting desperately to believe me, but finding herself far too bitter and frightened to embrace one single bit of what I said. Finally, when I paused to collect my thoughts, Rose quickly offered, "Ellis, you know what? I don't think I can take any more of this right now. Would you mind awfully leaving me to think about it all?"

"Of course not. You've been far more patient with me than I have any right to expect. If you will permit me, though, I would like to say a couple of things, neither of which is related directly to Hershel. Do you mind?" I really expected her to decline.

Rose inhaled deeply, then answered, "I guess not, if it's not too lengthy."

"I'll make it quick," I said, and then continued, "I merely wanted to tell you how much meeting you has meant to me. It must have taken a lot of courage on your part to allow me into your presence, and I truly appreciate it. I find you thoroughly charming and attractive, and can't for the life of me understand how anyone, even Hershel, could have the temerity to treat you in the way he has been doing. Meeting you and speaking with you this afternoon has brought me to the point where I'm tempted to switch allegiance. I don't really mean that, of course, because I find, actually, that I'm becoming quite taken with both you and the new Hershel Feldman. I want you to know that I will do anything in my power to help you both get past this crisis and back together again if, of course, that's what you both end up wanting. In the meantime, I plan to pray my heart out for both of you. That's the least I can do—or possibly the most I can do, depending on the way you look at it." Rose offered me her hand and rather than shaking it, I kissed it. It smelled of rose-perfumed soap. Hmm.

While I awaited the taxi's return, I spent some valuable time with Mrs. Bridges, gathering valuable insight into the Mandel-Feldman marriage. Even with what Hershel had told me in his narrative, I had not grasped the scope of his tyranny against Rose. Apparently his ire was unrelenting and, if it was, this gives full justification to her anguish during the time I was trying, moments before, to describe to her Hershel's transformation. I came to the conclusion that if their marriage is to be salvaged, it must be through the power of Almighty God; and that I must pray for His wisdom and mercy.

The taxi arrived in due course, with a different driver, who took me back to the cabstand without uttering a single word. Wonder of wonders. Even as we approached the building, I spotted Hershel's BMW parked in what appeared to be the same spot in which it had sat when the taxi and I had left him. When I attempted to pay the driver he informed me in as few words as possible that the bill, gratuity included, had already been settled. He walked briskly, cigarette smoke swirling around his head, into the cab company office. Scanning the area for Hershel, I found him at the rear of the parking lot, one foot propped on the steel guardrail that surrounded the lot, elbow on his knee and chin in the cup of his hand, staring into space. Even though my shoes crunched on the gravel of the lot, he failed to hear me until I was almost on top of him. He jolted at the sound of my approach, "Oh, you're back, Ellis. How'd it go?" He looked tense indeed.

"Better than we had any right to expect," I answered, "but naturally Rose is skeptical and afraid to commit to anything just yet. I found her totally charming and quite lovely and can't, for the life of me, understand how anyone could bring himself to treat her the way you have. For some reason, I remembered you as being halfway intelligent, but I guess it must be much more complicated than that. Anyway, she gave me permission to phone her in a few days, after she has thought things over, to see if we can meet again. I'm guardedly optimistic."

Hershel turned to face me and said, "That's great; but how is she? Is she in a lot of pain? I can't stand to think about how I've been to her. How in the world am I ever going to get her back, Ellis?" He turned quickly away from me but, before his eyes left mine I saw, for the first time ever, true contrition in his expression.

I was hard pressed to answer, but attempted by saying, "I don't know that it's even possible for *you* to do that, Hershel, but I also know that, with God anything is possible."

He turned to me again, an odd expression on his face, and said, "I was hoping you would say something like that, Ellis. I've been giving him some thought lately—God, that is. I've come to know that the answer to my problems is not in making a deal with Mr. Abaddon, but in getting to know God myself. I'm counting on you to help me with that, you know.

I think I know now why you said before that it's not the time yet to go and see the old dragon. There are some other things to be settled first." Stuffing one hand in his pocket, he jingled some coins together before he added, "Oh, yeah, I had a call while you were gone. It was from Detective Horne, one of New York's finest. He wants me to come in to the precinct office as soon as possible. He sounded none too pleasant, if you ask me; but then, I've never heard him sound any other way."

"Do you need me to go with you?" I asked.

"Thanks for the offer," he replied, "but I think I'd better do this one by myself. I'll let you know how it all turns out." With that, we climbed into his car and headed for Manhattan.

Chapter Thirteen

[in which I recount some events
randomly revealed to me]

Detective Vincent Horne was a methodical man, one who deplored the leaving of loose ends. The fact that Karen Boschert had cleared Hershel Feldman of any culpability in the murder of Lee Min-jun, as well as in the matter of her own close shave with death, gave Horne little solace. To his ordered mind, there must still remain some misdeeds on the part of this Feldman character that he, Horne, could use to put his mind to rest on the subject of the former's errant character and behavior. Even though Hershel was still under investigation for possible embezzlement in his position as accounting manager at Mandel Family Apparel, this afforded Horne no comfort either because he was assigned to a homicide squad and therefore no longer had jurisdiction over Hershel's case. In addition, Horne had been ordered by his chief to call Hershel Feldman in to the precinct office and inform him that he was no longer a murder or assault suspect. This added further to Horne's chagrin. It was, therefore, with great effort that he addressed Hershel with what little civility he could muster under the circumstances, "Well, Feldman, I guess you've dodged the bullet for the time being, but I warn you, I have a buddy that I graduated with who'll be only too glad to take up your case; and we'll see if he can't pin something on you that'll stick. Until then you'd best dot all your Is and cross all your Ts, if you know what I mean. And, by the way, I wouldn't leave town if I were you."

Hershel had nothing to say to all this, but merely answered, "Rest assured, Vince, I'm not going anywhere until this is all cleared up one way or the other." He left Horne staring after him.

Softening just a little, Horne called out, "Oh, yeah, Feldman, one more thing." As Hershel turned back, Horne went on, "We've brought in your friend Klausman—the jerk was in the act of skipping out of the country—and we found out you were right about him being that Rolf character's employer. After we finally broke Klausman down, we got a pretty good lead on Rolfy Boy and should have him in custody in a day or two. Seems he's a German citizen so it's going to get a little messy but, once pretty Miss Boschert puts the finger on him, it's curtains for him, no matter where he hails from. By the way, have you heard anything about Miss Boschert's condition?"

Gratified at Horne's apparent resiliency, Hershel said, "I was with her this morning and she's improving steadily, thanks. And, Anton Klausman's no friend of mine and never has been—more of an enemy, I'd say. Thanks for the information, Vince." This time he left Horne speechless as well.

The suspicion of Anton Klausman for complicity in the murder of Lee Min-jun and the assault on Nhung Karen Boschert created a scandal that spread through Klausman, Walther, und Hahn, GmbH like wildfire. There was even some speculation, after the fact, that Klausman may have had some involvement in the sudden death of Horace Daemon, although this was pure speculation; certainly no more than that. But, the most damaging implications, with respect to the company, were the outrageous advances Klausman had made against one of his own employees, the aforementioned Miss Boschert. It was revealed to the press by a local female restaurant owner, no less, that Klausman had made highly improper propositions to a young lady less than half his own age, and one who was in his own employ. In view of this debacle, the company's managing board in Zurich advised a hasty and discreet withdrawal from New York, including the entire Swiss entourage, minus Klausman, who had once again disappeared. In this way, the status of the audit of Mandel Family Apparel's accounting department remained just as it had been left by Aaron Ginsberg who, incidentally, also had vanished. Officially, at least, the embezzlement case against Hershel evaporated along with Ginsberg and all of the Swiss. The only means by which it could be reinstated would be by the filing of a complaint by Rose Mandel-Feldman against her husband, or by the disclosure by Karen Boschert of the results of her own comprehensive audit of the accounting department at Mandel Family Apparel. Whether or not either of the young women realized that Hershel's fate hung in their respective balances is moot. Certainly neither seemed wont to exercise her option. The fact remained, however, that the books of Mandel Family Apparel were beyond reproach due to the efforts and skill of one Aaron Ginsberg.

Barely a week later, the Hon. Anton Klausman was declared missing by his board of directors. All of the combined efforts of the various New York City Police departments failed to turn up any evidence of the whereabouts of the Swiss statesman *cum* business executive. The grand jury that had been preparing to indict him was left with an open court date and no one to examine. Detective Horne was particularly frustrated since he finally had believed he was on the cusp of filing charges for the murder of Lee Min-jun and the assault on Karen Boschert. His only recourse at this point was to continue to search for Rolf, whose description at this point was hardly what one could call accurate. Being the Irishman that he was, Horne persisted relentlessly.

After finally having managed to fall asleep well after midnight, Hershel was awakened by his phone early in the morning on the day after he had visited Karen in the hospital.

He tried feverishly to find the right button on the phone, struck two of the wrong ones, and then finally got it right. "H'llo," he answered in a muffled voice.

"Hershel! How are you buddy?" a familiar voice said, "This is Kevin. Where are you, anyway? I hate cell phones—you never know where the person is. Are you okay?"

"Kevin? I ugh, I don't know who..." Hershel's voice trailed off.

The reply came back, "Kevin, you know, Kevin Sheehan, your erstwhile assistant. What's the matter, Hersh, you sick or something?"

Hershel sat up in bed and rubbed the back of his neck, saying, "Oh, Kev, I'm sorry—dreaming, I think. What's up? Why are you calling me at the crack of dawn?"

Kevin laughed into the phone and said, "You never did like to get up early, did you? Come on, man, it's after eight thirty. I need to talk to you."

"I'm sorry, Kev, I didn't get to sleep until really late and I'm bushed. What's up?"

Kevin replied, "Well, we really need to talk, Hersh. Can you meet me this morning, somewhere close by?"

"Sure, how 'bout at Duggan's Coffee Shoppe at nine thirty? I need to shower first." Hershel had begun to perk up.

Kevin laughed again and replied, "Duggan doesn't serve scotch, you know. Are you sure?"

"We really do need to talk, Kev. I think I'm giving up the hooch for good. See you at Duggan's. 'Bye." Hershel hit the 'END' button on his phone.

It felt really good to shower and even better still to ride the subway the ten or so blocks to the street that Duggan's Coffee Shoppe fronted. Hershel had begun to hate driving in Manhattan, and despised even more riding in cabs. What in the world was happening to him? He had hardly *ever before* ridden the subway. Looking all around the car he was in, he was astounded at how interesting and non-threatening the other passengers appeared. He wondered what Rose would think of him now.

Business at Duggan's was just beginning to pick up for mid-morning breaks and he began to despair of finding a table when he spotted Kevin already seated at a cramped table in a rear corner of the shoppe. Hurrying over to Kevin's table and flopping down in the only remaining chair, he spoke as best he could over the din, "Hey, Kev. It sure is good to see you. How're things?"

Kevin simply stared at him a moment before asking, "Do I have the right Hershel Feldman? What happened—you don't look or sound like the old Hershel I knew and hated." He grinned, jumped to his feet, and gave Hershel a big bear hug.

"It's a long, long story, Kev. I'll fill you in later, but I'd like to know what's on your mind first. You look a little different yourself—not as relaxed and amused as usual." Hershel eyed Kevin critically as he said this last.

Resuming his seat, Kevin began, "There's lots going on at M.F.A., Hersh. First of all, they put me in charge of the accounting department on an interim basis until this mess is all sorted out—they being the managing board. It seems your wife has more or less given them temporary control until she gets better from her surgery. Have you seen her, by the way? I've only talked to her on the phone, but it's been like a zillion times. She calls me every morning and asks if there have been any auditors horning in. I believe she asked her lawyer to get a state audit called in and then wished she hadn't done it. Anyway, Bruce has been dragging his feet hoping she *would* change her mind. I told him we've enjoyed about all the audits we can stand. That Ginsberg character— what a creep! None of us could ever figure out what he was doing; but I'll say one thing for him. He sure knew how to cover tracks. Now, all of a sudden, our department is squeaky-clean, thanks to him. Poor little Karen—all that work, and this Ginsberg nut just undid the whole thing.

She'll be furious, I guess." Kevin took a sip of his Turkish brew and went on, "Anyway, your wife calls me yesterday and makes me promise not to tell anybody anything about the department until she is able to come down to the office and get with me so we can get our stories straight. Hershel, I think she's hoping either that you'll somehow be able to come back or that she can talk Karen into running the department. She told me to just continue to hang loose and do my job the best that I know how and not to rock the boat. I hope she can work something out. This job is driving me up the wall. I was never cut out to be a manager type; I just want to sit at my desk and do my thing, that's all." He sighed deeply and looked at Hershel expectantly. Then he added, "So, that's why I needed to talk to you. Do you think there's any chance you can come back? I mean, the last I heard, you're living in a flat uptown and not allowed in your own house, prime suspect in a murder case, being investigated for fraud or embezzlement or something, and suspected of shooting Karen, for gosh sakes. Heck, you wouldn't dream of hurting a hair of Karen's head. And Rose, she loves you like crazy and always will—I know that for a fact, even though she makes out like she hates your guts. So, what's the scoop? Are you a murderer, a crook, and a wife-beater or what? I know I've always had a love-hate relationship with you—mostly hate—but that's because you're always such a jerk." He reached across the table and punched Hershel gently on the shoulder.

"Too many questions, Kev, most of which I don't know the answers to," Hershel replied, "but I can tell you one thing: I haven't seen Rose yet; not because I don't want to see her, but because I'm not allowed. Her mother, you know, Yetsye Mandel or whatever name she's using at the present, is guarding her daughter like a Doberman and won't let me near my own home. Normally I'd raise a stink about it but I'm not normal anymore, I guess. At least I don't seem to be able to work up any malice or hostility to anyone, not even

Yetsye. But, that's another story I don't have the answer to just yet. I *do* know that Karen has talked to the police and has told them I was telling the truth. Believe me, there are those who didn't like that one bit; like a certain detective I know. And, she also identified Klausman's driver, Rolf, as the shooter; and they're searching for him now. I suppose it's only a matter of time. Another detective is on my tail about the books at Mandel Family Apparel, but he seems to have no evidence against me—just suspicion. After hearing what you've just told me, it looks like it's up to either Rose or Karen to turn me in, if they want to. Kevin, I can't, at this point, imagine why both of them wouldn't be falling over each other to put me behind bars for good. I swear, I'll never understand women; but I love them all the same." Hershel colored when he said this last and was quick to add: "I love Rose as my wife and Karen as a friend, I mean."

"You *have* changed, Hersh!" Kevin exclaimed, "The last I remember, you were ready in a heartbeat to dump poor Rose and run off into the sunset with delicious little Karen. What in the world has happened to you?"

Smiling weakly, Hershel answered, "As soon as I figure it out, I'll let you know, Kev. But, in the meantime, I need to get going. I have a ton of errands to run this afternoon. Let's stay in touch, okay? Oh, yeah," he added as an afterthought, "Why don't *you* hate my guts? I've always treated you pretty much like garbage and you have always put up with me for some reason or other."

Kevin laid his hand tenderly on Hershel's shoulder and replied, "Don't you know? I'm commanded to love others, even those who hate me or mistreat me. And, besides, I've grown used to you, you jerk." He grinned and squeezed Hershel's upper arm.

They parted with a handshake and a promise from each to call the other in a day or two. Hershel rode the subway back to the garage where he had parked his BMW at a greater cost per week than for his apartment. He hated to even think about where he would get the money to pay all of the debts he had accrued, but he also was determined to try his best to do it. Once he retrieved his car, he set about visiting all the bars, lounges, and restaurants in which he had run up big tabs, and paid off as many debts as his bank account would cover. Then, with a determination that surprised him, he drove the BMW to the dealer from whom he had purchased it and sold it back for whatever he could get for it. As he rode the cab back to his flat, he regarded the meager check the dealer had given him as poetic justice. Hadn't he spent the better part of his life exploiting others? Why not a little of his own medicine?

A shower, and then a frozen dinner splattering in the microwave seemed to make Hershel feel a great deal better; especially the shower. He had left the BMW dealership feeling as if he had had a load of something foul dumped on him. He lay on the couch across from the TV, belching from the powerful onions in the frozen dinner, and tried to watch a really stupid sitcom, but he just could not get into it. The previous tenant in his flat had left a few cheap paperback novels on a shelf in one of the end tables, and he picked through them, hoping to find one he could stomach. At this point in his former life, he would have succumbed to the craving to have a drink; but at the present he had no such desire. Finally, with nothing else to tempt him, he shuffled into his bedroom and undressed for bed. It was only nine thirty, but he was dead tired and fell into a deep sleep as soon as his head touched the pillow.

Hershel lay on his back on the plush living room carpet and held Isabelle at arms length above him, jiggling her plump little body and causing her to laugh hysterically. The more he jiggled, the more the child begged him to: "Do that again, Abi!" and the more he did it again, the wider her mouth opened with glee, exposing tiny baby teeth scarcely larger than grains of rice. Isabelle squealed with glee as her Abi lowered her to his face and gave her a sloppy kiss on the cheek. His heart swollen with love and gratitude, Hershel shifted his gaze over to Rose, who was seated at a small table, her laptop before her, presumably doing what she normally did to run Mandel Family Apparel. Looking up from her computer, Rose smiled at her husband and blew him a kiss. Abruptly, with no preamble, a voice began calling his name: "HERSHEL LEVY FELDMAN! HERSHEL LEVY FELDMAN!"

He sat up in his bed, awake now, but with his skin crawling in fearfulness. Who or what could have been calling him; or was it merely a dream? Hershel groped for the bedside lamp, turned the little switch, practically blinding himself, then squinted through his nearly closed eyes in order to be able to see the clock face. A little after two, and he was sure the voice had been only a dream. He tried and tried but sleep was denied him; at least for an hour or so. At long last, he dropped off, only to hear almost immediately the same call. This time, however, the voice sounded close by and much softer: "Hershel Feldman, Hershel Levy Feldman."

"Yes, who is it?" Hershel responded. As he spoke, he also opened his eyes, and there beside his bed stood a man, one whose dress and mien shocked him. The man's face was fully bearded in soft white, and he wore a robe of such vivid whiteness that Hershel could not look straight at it. The man's eyes burned like bright flames and he held in his right hand a gleaming sword. Presently, he vanished with a sigh of rushing air. The room, which had been fully illuminated by the man, fell dark again. Hershel found he could no longer sleep and got up, put on his robe, went into the living room and, taking a pillow and blanket with him, settled onto the couch. He tried to read one of the dreadful paperbacks, failed to get into it, and eventually slept fitfully. He saw the same man again, but this time differently. Hershel slipped out of half-sleep due to the brightness of the room and there, facing the couch on which he had been sleeping, were the lower legs of the man whom he had seen earlier. The legs were shod with boots of gold or brass, boots that extended upward and upward until they reached the hem of the man's white robe. It seemed to Hershel that the man's knees were hundreds, perhaps thousands of feet up in the air, and that he was seated on a high, high seat, or probably a throne, and that his hands on the arms of the throne were at a height so great as to be barely visible. This time he saw about the man's chest a sash of gold, but above that he could barely see, making out only the bottom of the man's snowy beard. There coursed through Hershel such a thrill of wonder that he all but cried out in ecstasy. He lay awake reliving the picture of the man so high and lofty that he extended to the heavens, until dawn came and roused the confused Hershel out of bed.

It was three days more before Hershel could muster the courage to call Karen's room at the hospital and ask permission to visit. She agreed readily to his coming, so he hailed a cab, which took him fully to the other side of Manhattan to the hospital. When he entered her room, Hershel was astonished to see the extent to which Karen's condition appeared to have improved. Her olive-gold complexion was restored; her hair, recently shampooed, spilled over her shoulders in shining blackness; and best of all, her smile was once more bright and captivating. If her pain was not much diminished, she was deceiving everyone by her appearance.

Extending a lovely hand to Hershel, Karen greeted him with a brightening of her smile, saying, "Hershel, I am so glad you've come! Are you well? Please take a seat over there." She indicated a chrome and plastic chair under the window by her bed.

Hershel took her hand and held it briefly, marveling at the fact that he could look at this lovely creature with pure admiration, and without the lust he had previously felt for her. "You look wonderful, Karen," he exclaimed, "Is the pain lessening?"

"Just yesterday and this morning," she replied, "it has begun to be much eased. I am so grateful." Pulling a coverlet up to her chin, she remarked, "Ah, but, it is so cold in this place I think I shall freeze into a piece of ice. However, nobody else seems to mind and they—the nurses and the other staff—keep me well supplied with blankets, so I have no complaint. You are looking well. Tell me, what have you been doing?"

"Worrying about you and Rose, mostly," Hershel answered.

"Rose! Oh, yes, she called me this morning and I was so excited to hear from her! We must have spoken for an hour at least." Karen, flushed with excitement, continued, "She speaks of you frequently and is quite transparently wishing to hear from you as well. Tomorrow she is to return to her doctor for more treatment and instructions. She has such courage, Hershel. Will you not go to her soon?"

He replied, "Well, I'm forbidden by her mother at the present time. And besides, I feel so unworthy that I don't dare ask her. I want her to know that I've changed and I want desperately for her to believe it, but I don't think I have the slightest bit of credibility with her. I mean, why on earth should she believe me after all the years I've lied and deceived her? And even hit her, too—I've even hit her before, Karen—so I'm sure she's afraid of me!" He covered his eyes with his hand so that she could not see the tears welling up in them.

"Come over here, Hershel, and let me tell you," she said, as she took his hand and held it firmly. "You cannot expect Rose to put your past behavior behind her if you will not do the same yourself. Why do you not begin all over again with Rose? I can see clearly that you wish to do this, but that you are afraid. Rose is afraid as well, but you must assure her that you are a different person now. You must not fear, Hershel, but you must trust Jesus. If you will relinquish—oh dear, is that the right word?—yes, relinquish yourself to

Him, He will give you the wisdom and strength to go to Rose in spite of her mother's objections. The thing I must tell you is this: Jesus, who is God as well as the Father is God, will give you a completely new life! Yes, He is the only one who can do this. Oh, Hershel, you must ask your friend, Ellis, to explain it all to you! It is so wonderful—so full of wonder— that is to say! I know for certain that he wishes to help you, Hershel. You must call him and talk to him soon. Only when you understand that your life can begin again with new birth will you see that *anything* is possible with Jesus!" Karen, coloring with excitement, regained a significant measure of her normal sublimity.

"I would, I suppose," said he, "but Ellis will just sound like he is preaching not only to me but to an audience on television. I would much rather hear it from you, Karen. You, I know, are absolutely sincere and would be speaking to me directly and for no other reason than to help me. But, Ellis, I don't know; it seems to me that he would have a dual purpose, sort of. Maybe he would at the same time be wondering about his ratings or about whether or not he was running out of time. Please; I would much rather you told me how you feel about Jesus since you seem to know him so well." After he had said this last, Hershel almost regretted having said it. It was at this point that he suddenly became aware of the softness of Karen's hand, the sweet curve of her cheek, and he felt he must leave at once before he might lapse back into his old ways of wanting her. He pulled his hand from hers quickly, smiling nervously. "You know," he added, "I think you're right; and, besides, I don't want to tire you out. I'd better leave now, but I hope you will let me come back in a day or two. May I?"

"Oh, please do!" she declared. "Do you know, I am a bit fatigued just now, but I shall be much, much better when you come back day after tomorrow. Please do not forget to come, will you Hershel? I should miss you if you did not come. Goodbye for now."

Isabelle Feldman had been a bit fretful and cranky for several days and her mother, Rose, was hard pressed to uncover the reason for this. The child had no high fever or any of the other childhood indications of malady. Her eyes were bright and clear, her skin smooth and cool, and her pale pink throat normal looking. Still, Rose was a bit concerned because Isabelle was normally a cheerful and happy child, in spite of the constant presence of marital and emotional stress between her parents. This recent moodiness had come upon the three-year-old out of nowhere, especially since it had begun *after* her father had been absent from home for some weeks. Was it due to her mother's illness? Rose did not believe so; Isabelle seemed to look upon Rose's confinement to bed as a sort of adventure in which her mother, a beautiful fairy, would emerge from her sick bed and her Abi would come back home and all would be as it should be; only better than before. Although she never mentioned it, Isabelle appeared hopeful, and impatient, for the inevitable restoration of her family situation to occur. She moped about the house, hardly attentive to Puffy the poodle; and practically scornful of her giant stuffed tiger. She would brighten only occasionally when her thoughts ran to the eventual reunion; then she would fall back into her malaise until the next recurrence of her hopeful mood.

"Izzie, Darling, where are you?" Rose called from her bedroom. The trip to the doctor's office was dreadful, and the chemo treatment was beginning to make her feel horrible. All she wished to do was to gather her daughter up into bed with her and for the two of them to be pals. She would not even mind having that monstrous stuffed tiger take up half the bed, as long as she could cuddle with Isabelle under the covers. She astounded herself by thanking God out loud for giving her a child like Isabelle. In spite of her skepticism about Jesus, Rose was finding that she would often think of Him as being very close by. Could Karen have been right about this Jesus being God? She, Rose, was running short of arguments against Karen's assertions to that effect. And then there was this perpetual **presence** that seemed to be so personal, so very authentic. She often found herself conversing with Him extemporaneously, as though she had known Him all her life and as if He were part of the family.

Her thoughts of Him were interrupted by the appearance of a mop of curly, dark hair in the doorway and the sound of a tiny voice telling Puffy she couldn't get into Ma's bed, but that she needed to go outside and tee-tee anyway. The stuffed tiger, being dragged along by one ear, was more fortunate than the poor poodle and was allowed into Ma's bed as long as he behaved himself. "Wead me a stowy, Ma?" the child pleaded.

Rose was only too glad to oblige and picked up from her nightstand the volume of The Chronicles Of Narnia that Karen had brought her to read to Isabelle. Much to Rose's delight and astonishment, Isabelle was totally captivated by the stories, and rarely fell asleep during the reading of them—usually shortly thereafter, however. Rose discovered that she herself was no less fascinated by them than was Isabelle.

On this occasion, as on most others, Isabelle did not succumb to slumber, but began an urgent discourse right in the midst of the reading: "Ma, when Abi gonna come back home? He sawwy he been so bad to you. Abi dint mean to make you cwy, Ma. He used to be bad, but he not gonna be bad any mowa, you'll see, Ma." She looked as if she were going to cry herself.

"Do you really think so, Darling?" Rose found to her delight that it was completely impossible to smooth Isabelle's unruly mop of hair, so she contented herself with stroking the child's cheeks with the backs of her fingers. Isabelle had no apparent objection to this. Rose added, "Why do you want Abi to come back, Izzie?"

"Abi funny when he not being mean," the child giggled. Turning to her tiger, Isabelle asked, "Why Gwam so mean to Abi?" Apparently the question, though seeming to be directed to the tiger, was actually meant for Rose.

The latter answered, "Ma is sorry, dear, but your Gram doesn't like for Abi to be mean to you, or to me either, so it makes her mad at Abi. Why don't you go and ask Gram to be nice to Abi for a while and we'll see if she'll let him come back home. Maybe if we just love him a lot, like you do, he'll stop being mean to us. What do you think, Izzie?"

Without a word Isabelle threw off the blanket covering her, slipped out of the bed, and shot out of the room as fast as her pudgy little legs would carry her, shouting, "GWAM, GWAM!" at the top of her shrill little-girl voice.

"Shh, Baby, you'll wake your ma," Yetsye hissed. "What is it you want, Izzie?"

Clutching Yetsye's apron in her tiny hand, the little one whispered, "Ma want us to let Abi come back home. He won' be bad anymowa, Gwam, we pwomise." Isabelle was sure that tugging on Yetsye's apron was by far the best method to give poignancy to her request.

"I don't know about that, Baby," Yetsye replied, "We don't want your Abi to hurt you or your Ma, do we?" Swiftly checking Isabelle's ruffled panties, Yetsye remarked, "We'd better get you into the bathroom before you have an accident."

"No, no, Gwam, Izzie don' have to tee-tee." Squirming out of Yetsye's grasp, the child took off for Rose's room with Puffy, who had rejoined her human pal, leading the chase down the hall.

The remainder of that afternoon was consumed by spirited discussion between Rose and her mother relative to whether or not leniency should be extended to Hershel to the point that he would be allowed back into his own home should he happen, once again, to communicate with his family. At one point Rose asked Isabelle, "Darling, why are you so sure your Abi won't be bad and mean to us anymore?"

Isabelle, who did not appear to have been listening to the debate between her mother and grandmother, answered simply, "'Cause he tole me so."

Yetsye, who was indeed skeptical, asked, "When did Abi tell you he wouldn't be mean anymore, Izzie?" She had to take the child by the shoulders to draw her away from the stuffed tiger's attention. Holding Isabelle's notice to her with her eyes, Yetsye repeated the question: "When did you talk to Abi, Baby?"

Almost casually, Isabelle replied, "Last night, in the middle, Izzie talk to Abi."

With a patient expression on her face, Rose exclaimed, "You must be mixed up, my Darling, Abi wasn't here last night. Wasn't that a long time ago that you and Abi talked?"

Isabelle smoothed the striped back of the great tiger; carefully skirting the chocolate milk stains, concentrating wholly on the task. It was a short while before she answered her mother, "Uh, uh, Ma; he come into my woom an' it was dawk. Missy Cawmen saw him too. She gave me a dwink."

After supper, when Isabelle and Puffy had retired to their room and were tucked in, Rose and Yetsye resumed their discussion about the possibility of allowing Hershel, at the very least, a return visit. Yetsye was adamant against it; Rose was not so sure. A part of her wanted Hershel back with her more than anything else, but another part of her was terrified on its account.

"I'm telling you, Rose, it'll be the same thing all over again, and I won't have you and Isabelle going through that hell anymore." Yetsye was determined and unrelenting.

"But, Ma!" Rose returned, "How do you explain the strong feeing I got when Hershel was here, that he had changed very significantly?" She wrung her hands in distress and frustration.

Arms akimbo, Yetsye insisted, "Never mind about *feelings* and that sort of nonsense! Use your head, for goodness sake. The man is no good and never will be! He'll never change and right now you've got a chance to get rid of him once and for all. You've still got your baby, your ma, and your business. Forget about men; forget about this man!" From the emotions of the moment, her mascara had begun to run and her rouge was becoming blotchy. She had no intention of softening toward Hershel, or *any* man, for that matter.

"But, Ma," Rose said, "You never heard what that nice Dr. Keaton said. He truly believes that Hershel has been touched by God and God has changed him. So, you see, it's nothing that Hershel himself has done—it's just the work of Almighty God!"

"Whaat God?" Yetsye spat out. "That man is nothing but just an ordinary man of the cloth. What does he know of God?"

Rose had to smile, "Well, a good deal more than most, I should think. He's a highly respected and well-known evangelist; a man who has spent his entire adult life studying the Bible and many other things about God, I'm sure. Anyway, what do you have against Ellis Keaton? He sounded to me like his main concern was for Hershel and me to be happy, whether or not we ever get back together. What's wrong with that?" When Yetsye said nothing for a bit, Rose continued, "And, don't forget about Isabelle's dream. Dreams are important, especially when they come from little children who don't know how to be conniving and deceiving; and you know there is not an insincere bone in Isabelle's body. And, and, there's Carmen—don't forget about Carmen; how she backed Isabelle's story completely, how she heard Izzie talking in her room and, when she went in there, Izzie told her that her Abi had been there and they had been talking together. What's so hard to believe about that?"

Yetsye, pressing her lips so tightly together that they all but disappeared, replied, "All I'm saying is, the man has a record of being abusive and unfaithful, and I think you should drop him while you have the chance. Men are all scum; you know that."

"No, I do not *know* that—I don't even think that. There are a lot of decent men, men like Kevin Sheehan, Ellis Keaton, and a lot more. Oh, I don't want to argue about this anymore, Ma, I just think we ought to give Hershel a chance—or maybe we shouldn't—I don't know. I'm just so confused and frightened!" Rose burst into wracking sobs, but almost immediately checked herself. The heaving of her chest from the sobs brought back terrible pain from the surgery. She looked pitiably at her mother.

Yetsye sighed impatiently and asked, "Which is it, Rose? Do you want Hershel to come back or do you not? I can't figure you out."

"Yes, yes, I want him back, Ma; but I don't want him to see me this way, either!"

"Well then, let's call him and tell him to come and talk a while. How about that?" Yetsye was beginning to lose patience.

"NO, NO, Don't bring him back! I don't want to see him!" Rose cried.

"Then what, what *do* you want?" Yetsye asked in exasperation.

"Ma, can't you understand?" Rose stormed, "**I only have one breast!** Hershel would *never* want me back this way!" She wept bitterly in spite of the pain.

"There, there, don't think about it anymore, Honey," Yetsye soothed, "You need to rest for now. We'll discuss it sometime soon when you are better. Let me bring you some chicken soup." With that, Yetsye left her daughter alone to wrestle with her emotions.

Two full weeks passed before Hershel was able to ramp up his courage and boldness to the level that he could force himself to call his own home and ask to speak to his own wife. The phone rang multiple times before he remembered that Rose had insisted that they have caller I.D. Determined, he allowed the ringing to continue, hoping that Yetsye would ultimately relent. Finally, she picked up the phone and grunted something unintelligible into it.

"Yetsye, it's me, Hershel," he pleaded, "May I please speak to Rose?"

"I know who it is—I can read," Yetsye hissed, "You gotta nerve calling here."

"I know, I know, but please just let me talk to Rose." Without even putting on his usual airs, he sounded plaintive and contrite.

When Yetsye tapped the HOLD button on the phone and, taking her sweet time about it, carried it to Rose's room, Hershel was afraid she had hung up on him.

He was relieved when he heard the 'beep' and Rose's voice question, "Hershel?"

"Rose, I really need to talk to you. Do you think there's any way I could be allowed past your mother and into the house? I could come while Isabelle is taking her nap so she wouldn't see me and be afraid. Would that be all right?"

Rose discovered that she was not really all that shocked at his conciliatory tone of voice. She answered, "I think that would be a good idea. We definitely need to clear the air. Can you be here in an hour?" She could not conceal the tremor in her voice.

"I'll do the best I can," He replied, "but I'll have to grab a cab. I'll explain that when I get there. Be there as soon as I possibly can. 'Bye."

When Hershel arrived at his own home, even Puffy the poodle was suspicious. As Hershel strode up the driveway toward the back door, the little dog lunged at him, from a safe distance of course, yelling at him with her shrill little bark and scampering a secure space away when he called her by name and put forth his hand for her to sniff. Declining the offer, Puffy scuttled through the doggy door to the garage and stood her ground from that strategic location. Before Hershel could press the doorbell, Yetsye appeared and opened the door for him, scowling beneath her ample brows. She surprised him by allowing him to proceed down the hall to Rose's room without accompanying him and dressing him down as they went. He concluded, rightly, that she and Rose had come to some sort of agreement about her behavior while Hershel was present. Just her facial expression gave him to know that this entire venture was against her better judgment.

He found his wife propped up in bed, a calf-cup of tea getting cold on the nightstand and a book open on her knees. "You made it in fifty-eight minutes!" she exclaimed. "You really have changed, haven't you? Don't sit on that stupid thing, Hershel; bring that nice chair over here and sit. How've you been?"

Smiling sheepishly, he replied, "In some ways I've been better and in other ways, worse. Really sort of mixed up, I guess. Are you in really bad pain, Rose?"

"The pain from the surgery is tolerable, but the other pain in my life is really, really hard," she answered. She fell silent then and said nothing, waiting for him to speak, apparently. Actually, she was afraid if she were to say anything else, she would begin to cry.

Looking even more miserable, he said, "Rose, I can't tell you how sorry I am about the way..."

"Please, Hershel, let's not go over all that right now," she said in obvious anguish. "Please, let's just do this: Let's just say what we have to say and not try to undo what has already been done. There are some things you must know before we can even start trying to reconcile what has happened in the last few months, so please just let me talk for a few minutes and then you can have your say, alright?"

"Of course, sure," he said.

"As you may or may not know," she began, "I was diagnosed five weeks ago with acute breast cancer, and have gone through a partial mastectomy. This means, Hershel, that I now have only *one breast*. I want to be sure you heard me correctly; I am now disfigured by virtue of having had one of my breasts removed surgically. Are you perfectly clear on that point, Hershel?"

"Yes, I understand perfectly," he replied.

"And?" Rose asked.

"And what?" asked Hershel.

"And, does that fact have any effect on your purpose in coming here today?"

"No. Should it have?"

"I don't know. That's why I'm asking." Rose was having difficulty maintaining her composure, but she pressed on: "So, you're saying that, now that you know I am disfigured from breast surgery, your mind has not changed regarding coming here today?"

"I'm not going to play games with you like I used to, Rose," he said. "I'll admit I am shocked to hear that you have been through such an awfully traumatic experience and I was nowhere in sight to support you. Yes, about that I'm devastated for you. But, as far as whether or not the fact that you have had a partial mastectomy affects the way I feel about you, I have to tell you that it hasn't changed a thing. If there's one thing I have discovered in the last five weeks it is that I miss you terribly when we're apart. Please don't ask me how or why that has happened, because I really do not know. I'm hoping and praying—yes, I said praying—that Ellis will be able to help me come to terms with this whole change in my life. As it is now, I seem to be just feeling my way along. But, I *am* telling you the absolute truth when I say that the way I feel about you, Rose, is not at all governed by the number of breasts you have. Beyond that, all I know to tell you is that I came here to ask you—no, beg you—to take me back in spite of all the detestable things I have done in the past, and to do that without regard to the past, but with regard to our future. In short, I want desperately for us to start over fresh so I can show you how the *new* Hershel Feldman can behave."

Rose had not prepared herself for this development and could formulate no immediate reply. Instead, she invested at least three full minutes in examining Hershel from head to toe, uttering not a sound herself. She visually scoured his entire form, from the color of his eyes, the wrinkles in his forehead, the taper of his fingers, the crease in his trousers, the style (if one could call it that) of his hair, the breadth of his shoulders, and every other characteristic that identified this man as Hershel Levy Feldman. In every single way, every facet, he remained exactly as she had always known him to be; and yet, he was an entirely different person. How could this be? What force, what influence, had engulfed Hershel so that he was utterly and truly transformed? At last she could contain no longer the emotional tempest that she had been enduring; and she burst into tears. This was not simply weeping, but a veritable eruption of her self into a completely different state. Her face became grotesquely contorted, she wailed piteously, she dragged and pulled at her hair, she flailed her arms over and around her head, she screamed at nothing in particular, and finally, she simply moaned and moaned, rocking to and fro as she hugged her torso in defense of the fierce upheaval of internal emotion taking place inside her.

Before he realized what he was doing, Hershel found himself at her side, catching her up in his arms, cautiously so that he would not hurt her, and rocking her in unison with the motion she had set up herself. "There, there, Rosie, don't worry, Dearest, it's going to be alright, you'll see. I'm going to take care of everything now. I'm going to make it up to you by showing you how much I care about you and how much I truly love you! Please don't be afraid to trust me. I will *never* let you down—not anymore—not like I used to do. I finally know now how to love. Don't ask me how I found that; I just know that I now know how. Don't cry anymore, Sweet; that's right, just lean on me, my love." Rose then began to weep intensified, bitter tears, tears that evolved into deep, wracking, wrenching sobs; and all the while he, Hershel, stroked her feverish forehead and cheeks with gentle hands; rocking, rocking and murmuring soft endearments, smoothing her damp hair, declaring his love over and over. He took to kissing her hot face ever so softly; then murmuring some more. At times she would look wildly about; and then she would search deep into his eyes, but all the while sobbing, sobbing pitifully. He rocked his newfound love until at last her sobbing subsided and she fell into an exhausted sleep of peace. When he kissed her forehead one last time, then laid her back on her pillows and turned to leave the room, he nearly ran over Yetsye in the doorway. Before she could turn away from him, Yetsye inadvertently allowed her son-in-law to glimpse the rivulets of garish mascara creep slowly down her cheeks.

Chapter Fourteen

When Hershel phoned me and asked if we could meet somewhere and talk, I feared that he might have fallen back into his old ways, but his suggestion that we adjourn to Giordano's for lunch put me back at ease. This really was the new Hershel Feldman! And, to top it all off, when I arrived at the aforementioned *ristorante* ten minutes early, Hershel was already seated, sipping coffee and chatting with Luigi. It seemed that, with Luigi, all was forgiven regarding our last visit wherein we had monopolized his favorite table by the window for an entire evening. Luigi, uncharacteristically cheerful, bowed and smiled at me, leaving Hershel and me to occupy table number two for as long, this time, as we wished. Even though he had lost a little weight, and perhaps a bit of tan, Hershel looked better than I could remember ever having seen him. He sat straighter, gestured more calmly, as opposed to frenetically, and smiled often. "Sit, Ellis, sit," he said jovially, "And, before we go any further," he added, "this one's on me."

"What's the occasion?" I asked.

I could tell he was trying not to sound presumptuous when he replied, "Well, for starters, I think Rose and I might get back together again, and for good, this time." His grin gave away his excitement. "She is cautious, of course, but we're both trying really hard to put the past behind us and get on with our life together."

"Hershel! I think that's truly wonderful!" I exclaimed, then added, "Is there anything I could do to help?"

"Not that I know of; unless, of course, you could have a little talk with Isabelle. She's not entirely convinced that her

'Abi' is a changed man—still a little afraid at times. Who could blame the little thing? She's seen me at my worst, slapping her 'Ma' around and falling down drunk. But, you know, I think we're making progress by me just visiting casually and being consistently loving and gentle with her and with Rose. Given some time, she'll come around, I'm sure. I'm not rushing things, though." His grin broadened and then faded somewhat as he appeared to lapse into thought. "Besides, I need some time myself to get things straightened out." He looked away from me; sort of into the distance, and I could see the muscles working in his jaw. He said nothing more but watched the cars swish by in a chilly drizzle outside the window.

"There's something you haven't told me yet, isn't there, Hershel?" I could see he was struggling with some issue.

"It's that obvious, is it?" He tried to smile at the question, but his thoughts squelched the grin into a quiver of the lips. He added, "There's something that's really bugging me and keeping me from working this thing out in my own life." A little of the old Hershel returned briefly as he apparently contemplated something distasteful or fearful; and he shuddered to himself before continuing: "It's really hanging over me, Ellis, this deal I made with the devil. As I recall, the penalty for welshing on the deal was pretty stiff—at least by implication it was." Returning his gaze to me, he fastened his eyes upon mine and grimaced with anxiety.

"I don't know; I wouldn't worry too much about that, Hershel. At the time, you didn't really know what you were saying. Are you really afraid he'll carry out his threat?" I dreaded his answer.

"I'm not only afraid he will, I'm sure he will." His anxiety grew as he went on, "I really don't know what to do. I know I have to go back and face him, but I can't do it by myself—I don't have the strength or the self-assurance. And, that brings us to the reason I asked you to meet me today."

"Oh, God, here it comes!" I thought with horror. *"How am I going to get out of this? There's no way I'm going to go face-to-face with Satan!"* I began to tremble and did my utmost to hide the fact from Hershel. I doubt that I was successful.

"Ellis, we need to go and visit Mr. Abaddon right away! I can't stand to wait any longer—it's eating away at me—not knowing what to expect. But, you, you know what to do. After all, you've studied all about the devil and you have God on your side. Me, all I've done is read about him in the Bible, and it scares me half to death." Hershel had paled and was trembling himself.

"Oh, I, I wouldn't get all upset about it if I were you," I stuttered, "We could just as easily go tomorrow, or the day after—there's no hurry." I couldn't meet his gaze, but I went on, "You don't really *have* to actually go there at all—I mean—what makes you think he even *knows* you aren't going through with the promise?"

"Oh, he knows alright," Hershel nodded, "He seems to know everything that's going on, I remember. C'mon, Ellis, we gotta go! I gotta go, and I need you to go with me, please!" Now, even his voice shook.

I swear, I just didn't know how to refuse. Even though I was terrified, I just did not know what to say to dissuade him. Finally, with a gulp, I said, "OK, man, I'm with you, I guess, but I really don't know what good it would do to drag me along. Why don't you just tell him you didn't know what you were saying and you've changed your mind? He'll understand, won't he?" I knew Abaddon would do anything *but* understand.

The cab driver, surly and irascible, managed to take a circuitous route from the *ristorante* to the warehouse area that added several miles and dollars to an otherwise more or less direct ride; and we arrived at the abandoned warehouse building fully half an hour later than planned. In addition, he refused to take us down the alley to the stairwell, but dropped us off summarily at the corner, from where we were forced to walk in the filthy and cluttered street to our destination. As we faced the old rusty door, and Hershel raised his hand to knock, the door swung open, apparently on its own, revealing a ghostly face illuminated by the oil lamp held beneath it by two brown-skinned hands. The face, surrounded by total darkness, appeared to be hovering in space above the sputtering lamp. Scarcely moving, the face's lips formed the words, "You come."

We stepped into the darkness and followed the now barely discernable form of a man; a man who led us to the left along the wall to another flight of stairs that descended to the level below. As we crept along in the near darkness, Hershel whispered in my ear: "Yong Se."

"Ah," I replied. The name certainly did sound contrived just as Hershel had described to me a few weeks earlier.

The steps were treacherous going due to their crumbling condition and I nearly lost my footing several times before we actually reached the floor at the bottom. Yong Se was no help at all, holding the lamp in front of himself where it provided virtually no illumination for Hershel and me to guide our steps. The first thing that hit me was the strange odor that seemed to pervade the entire cellar room. It reminded me of the reptile building at the zoo. Yong Se led us to the right toward the only apparent source of light in the entire chamber, a single candle in a holder on a battered and splintered oak table. The flame began to dance atop the candle as our approach produced air currents sufficient to agitate it. The light thus produced was so erratic that neither Hershel nor I noticed at first the figure seated at one end of the table. The figure spoke: "Good afternoon, gentlemen. Please be good enough to take a seat. I shall be with you in a moment." The voice was cultured and was delivered in a measured European accent; while the owner of the voice, a man, seemed to fuss about for a minute or two, doing absolutely nothing, before he finally turned to face us.

Hershel and I breathed the exact same name simultaneously: "Klausman!" Then, also simultaneously, we looked at
each other with alarm. Anton Klausman had around his neck
a collar of iron with a chain attached, a chain that extended
about ten or twelve feet to a steel pole to which it was
affixed with an eyebolt. Klausman appeared to be oblivious
to the presence of the collar and chain because, as he moved
here and there, the chain rattled as it dragged along; but he
paid no notice.

"I must say," Klausman said cheerfully, "I am highly
gratified to see you gentlemen arrive so promptly, and I am
proud to say how pleased I am that my staff have completed
the necessary preparations in such a timely manner. If you
will just make yourselves at home, we shall be ready to
commence the proceedings directly." On and on he prattled
for some five minutes before Hershel and I were able to pry
our eyes from him long enough to take note of our
surroundings.

As my gaze traveled to a far wall, I caught sight of an
object that I was, at first, unable to identify. Perhaps it was
the unlikely color, pale gray-green, that put me off, but it
was only after considerable scrutiny that I was able to make
out the shape of a huge snake. The thing must have been at
least twelve feet long and it lay in the semidarkness along the
base of a far wall, eyes staring but unmoving, and tongue
flicking occasionally, tasting our presence. Presently it
seemed to notice my stare and, as I nudged Hershel and
pointed, the creature began slowly to make its undulating
way toward us. It was so huge that we could actually hear the
scuffling sound of its body as it squirmed along across the
stone floor, and the strange lapping sound of the flicking of
its enormous tongue. We were both transfixed at the sight of
it and hardly noticed that it began to change in appearance as
it neared our table. Gradually, the nature of the mouth and
tongue went from serpentine to crocodilian as the monstrous
thing morphed into a stinking, steaming, flaming dragon.

The smooth shuffling of the snake became the rattling and hissing of the dragon and then, once more, as it reached the table and scuttled up into the remaining chair, it was the filthy and sordid, snaggle-toothed ogre. Through each progression the stench grew more and more repugnant until Hershel and I could hardly catch our breath. Klausman appeared not to notice the ogre or its fetid aroma.

Before the odious thing spoke, it transformed itself once more into the slick and oily Lucifer Abaddon: "Aha! Here we have the intrepid Hershel Feldman and, 'pon my soul, the illustrious Dr. Ellis Keaton, of television renown," he began, as residual tongues of flame played about his lips and tiny tendrils of smoke snaked from his nostrils. He continued, "I must say, gentlemen, I am touched by the sight of you both. It is no shock to see Feldman come cringing back, but to bring along the mighty and famous TV evangelist as I had requested seems to me more than I could have asked. Let us celebrate, shall we? A chalice of gore, either of you? Ha ha ha ha ha…" The cackling laugh followed his pushing toward us each an ornate cup containing—well—blood, or so I assumed.

While I shook my head vehemently in repulsion Hershel, simply ignoring the offer, said, "Let's get down to business."

"My my," oozed Abaddon, "We *are* brave, aren't we?" He chuckled loudly, emitting little smoke rings from his nose. "You seem to be in a mighty hurry to get your just desserts. You haven't, after all, fully satisfied the commitment you made to me in exchange for your life. While you have indeed brought Keaton here to me, neither his presence nor yours, for that matter, are in keeping with the spirit of the agreement. I perceive that you have no intentions of leaving him here with me, nor do you harbor any real plan to relinquish Miss Boschert to me. This entire visit is being conducted under false pretences. Accordingly, I propose to exercise my prerogative and exterminate you immediately. Unfortunately for you, good doctor, since you are close at hand, you will be unavoidably involved in the disaster. What a pity! Ha ha ha ha ha ha ha..."

"I thought you would welsh on the deal!" declared Hershel. "You're nothing but a phony, powerless clown. Your huffing and puffing, and changing into all those disgusting beasts, they don't impress me one bit." To my utter and complete surprise and admiration, Hershel actually leaned toward Abaddon, shaking his fist and glaring menacingly right into the monster's eyes; the result of which was a series of Abaddon's rapid-fire transformations into first one and then another of his full repertoire of hideous beasts.

At length Abaddon seemed to have exhausted both himself and his assortment of boogies, at which point he resumed his previous manifestation, that of Abaddon himself. Turning to me, he asked, "Why are you so silent, Keaton; having second thoughts about coming here, are you?"

Paralyzed with consumptive fear, I stuttered, "Well, I certainly—that is—I am in complete accord—you know—of—I mean—with Mr. Feldman here. You have no right to—ah—retain us—well—to keep us—in this place without our..." I completely fell apart and lapsed into silence, looking down at my hands trembling on the table.

When, after long moments, I was able to lift my eyes to Abaddon's face, he was smiling through gleaming white teeth, sparks playing across his lips while the obligatory smoke drifted toward Hershel and me. "Well, now," he remarked, "This is quite an interesting turn of events. When you two arrived, I just naturally surmised that you, Feldman, had brought along our friend Keaton for support; but this does not seem to be the case. In fact, I do not believe Mr.— or rather, Doctor—Keaton has the stomach for this sort of thing. Perhaps I shall alter my plans for him. Yes, I think I know just the perfect role for him to play." He paused, looking quickly, first at me and then at Hershel. He went on,

"So, I have decided, then: brother Keaton shall remain with me where he can keep company with our other friend, Herr Klausman, while you, Feldman, shall journey to oblivion. Yes, yes, I have decided! Klausman and Keaton will make a perfect pair, pawns with which I may amuse myself; and back to dust it will be for Mr. Feldman. How wonderful! Ha ha ha ha ha ha..." For a brief flick of time, Abaddon the father became Abaddon the handsome and dashing son—for celebratory reasons, no doubt—then returned to the form of the father once again.

"You'll do no such thing!" Hershel shouted, "You forget one important thing, Abaddon: Even though Ellis may not be asserting himself just now, that doesn't mean he isn't under the protection of Jesus Christ! You forget, Ellis has surrendered himself to Jesus and therefore you're going to have to battle Jesus, not Ellis, before you can have your way. You're no longer in charge of Ellis's fate—Christ is! And, He's in charge of mine, too. Yes, that's right; I have given my life to Jesus as well! So, you are beaten, Abaddon! You have no power whatsoever over either of us, and you certainly have absolutely no power over the Lord Jesus Christ, Son of the Living God!" Hershel had raised both arms above his head, hands turned toward each other, his eyes ablaze with passion, and his voice ringing with power and emotion. In a much softer voice, he added, "C'mon, Ellis, let's get the hell out of this stinking place!"

"Eh? What is this you say?" The devil, sounding incredulous, bleated, "Now, all of a sudden, you are an upstanding Christian? Why, you are not even a good Jew! This is utter nonsense, of course—a feeble attempt at bluffing. Admit it; you are doomed to die and your supposed 'friend' is now my exclusive possession."

At long last, I found my tongue: "You haven't changed one bit, have you, Satan?" I shouted, "Always the deceiver, even deceiving yourself when it serves your purpose. It's not going to work this time, however, because you cannot trump the Lord of Glory! He has indeed heard the prayers of a penitent Jew named Hershel Feldman and has poured out His grace and protection on him. And, as for me, He has taken me under His mantel years ago where I am still safe in His presence. Now, the two of us come against you in the name of God the Son, Jesus the Christ! We rebuke you! We have no fear of you whatsoever! You are defeated already by the power of the Lion of Judah! **To hell with you!**"

The room split open with a tempestuous roar, the sound of the ear splitting, panicked voice of the devil, shrieking: **"AAAAAAAAHHHHHHH! NO, NO, Not Jesus Christ! AAAAAAAHHHHH!"** The figure of Abaddon began to melt into what appeared to be lava; smoke, flame and steam gushing from the pathetic mass of stinking flesh and gore as the thing flashed from snake to dragon, to ogre, to slick, greasy gentleman, to hideous raptor bird, to snake again, to dragon once more, and back through the entire assortment of ugly, ghastly, fetid abominations.

Presently, the entire building began to tremble, then shake violently, with debris falling from the ceiling above us. Then, the floor below us began to crack and part, fire and smoke coming from the crevasses, along with a dreadful roar like rolling thunder. Soon, the shaking became so violent that we could scarcely keep our feet. I was mesmerized into immobility, but Hershel yelled over the calamitous cacophony, "Come **on**, Ellis! Hurry; let's get out of here before the whole thing comes down on our heads. **Come on, man!**" He grabbed hold of my arm and began to drag me toward the stairs leading up to the main level. He was too late: with a tremendous crash, the whole ancient building started to crumble! The lone candle was extinguished almost immediately and, with the darkness there came even more chaos. Although I could see nothing at all, Hershel continued to drag me toward what he obviously believed to be the stairs. I felt, as much as saw, a huge slab of masonry come hurtling toward us and fully expected to feel a horrendous impact and, of course, certain annihilation. Instead, after a dizzying rush of wind and motion, accompanied by a deafening roar, I found myself standing across the street, alongside Hershel, witnessing from a safe distance, the collapse of the old building. Clouds of dust, smoke, steam and debris billowed upward into the evening sky, accompanied by a strange roaring, whining commotion, until the entire structure settled into a fitful pile of slabs, beams, pipes, wires, and a scrambled assortment of random shapes. Strange, I thought I could hear the sound of poor Klausman screaming.

Minutes later we were being swept away hurriedly, for reasons known only to the taxi driver, when Hershel tapped my shoulder and pointed outside the cab's rear window at the huge gray-green snake as it slithered silently into a storm sewer.

Chapter Fifteen

During the next four weeks, while I was engaged in a preaching tour on the West Coast, I played back in my mind, on practically a daily basis, Hershel's and my confrontation with Satan. I returned over and over again to the same conclusion: I had acquitted myself very poorly in that encounter. Furthermore, prior to the event, I had steadfastly attempted to circumnavigate our meeting with the devil. Why, I asked myself repeatedly, had my faith failed me so abysmally? What became of the Ellis Keaton who was supposed to be, by virtue of decades of study and worship, an effective adherent of the Lord Jesus Christ? Throughout the entire tour I gained not the slightest insight into the cause of my apparent collapse in the face adversity. To state that I fell short of my own expectations, as well as those of the ones who witnessed my sermons, is a gross understatement. I don't believe I have ever in my life received so many perfunctory and bogus accolades as I did following each message. The last evening of the tour, I sat in my hotel room and watched the news coverage of my final sermon on TV. As far as I could determine, I did not make one single definitive statement throughout the course of the entire 'message'. My pale visage, the source of endless blather, reached no conclusions and made no firm declarations. Never have I seen so many wooden smiles, so many avoidances of eye contact, as I did in those weeks.

In the period subsequent to that ill-fated tour, I could not think back on that dreadful debacle without cringing with humiliation and dismay. Furthermore, I found that I could no longer write a sermon, let alone face a congregation and deliver one. Speaking into a television camera was entirely out of the question. At length, I informed my church's elders and board of directors that I must take an extended leave of absence, that I seemed to be experiencing some sort of breakdown, and that I was unsure when, indeed, whether or not, I would return. Had it not been for the kind hearts of this group of saints, I am certain I would have been asked to resign my pastorate. As it was, we agreed that I should take a month in seclusion and then reassess my situation, with the hope that I could then return to my position as senior pastor.

On my return from the Coast, I discovered in my personal mail accumulated during my absence, an envelope postmarked the undecipherable name of a city in China. Inside the envelope, written in the most intriguing hand I had ever seen, I found a lovely, short letter from Karen Boschert. In her quaint English, she assured me that she was in the presence of her loving parents, on holiday in the city of her mother's birth, and mending very well after her ordeal in New York. She further stated that she had severed her employment with Klausman, Walther, und Hahn, GmbH; and that said company had gone through dramatic changes since the loss of its principal director, Anton Klausman. In addition, she stated that she had, with considerable compunction and abundant tears, refused Rose Mandel-Feldman's offer of an executive position at Mandel Family Apparel; and that she had thereafter been offered, and had accepted, a similar position with a prestigious Hong Kong firm. She closed with the most moving regrets concerning the unlikelihood of our ever meeting again. I doubt that her disappointment could have been any more poignant than my own.

The very next day, as I put my church office in order for my departure, there appeared in the 'IN' box on my desk, the financial section only of the current issue of the New York Times. An article on the first page featured the newly reorganized company, Mandel Family Apparel. Above the text of the article, there appeared a large photo of Rose and Hershel holding hands and gazing into each other's eyes and, standing between them, a captivating, mop-haired three-year-old girl holding a toy poodle and mugging into the camera. The caption read:

"CEO Rose Feldman and President Hershel Feldman, with daughter Isabelle holding family pet"

I took this to mean, in part because Rose had dropped the use of her maiden name, that the Feldman family was currently functional, with the past firmly put behind them. Both Rose and Hershel appeared happier than I had ever seen them before. I could find no cause, either, to be concerned about the state of their souls. Were my eyes deceiving me, or was the formerly restive little Isabelle seen voluntarily snuggling against her Abi?

As I strained to stay in place on the grimy and damp plastic backseat of the cab, while the driver see-sawed through Manhattan traffic, I pondered the events of the last few months; how I had taken more or less for granted the fact that God had sent Hershel into my life to teach me something, and how I had persistently refused to attend to His voice. I struggled to apprehend, perhaps reluctantly at first, the reason He had allowed me to fail so abysmally in confronting Satan. There had to be some issue in my life, some point of attitude maybe, that was draining away my effectiveness as a preacher and as an evangelist. Ought not I to know, after all these years of preaching, when or how I was falling out of tune with God? Apparently not. Working my way to one end of the seat, I tried to position myself so the driver would be unable, through his mirror, to see me in prayer. It was not that I felt ashamed; I simply did not wish to answer any questions or to engage in any sort of conversation at this point. The prayer I mumbled came out so impersonal and obligatory, that I felt as if I should retract it and replace it with a real one. I needed to be alone.

Whatever I was going through was sapping the strength from my body. Had the two short flights of stairs to my front door suddenly become steeper than before? After having trudged up the initial nine steps to the first landing, I paused there to catch my breath before continuing to climb the remaining steps to the second landing upon which my front door opened. Through the thin walls of the stairwell, I could hear the wavering strains of my landlady attempting to sing an unfamiliar aria from an obscure Russian opera. She was a dreadful vocalist, but seemed able to entertain herself thoroughly. I rather envied her that ability. Unlike during the first fifteen years of my living in this place, this evening I experienced no satisfaction whatsoever in arriving home. My old, friendly furniture now came across as hostile and not at all accommodating; and even the smell of the place offended me. Reaching down to switch on a table lamp, I was startled half out of my wits when the light bulb, burning out with a sharp click, flashed like a photographic flashbulb. Were those pesky photographers out to get me? The bedroom wasn't much of an improvement. It seemed that, in my haste to meet with my church officials, I had forgotten to make my bed. Ordinarily, that would not have been such a heinous crime, but this evening it was unforgivable. Now, the bed that I usually enjoyed falling into was downright inhospitable.

Perhaps I was hungry and therefore grouchy and out of sorts as a result. The refrigerator provided no balm whatsoever to the wounds to my disposition. Any items that might initially have borne some merit had long since yielded to growths of the most disgusting nature and were therefore no longer edible, but downright offensive to my palate. To be sure, even those dishes that had not spoiled held no attraction for me. On second thought, hunger must not have been the issue. What then was the problem? Well, I knew what it was, of course. I had lost touch with God and therefore could not function; not on any level. If I, a preaching evangelist, could not preach and could not evangelize, what *could* I do? The obvious remedy was fasting and prayer, which explained my rejection of food. All right, I would fast and I would pray.

The fasting proved to be no problem since all food was abhorrent to me, but prayer was another matter altogether. My prayers began as a series of accusations against God, but ultimately became demands for answers to myriad questions; questions that continued to crop up in my mind as I contemplated all the failures I had experienced while I was supposed to be ministering to Hershel. I began to pace the floor of my apartment, shouting and raving at God, demanding explanations, demanding His assistance. This would never work; there were too many distractions. How long could this rain persist? I took time out from my ranting to shut the blinds and pull all of the drapes closed in every room in the place. It was a start, but I could still hear the storm beating at the window glass and roaring against the roof. In addition, I extinguished all but the very least effective lighting, leaving the apartment in near darkness— exactly the effect I was after. This was supposed to allay my depressive mood? I cared not in the least, but sought other means to darken my frame of mind. Due to the wind and rain, the place was becoming cold and damp. Leave it that way; don't turn on the heat. I tramped around in the dreary rooms, famished but not hungry, freezing but sweating, half blind in the dimness but wanting total darkness, drowsy but finding sleep out of the question. I shouted out in rage. I cried out to God. I sobbed in frustration. I argued with and debased myself. I tried over and over, with all I had, to pray; but nothing came. What few prayerful beginnings I made slipped into the most perfunctory and insipid utterances imaginable.

For some inexplicable reason, I set out to obliterate all evidence of the passage of time. Everything containing a timepiece was disabled: I unplugged the microwave, took batteries out of wall clocks, stilled the pendulum in my antique mantle clock, and threw my wristwatches into my sock drawer. Then, carrying my senseless tirade still further, I switched on the TV, turned the volume up loud, and tuned in an obscure cable channel that was broadcasting in some foreign language I could not identify. Finally, I put on an old, disgustingly stained and tattered robe over my underwear, slipped a pair of dirty socks over my icy feet, and padded about the place, my entire frame trembling with the cold while the TV blared and illuminated the place with its constantly changing and flickering light. Outside, the rain persisted in earnest. It was at this moment in time that I believe I lost touch with reality; a condition that persisted for a span of time that I later calculated to be three days and three nights.

What scant recollections I have of that period are sketchy at best and consist of images of myself lying on the floor before the TV trying to converse in a strange language with the people in the mistily glowing box. I truly believed that, in the space of a few intense moments, I had achieved fluency in their tongue and felt right at home with them. I recall later, finding myself trying to sleep on the floor in the hallway, out of my head with the cold and huddled in a position resembling the fetal. Another recollection involved a food fight in the kitchen, wherein I found myself hurling the rancid contents of the refrigerator at a foe of unknown identity; or was it my bitter grade school enemy Bobby Hill, the creep who lived next door to us? Well anyway, he deserved the killing I gave him. Other flashbacks were phantasmal, and they were many. What amounted to hallucinations and nightmares, the phantasmagoria continued for three days and, on the third night, led into a dream or vision that lasted for quite some time; perhaps eight or nine hours, for all I know. I lay on the floor in my living room and pulled a throw rug over me to attempt to quell the shivering, a pile of magazines and newspapers serving as a pillow. Apparently I dozed off for a time because I seem to have spent some considerable time in my leaky boat out on the lake where our often-rented vacation home nestled among hemlocks and yellow pines overlooking the warm, shimmering waters. The interval was a mix of sweet pleasure and bitter sadness. I loved to sit alone, out on the lake, and read by the hour, the only interruption being the necessity to bail out the boat now and again. Strangely, the sweetness of this particular time was haunted by the knowledge that my mom would soon be taken from us. Strange because I had no hint of that dreadful event until our last vacation was ended.

Since all the lights except the infernal TV were turned off, I had to feel my way into the small room I called my library. Maybe my old, sagging couch would be less uncomfortable for sleeping than the living room floor. But, what is Dad doing in New York sitting on my old couch? Oh, no, that can't be my dad; this old fellow has scraggly white hair and an equally white beard and Dad is nearly bald and he would never dream of growing a beard—especially a white one. It sure looks like him, though. See the way his eyes kind of crinkle up when he smiles? And, the mouth—how about the mouth?

"Hey, Dad. What brings you to the big city?" I asked, in considerable discomfort. Could this possibly be Dad? I thought Dad had died eight years ago. But, the eyes and the mouth, they were hard to ignore. "I hope you came to help me because I really need your wisdom this time," I added.

"That's what dads are for," the old man said. His voice was poignantly familiar, but then it wasn't, either.

It seemed to me that I might as well take advantage of his being there, even if this wasn't really Dad, so I said, "I've got all these knotty questions bothering me, Dad, and I wonder if you would give me some answers. You know more about God than anyone else I know of."

The old man chuckled and replied, "Well, I *ought* to know a lot about Him, wouldn't you say?"

"Yeah, I guess you're right," I answered, "but I don't want to take up too much of your time; maybe you have to get back."

He chuckled again and said, "No, no, I'm in no hurry. Fire away." He settled back on the old couch while I pulled up my squeaky desk chair and turned it around backwards so I could rest my arms on the back while I sat facing him. Arms akimbo, the old man regarded me with a blend of amusement and gravity that unsettled me.

"Well, here's the thing," I began shakily, "I've gotten involved with that Hershel Feldman character—you remember, the one that used to treat me like dirt until we lost track of each other? Well, he called me several weeks ago needing my help and I've spent a lot of time and effort trying to help him, and finally he's sort of out of the woods but now I'm all mixed up, and I don't know what's wrong."

Shifting himself around on the lumpy couch, the old man (or Dad) interrupted, "Yes, I know all about it. So, what are your questions, my son?"

How could I not be surprised that he said he knew all about my renewed relationship with Hershel? How could he know about this all the way from Atlanta? Better not to dwell on these things and just get on with it: "The first thing that comes to mind is why did you send Hershel to me in the first place? I mean, what was it I was supposed to learn from that?"

"In order to answer that, I will ask you a question: Why did you agree to help Hershel?" His eyebrows, much bushier than Dad's, arched over his eyes when he queried.

I was a bit put off by this, but I did my best to answer truthfully, "Well, I thought it was the right thing to do; I thought God would want me to."

"So, it wasn't love for Hershel, then?" He asked.

"No, I guess not—just love for God," I said sheepishly. Why should I feel sheepish, I wondered?

"But, anyone can love God, because He is good," the old man said, "but, not just anyone could love Hershel. God would have wanted you to help Hershel for love's sake. Jesus said, *'But I say to you, love your enemies, bless those who curse you, do good to those who hate you, and pray for those who spitefully use you and persecute you,'"*

After ruminating on this a moment, I was moved to say, "I understand what you are saying, and I believe you are right about Jesus' saying this, but why was it necessary to remind me of this at that particular time?"

Dad smiled his crinkly smile for just a second, and then grew serious as he replied, "The Apostle John put it this way: *'If someone says, 'I love God,' and hates his brother, he is a liar; for he who does not love his brother whom he has seen, how can he love God whom he has not seen? And this commandment we have from Him: that he who loves God must love his brother also.'* And, our Lord spoke it this way: *'A new commandment I give to you, that you love one another; as I have loved you, that you also love one another.'* To obey God is to love Him, but that is not the completion of it. Putting that obedience into practice by living in accordance with His commandments is true godly love."

I sighed and said, "All right, I see what you're saying, but why do you perceive me this way, Dad? What makes you think I don't do my job with love?"

"You are getting away from the work of God," he replied, "by not believing in Him and the One He sent. Remember, Jesus said, *'This is the work of God, that you believe in Him who He sent.'* You're working at too many things; putting too much trust in yourself and neglecting to put *all* your trust in Jesus. Do *only* what He leads you to do and, for heaven's sake, preach only Jesus, and Him crucified. Remember what

Isaiah said: *'These people draw near to Me with their mouth, and honor Me with their lips, but their heart is far from Me. And in vain they worship Me, teaching as doctrines the commandments of men.'* You perceive that you know too much, so you aren't humble enough to really pray and to sincerely seek Him in what you are doing. Remember your Beatitudes, my son."

These sayings of the old man cut me to the quick—not that he had offended me but that I had offended God and myself. I asked him, "How did I get to this point? I mean, I thought I was doing everything according to His will. What's wrong with me?"

"I will answer you," the old man said, "in the words of the Lord Himself: *'Nevertheless I have this against you, that you have left your first love. Remember therefore from where you have fallen, repent and do the first works...'* So, you see, you must forget about making a name for yourself, and go back to working for Him and for Him alone; and, most of all, in love. Remember: *'And now abide faith, hope, love, these three; but the greatest of these is love.'* Practice this and you will please God."

I was only partially satisfied with this, and questioned further, "Do you think, then, that Jesus sees me as having turned away from Him?"

"Not completely, perhaps, but we can and do sometimes take our eyes from Him on occasion; we let Him get out of our focus," the ancient one answered. After favoring me with a kindly smile, he continued, "We let our eyes stray from the Blessed One and let them become focused on that which we ourselves are engaging. All too soon we are wrapped in our own schemes and follies and only now and then do we glance His way; and even then we are not totally absorbed in Him. Do you not remember what the psalmist wrote? *'Behold, as the eyes of servants look to the eyes of their masters, as the eyes of a maid to the hand of her mistress, so our eyes look to the Lord our God, until He has mercy on us.'* Pray let your mind dwell on this and your eyes fix on God."

"Yes, I see that much more clearly; I see now what you mean by my not staying focused on Jesus," I said. "But, how does that relate to the fact that I was so afraid to confront the devil; to even be in his presence? I was terrified of the prospect even of going to meet with Mr. Abaddon. Why?"

There was that sweet smile once more; and again Dad had the answer: "Because there was no love there. The apostle that Jesus loved knew much of love, and he said it thus, *'There is no fear in love; but perfect love casts out fear, because fear involves torment. But he who fears has not been made perfect in love.'* You have only to look to the Spirit that is within you and you will find the knowledge of these sayings."

It was at this point that I took notice of something about the old man that had previously escaped me: there was a jagged scar that appeared to completely circumscribe the base of his neck, as if his head had been severed from his body and later restored. I was moved to ask him, "Are you Paul?" But, rather than answer me, he seemed to withdraw from me, growing fainter and less distinct, carried away finally by a frigid wind that knifed right through me as well. Immediately I was chilled into my bones and awoke with a snort, my neck and shoulders wracked in terrible cramps from having been twisted for hours at an odd angle. It took long moments for me to orient myself. I lay on the floor, the throw rug having unwrapped itself from me and my grungy robe having fallen open, my nearly naked body exposed to the chill and dampness of the unheated room. But, where was Dad; or was it the Apostle; or perhaps Elijah? It was none of these really, or maybe all of them, but it was a dream or a vision, and in it was an old man who was very close to God. How was I to remember which one it was? It didn't seem to matter whom I had encountered, but it did matter what he had said, and I vowed right then to treasure every word in my heart.

The rest of the third day I spent in prayer and thanksgiving to God, and only later that evening did I surrender to the needs of my body by shaving, showering, consuming half a box of cereal, and then rolling into my bed dead tired; falling immediately into a consuming sleep. Having relinquished all knowledge of the passage of time, I arose from bed many hours later, refreshed and revived, but having no inkling of the hour of the day. Throwing open the drapes and yanking open the blinds of my bedroom window, I beheld a gloriously beautiful and sunny April morning. Gone was the cold rain and bone-chilling wind, both of which had yielded to the warmth of the bright spring sun. Were those buds on that tree, the one I could never think of the name of, outside my window? Rummaging in my sock drawer for my watch and my phone, I resolved to make two urgent calls: I needed to call Hershel to thank him for allowing God to use him to awaken me; and I had to call the elders of my church in order to inform them that I was back in business.

He saved them from the hand
of him who hated them,
And redeemed them from the
hand of the enemy.

Psalm 106:10 (NKJV)

And the devil, who deceived them, was
cast into the lake of fire and brimstone
where the beast and the false prophet are.
And they will be tormented day and night
forever and ever.

Revelation 20:10 (NKJV)

END

Made in the USA
Columbia, SC
12 June 2019